call *michigan*

SAM DESTINY

CALL ME MICHIGAN

Second Edition
First published in Germany in 2016

Copyright © 2016 by Sam Destiny

Cover Artwork by Daqri Bernardo at Covers by Combs
Formatting by Leigh Stone at Irish Ink
Editing by Jenny Sims of Editing4Indies
(http://www.editing4indies.com)

www.samdestiny.com

dedication

*Sometimes your first love is your only
love.
Hold onto it.*

more by sam destiny

Morningstar – Series

Set In Flames (Book 1)

Set To Start (Novella)

Set in Sparks (Book 2)

Set In Burns (Book 3)

Romances

Tagged For Life

AJ's Salvation

AngelBond Trilogy

Raise The Fallen (Book 1)

prologue

Mason Stiles watched as his best friend pulled up in a truck and parked it right next to his black pickup. Though no one could see inside the darkened windows of the bar, Mason could clearly see the apprehension on his best friend's youthful face. Brad pushed the Stetson off his black hair, scratching his forehead before lowering the hat back into place. Mason downed his shot of whiskey and then signaled the bartender for another, adding a beer to mix up the flavor.

The run-down bar was really a hole in the wall with mirrored windows from the outside, a door with peeling moss-green-colored paint, and a brass handle. Inside, the oak bar, some tables, and a run-down pool table in the back had seen better days. The floor was imitation wood, but the excessive foot traffic had made the original color indistinguishable. The chairs were simple oak, no padding, and the barstools were leather-covered, even though not one was still intact. The walls were painted a muddy brown, making Mason think that bars often were designed to put you down even more. It was probably a tactic to get you to buy more alcohol. Left of the bar was a hardware store and to the right, a hairdresser. The only windows were the ones across from the bar, on each side of the door. It made the whole room even gloomier; especially since the green glass-covered lamps didn't do shit for lighting up the room.

"Gimme your car keys, Mase," Brad demanded the moment he stood next to his barstool. He held out a calloused hand, showing traces of hard work.

"Nope," Mason replied, making the 'p' pop. With surprise, he noticed that his words had lost their edge. How many of those honey-colored shots had vanished behind his lips?

"Yes! And then you'll pay your tab and get in the truck with me. You need to see Taylor before she leaves," Brad ordered, already patting him down.

"I didn't know you swung that way, buddy. I could've made ya happy a long time ago." Mason grinned, chuckling as Brad rolled his eyes while pulling the keys from his best friend's pocket.

"Taylor. Now," he repeated, and Mason shook his head.

"No. Collins made sure I knew she didn't want to see me anymore," Mason protested, his heart hurting with the truth behind those words.

"That girl just turned eighteen and finished high school. She doesn't know what she's saying," Brad insisted, waving over the bartender. "How much does his drunken ass owe you?" he wanted to know, and Mason saw the old man smile in sympathy.

"There ain't no way to pay for a broken heart," he rasped out, his voice hoarse from too many cigarettes and whiskey. His gnarly hands moved a rag over the polished top in an easy rhythm of habit. Especially since he didn't need to look down in order to wipe around glasses or bowls that adorned the wood.

Mason stumbled off his barstool, snorting. "I ain't got no broken heart," he slurred, seeing Brad and the bartender exchange a glance.

"It's two o'clock in the afternoon, son, and you're done. Totally and absolutely drunk. A woman is the only reason a man gets that wasted. And young Taylor is a pretty reason, too," the bartender remarked, going from cleaning the bar to polishing some glasses.

"But –"

"No 'buts' or 'maybes,' Mason. We are gonna go and see your girl now. In your current state, you might be brave enough to actually open that stubborn mouth of yours," Brad announced, reaching for him. It was a hard feat to get back to Brad's truck since the world kept tilting on its axis and sometimes even moved in waves just to spite Mason. Additionally, the falling rain made him think the ground had holes where there was none.

"I really love her." That statement didn't surprise him or Brad, but still, it cut deep. God, it was so true. He loved everything about Taylor Collins and had since the first day she entered high school, bringing the sunshine with her.

"I know." Brad's tone was somber, clearly stating how bad he felt for his friend.

"I'm twenty-one. I feel like my life's over. I don't know where to go from here. I could see it, Brad. Me and Collins on the farm, our children running around while I kiss her nose and tell her she's still as beautiful as she was when she was sixteen." Shaking his head, he wondered why the world hated him so much.

Brad started his truck, staying silent. Then again, what was there to say? The drive to the Greyhound station didn't take longer than five minutes, but the weather had taken a turn for the worse; black clouds rolled in and brought thunder and heavy rain. Still, Mason spotted Taylor as if she were a beacon in the darkness. Standing between two silver buses, she had just handed her one suitcase to a bus driver to be stored and therefore start her new adventure.

The moment Mason had heard that she planned to leave Sunburn, his whole life had been turned upside down. He had watched her for two years, being only her friend. He decided to give her time, make her experiences, always telling himself to give her just one more year until he told her that he loved her. She was sweet, charming, smart, and beautiful; so naturally, guys had swarmed her, but she still hung with him and his friends if she had the choice. A million and one parties had happened, yet he never had found the courage to take it one step further. His plan had been to watch her kiss a lot of frogs until sweeping in and making her see that he was her one and only prince.

"Get her to stay," Brad urged, almost pushing him out of the parked truck, and Mason moved, still having a hard time keeping himself upright.

The rain was soaking through his jeans and button-down as he approached Taylor. She was perfect in his eyes: brown leather boots that complemented her long legs, a yellow dress that ended mid-thigh, long blonde waves spilling down her shoulders, wild as the girl who wore them. She had her denim jacket in her hand, just pulling it over as he reached her side.

Her eyes had widened in surprise before they narrowed in fury. He deserved that look, too, and he knew it. At the news of her leaving, he had felt as if it had been a personal decision against him, so he wanted to hurt her back, having thrown a private party for him and Patricia, the girl Taylor hated most in the entire county. Of course, a small town had no secrets, and Taylor had basically found out the second Patricia walked out of his door.

"I don't need a good-bye from you, Stiles," she spat, her voice dripping with anger. She wanted to turn away from him, but he grabbed her arm, breathing in the rainy air to clear his drunken haze. Facing her buzzed was the worst idea Brad and he had ever had, and their track record of stupid ideas was long.

"Stay," he pleaded, keeping his voice low to maybe hide his physical state.

"Are you drunk?" she asked in utter disbelief, catching on to him instantly. After all, she knew him inside out.

"Stay," Mason simply repeated, and she stepped forward. He knew she was going to smell his breath, but that wasn't what he had in mind. Instead, he grabbed her shoulders, and then he was kissing her. His lips pressed against hers until she opened them with a gasp and he invaded her mouth with his tongue. She was soft, warm, and tasted of strawberry chewing gum. He knew it was a comfort thing for her, and she chewed it when she needed mental strength. He had always loved the scent on her breath, and now, he loved the taste of her on his tongue even more. For a few seconds, he even imagined she was kissing him back, her lips moving against his, almost compliant, but then...

"Fuck, Mason," she cursed, pushing away from him. "Fuck you thirty ways to hell!" She stepped back, her eyes on his face, pain twisting her features.

"Taylor, wait," he called after her, but she just shook her head, turning away. He took a step to follow her, but his own foot got caught on his jeans, and he stumbled to the ground. Closing his eyes, he wondered if getting up would change anything. He felt as if his world had come crashing down and he was sitting in the ruins with no way to ever rebuild it.

The bus passed him, and he looked up, letting the rain pelt down on him until eventually Brad pulled him back toward his truck. Mason didn't care; his heart had just left this town on a damn Greyhound bus.

one

Mason Stiles loved nothing more than the solitude and peacefulness his truck provided. He adored his family, his work, and his house, but sometimes, things just were too much, and he needed a break.

The day had started out sunny, and Mason had decided to head over after finishing work in Freedom, the next big town, to get the parts he needed to repair the leaking faucet at home and the broken fence at the end of his driveway.

He had just passed the Greyhound station that twelve years prior had taken his life away from him, and he figured in about another sixty minutes, life would swamp him again, chasing away the calm he had felt in the cab of his truck. Turning on the radio, he found his favorite country station, singing along to the familiar tunes while trying to avoid over-thinking things. His thirty-third birthday was coming up in a couple of months, and as much as Brad had insisted they needed a barn party, Mason hoped he'd be able to get drunk all by himself. He wanted to nurse his broken, lonely heart in the sanctuary of his home, without anyone bearing witness to his pity party. In front of him, the sun was shining brightly, but his mood more fit the black clouds rolling in behind him.

Sighing, he suddenly spotted someone walking up ahead on the road. Between their location and the next farm or town, there were miles and miles of fields and more fields, meaning hours of solitary walking until that person even met another soul.

Judging by the stature, Mason guessed it was a girl, and looking at her clothes, he decided pretty quickly that she wasn't from around here. Her curves, if you even could call them that, were barely concealed by a white blouse and hugged tightly by a pair of damn skinny jeans those urban folks loved so much. Mason preferred his girls the typical country style: boot cut jeans, plaid shirt, and real cowboy boots instead of those flimsy ballerina shoes this girl was sporting.

Her hair was in one of those fancy up-do's with not a single hair out of place. That wouldn't be the case much longer because, before long, the storm rolling in behind them would catch up with her.

She carried a sea sack; one Mason knew people owned if they once had been in the Army like he had been. Frankly, the luggage made her appear even smaller.

Slowing his truck to a crawl, he rolled down his window and saw huge and ugly sunglasses covered half of her face. Her cheeks were hollow, and he could see the bones at the base of her neck standing out more than he thought was healthy.

"Hey, lady," he called and then watched how she swallowed before looking at him. He couldn't make out much besides her pursed lips, but something about her heart-shaped mouth triggered a memory in the back of his mind.

"You need a ride? It'll rain soon," he continued, and her face turned from him to the clouds behind his truck.

"Crap," she muttered, her voice soft and warm.

"Wanna hop in?" *Great job, Mason*, he scolded himself silently. *It's not at all weird to invite a city girl into your truck since they were suspicious of everyone and everything*. Unlike the women he knew, those damn girls from the big towns didn't know the typical country friendliness; at least, that was what the TV always portrayed.

"If you don't mind," she replied without an ounce of hesitation, and Mason stopped the truck. She threw her bag in the backseat as if she had been riding in trucks all her life.

"Where are you from?" he inquired as she settled down in the seat next to him.

"Michigan," she replied, and Mason noticed that instead of looking at him, she stared straight ahead.

"Where to, Michigan?"

She lowered her head, her shoulders slumping, giving her an air of defeat. The truth was Mason had never seen a girl who looked as unhappy as she did. Her skin was pale, her body was way too slim, and what he saw of her face held no traces of a smile. In fact, she looked as if no happiness had grazed her features in way too long.

"The Collins' farm," she eventually announced, and he shifted gears, making the truck finally move again.

"They're nice folks," he observed, avoiding the last name. Twelve years later and his heart still hadn't forgotten the one who got away. The memories of the day Taylor had left were hazy at best, at least when it came to everything that had transpired after him entering the bar, and basically non-existent when it came to how he had left it again. "They just had tough luck with the dad runnin' away. The middle child, Tamara, is takin' care of the smallest one now, but I guess you know that. You're heading there to help?" He really liked that since Tammy was way too young to be burdened with something like that. While she never once had complained, Mason couldn't imagine it to be easy at all. The girl in the seat next to him simply shrugged.

"Something like that, yes." She trailed one bright red fingernail along his dashboard while studying the pictures Mason had long ago meant to take down.

Rain started pelting down hard, and he turned on the windshield wipers, but they barely made a dent as the heavy drops kept falling.

"It's a long way on foot to reach the Collins' house," he remarked, curious why she didn't take the glasses off even though it was now dark. She kept her face hid.

"I know," she gave back, and then added, "Ashley is a beautiful girl." Mason had a hard time not slamming his foot down on the brakes.

"What?" he asked, disbelief coloring his voice, wondering how she knew that name.

"It says 'love, Ash' on this one, so I just wanted to comment ... forget it." She waved it off, resting her chin on her palm after placing her elbow against the door, staring outside again.

"I'm sorry, that wasn't what I meant, Michigan. Ashley and I haven't been a couple in two years. I wanted to take down those pictures quite often, but..." He rolled his shoulder as if that said it all.

"You're having a hard time letting go?" She helped out, and he gritted his teeth as it got harder to see and even harder to concentrate.

"Funny fact ... when I kissed her the first time, I knew

she wasn't it for me. The one, you know?" It was weird putting it out there like that, but it was the truth. He only held onto the thing with Ashley for so long because, besides it being the wrong woman, the rest had been close to everything he'd ever wanted.

———

Taylor's heart was bleeding all over Mason's truck, and he didn't even see it.

"First kisses are a crucial thing," she stated, wondering if she was hurting so badly because he hadn't recognized her, or because in the pictures with Ash he looked so happy; she wished she could put that expression on his face just to bathe in the warmth his smile was radiating.

"You're absolutely right, Michigan."

For a short moment, she debated telling him who was in the truck with him, but then she decided against it. Coming home had not been her choice. When the lawyer had called in her mother's and father's name, she hadn't hesitated and sold everything that had defined her up in Michigan.

Life on the Collins' farm had always been tough. Her parents had loved her unconditionally, even after the farm had hit rough times, and while she didn't mind helping out every now and then, Taylor knew that it wasn't going to be her life. So once her mother had announced that Taylor was now old enough to take over the bookkeeping and help run the farm alongside her dad, she had grabbed everything she valued and had fled the sheltered life she knew. Five years later, her sister, Tamara, had called her in tears, delivering the news about them getting a baby brother. Add two more years and their mother had left the family hanging.

Tammy had never asked her to return, and Taylor had never offered. But now, with her father gone and Tammy left to raise an eight-year-old, Taylor hadn't thought twice. She left her party-planning business to help her sister and take on the responsibility that should've been hers in the first place. Neither of them had deserved that life, yet Taylor at least had gotten twelve years of more or less freedom away from North Carolina.

When planning her future, she had always thought that she'd be married by now, but three years into her new life, she knew she couldn't give her heart away because that day, in the rain at a North Carolina bus station, she had left it with a drunken boy.

If Mason had said different words that night, would her life have gone down a different path?

"I shared a memorable first kiss after I finished high school," she hinted drily.

Mason laughed, sending uncalled shivers down her spine. God, she barely recognized herself as the desperate need to crawl into his lap and let him hold her came over her like the storm she hadn't seen roll in earlier. She had lost weight, enough to scare her, too, but she hoped that some of her former curves would return eventually once she had settled down and found a new routine. She missed feeling like herself. Stress had taken its toll on her in the last months.

"You don't sound impressed." He grinned while she watched how he slowed down the truck more and more. It was almost impossible to see the asphalt through the heavy curtain of rain while thunder shook the car. While she couldn't even begin to explain how glad she was that Mason had picked her up, she still didn't want to spend any longer than necessary with him in here.

"He was drunk as a sailor, and it came out of nowhere. For more than a year, I had fantasized about being kissed by him, and then he tasted like the bottom of a whiskey bottle." She shook her head while secretly checking his face with her sunglass-covered eyes, but he seemed unaware of the memory. It cut deep, realizing that she was the only one haunted by that kiss. Then again, she had already suspected as much. The confirmation didn't sting any less, though. "Lucky bastard doesn't even remember it anymore," she finally added, and his expression turned serious.

"Lucky, indeed. He gets a second chance if that's what he wants," he concluded, and for a few seconds, she wondered if maybe she had been wrong about his lack of memory, but then he sighed. "First kisses are somethin' else. I'm still waiting for my last first kiss. The kind where you know there's no walkin' away from it, ever," he confessed, and it reminded her that a true cowboy was not only devoted but also honest. She missed the Stetson on his dark hair, yet she gave herself a chance to admire the scruff on his cheeks, his strong jaw, straight nose, and full lips. She found herself reaching out, only to change direction and fiddle with the radio instead.

"I think this storm makes listening to music impossible," Taylor pointed out, thinking of one too many storms she had spent inside of Mason's truck at one party or another. The groups would vanish inside vehicles at the first sign of thunder to wait out the rain. Somehow, she had always ended up in Mason's truck – without anyone else around.

"Yeah, that just happens," he agreed, reaching out for the radio as well.

"I guess you just have to sing by yourself, S ... singer." She amended the end of her sentence quickly as she noticed her almost slip.

He stiffened nonetheless, and Taylor cursed herself. She had said that sentence so often, it more was an inside joke now instead of a statement. She felt tears coming to her eyes at all the happy memories Mason's presence awoke in her. He had an amazing singing voice, and each time she'd heard it, she had been able to see him singing a child to sleep, softly brushing a coarse kiss across baby soft skin afterward. If he ever had a baby girl, she'd probably adore him. She could easily see it: All his children would focus on their dad.

The image of them sharing a house and having a family seemed so real in her mind; she could almost touch it.

"What did you say?" he questioned while bringing the car to a stop at the side of the road, his eyes focused out the windshield, as if in his head he was trying to work something out.

"I ... suggested you sing for us," Taylor stuttered, wondering if he would.

"Ashley hated when I sang," he started, turning toward her in his seat. Taylor swallowed a few times as her throat seemed to clog, then she looked away from him, no longer able to hold his gaze. His blue eyes were too watchful, and even though she still wore these stupid sunglasses, he seemed to look right through her pretenses. "She always complained that it reminded her too much of things long buried," he went on, and she noticed from the corner of her eye how he reached out and started to pull the hair pins from her chignon, dropping them onto the dash one by one. "Obviously, one of her friends—her best one, in fact—loved to be serenaded by me, and while Ash loved her like a sister, she didn't want the memory of another woman standin' between us."

Taylor squeezed her eyes shut as his movements,

precise and surprisingly well practiced, made her whole body thrum with need. Holding her breath, she couldn't deny that she wished that just once, accidentally, he'd brush her cheek.

Twelve years were between them, yet with every pin he pulled out, she had the feeling he made them vanish one by one. *If only that were possible*, Taylor thought as a tear left a wet trail down her cheek.

two

Mason had a lump in his throat. He had known something was off with this girl, but then she had been ready to call him Stiles as if it was the most natural thing in the world, and his body had gone into overdrive. He could hear the blood rushing in his ears, her silent acceptance of him freeing her hair saying more than a thousand words could. Eventually, long blonde waves tumbled down her back, and Mason reached out to pull them apart while his mind was doing a million miles a minute.

Touching her cheek, he took a fortifying breath before pulling those ugly glasses off. His breath caught in his throat as his eyes fell on her features.

She was the same kind of beautiful yet totally different. Her cheeks, hollow as he noticed before, made her cheekbones so much more prominent. He recalled the fullness of her lips, but they lacked the rosy color he remembered. Dark lashes framed familiar hazel eyes, but the typical happy glint was missing. His heart, galloping in his chest, left no doubt: The girl in front of him was Taylor.

"Mason." His name was a broken whisper on her lips as her voice trembled. He couldn't form one coherent thought, but she suddenly wrapped her arms around him, her face hidden in the crook of his neck, where only she seemed to fit perfectly. He moved until she sat on his lap, and while he wanted to squeeze her tight, her body felt breakable under his hands. He could feel her ribs underneath his palms, so he cupped the back of her neck with one hand and wrapped the other around her hips, careful not to hurt her.

"What the hell happened to you, Taylor?" he wondered quietly, feeling how she shook her head against his shoulder. He squeezed his eyes shut, soaking up her closeness while realizing that besides those long blonde waves, nothing was left of the girl he once knew.

"I'm terrified, Stiles. I returned, knowing I need to raise an eight-year-old boy and run a farm. I don't ... I couldn't eat much. Each and every time I took a bite, it felt as if razorblades were going down my throat. I've spent two weeks acquiring all the documents I needed after my father abandoned Timmy and Tammy. This town blames me for everything." She sobbed, and he swallowed all he wanted to say. He knew how small towns worked, but he remembered as well how much they had loved Taylor Collins before she had left.

Suddenly, as if stung by a bee, Taylor was back on the other side of the seat, her breath sounding labored as she looked at him, making herself small against the door. She looked even more broken than she had before, if that was possible.

He wanted to call her Collins again the way he used to, but the name didn't come past his lips. No matter how much he wanted to give her a piece of normalcy again, it felt too wrong. She wasn't his Taylor any longer.

"Call me Michigan for now," she implored as if she felt his apprehension.

"As of now, it fits you way better," he admitted, finally finding his voice. She had been gone for twelve years, and as he watched her now, he couldn't help but wonder if maybe, for more than a decade, his heart had held onto a girl who would never return.

———

Taylor wanted to break down and cry until no more tears came, but she told herself to wait until Mason could no longer bear witness to her pain. People thought that during high school, you formed bonds that would last a lifetime and wouldn't break from years apart. Taylor was no exception to that belief, but this encounter with Mason made it clear that it was nothing more than a misconception.

His eyes were wide, and he kept watching her with an expression that made her think she had just told him there was no Santa. She wished now she had kept her emotions in check instead of falling around his neck, but she couldn't take it back. His touch had been barely there; so light, it had brought the pictures of him and Ashley back to the forefront of her mind. She recalled too clearly how obvious it had been that he couldn't let go of them.

Ashley, her former best friend, had dated Mason, and he still wasn't over it.

"I'm sorry, Mase."

"What for?" he inquired, brow furrowed, and she shrugged. She honestly had no idea, but for whatever reason, she felt the need to continually apologize.

"I have no idea. So the rain let up and I need to ... I guess I should..." Nothing was left to say, and it scared her. She couldn't think of one sentence to utter, one question to ask, even though she hadn't seen him in forever.

Mason turned to her, studying her for a long moment before patting the spot next to him. She scooted closer, and he kissed her forehead, his lips lingering. "People need to get used to the new you, Michigan. You haven't been around in a very long time. Give them a chance. This is still a small town, and you know best how those are.

Maybe people will surprise you." He tried to soothe her, but she stayed silent as he turned the key and made the engine come to life again before easing it back onto the road. "Things changed around here, too, but you know that kindness goes a long way. You never had a problem with bein' kind, Michigan, so there's hope on the horizon." He gave her a smile and tugged her into his side, letting her soak up his warmth.

Somehow, though, no matter what, Taylor couldn't shake the feeling that she had just been friend-zoned.

———————

The last thirty minutes of the drive were quiet yet eventful. Mason was strangely aware of every breath Taylor drew, of how a sob caught in her throat every now and then even though she tried to hide it, and the way she fit in his arms so perfectly while she drew lazy patterns with her fingertips across his thigh, most likely worrying about her home.

He had so much he wanted to say to her, like how he had lost his heart to her when she'd been merely a sophomore, but he figured she had more than enough on her plate already, and all she really needed was a friend. He was ready to be just that for her until they figured out who she was exactly. Plus, he had his hands full with his own life, especially because Taylor didn't realize yet that Ashley might not be very fond of her any longer.

He parked the truck at the end of the driveway the

way she'd asked. She shivered next to him, and he reached to his backseat for his college football jacket. It was his everything, the one piece of clothing he never let go of, but since football jackets had somewhat been their thing in high school, he hoped that this would offer her some sense of comfort and home.

She slipped her skinny arms through the sleeves and then freed her hair from the collar while a small smile graced her lips. She grabbed her bag, making him wonder if it was a keepsake from one of her ex-boyfriends. She got out of the truck after wordlessly squeezing his arm. She had crossed only a few yards before her steps faltered.

He watched as Taylor stared at the house that used to be her home, and Mason was glad that her father had at least kept it well maintained. She froze where she was, and Mason slipped out, walking around the truck.

"Michigan?"

She spun back around as if he had promised to take her away again. "My cell number hasn't changed. If you need me, call me," he ordered and then watched as she took a few fortifying breaths before hurrying back to him. He caught her in his arms, watching her bag in the mud where she had just dropped it. As much as it killed him, he was glad that he couldn't feel her bones as much through the leather of his jacket and held her tighter now than he had dared to before.

"Stop bein' a wimp," he reprimanded. "Put on ya big

girl panties and rock that family thing."

She laughed, but her voice hitched at the end. "I just need to step inside. I'll be fine," she promised, and he had no doubt about it. Taylor had always been strong. She pulled back, nodding before walking up to her bag, grabbing it, and marching to the house. Now, that was more the Taylor he recognized. The moment she vanished inside, he got back into his truck and finally began his way home again.

He wished he could go to Brad's house and have a few beers to sort his thoughts, but obligations were calling. He drove straight home, finding his mother on the front porch. Dusk had settled over the farmhouse, and she had lit only a few of the decorative lanterns.

"I was gettin' worried, son," she stated, crossing her arms in front of her body. Stella Stiles still was a beautiful lady and his savior most days. Her dark hair hung in a braid down her back, her figure womanly and showing traces of age. On her face, it was obvious that she'd had a good life so far; laughter lines around her eyes and her lips made her seem younger. Her blue eyes were hooded, a silent accusation in them.

"I got in a storm and then picked up a girl on the side of the road. Mom, Taylor Collins is back." His voice was barely above a whisper, the shock at seeing her finally hitting him. His mother knew all about his regrets of never having told her how he really felt. To his surprise, Stella nodded, her face suddenly laced with sadness.

"I met Ashley in town, and she mentioned that it was likely to be today. I had no idea how to tell you, so I didn't. I hoped you'd have some time before meeting her and ... I know it was the chicken way out, but I couldn't let myself see the hope on your face before realization would crash in, ruining it all," she admitted. "How do you feel?"

"She's not the same girl she was when she left."

His mother nodded again. "She gave up everythin' in Michigan, including her event management business. I know you avoided hearing about her life away from you, but she did very well there. The girl who left turned into the woman who returned. Plus, you aren't the boy you used to be," she reminded him, and he swallowed. It was crazy how even though he and Taylor were back in the same town, they suddenly didn't seem to be on the same planet any longer.

three

Taylor had never been afraid to walk into business meetings, no matter how many sharks sat at the other end of the table watching her as if she was their next meal, yet she was terrified of crossing the doorstep to the house that used to be her childhood home. It fazed her that Mason just assumed she'd still remember his number and therefore hadn't bothered to tell her again, but even worse was that she indeed recalled every single digit with ease.

The rain was gone, and while the encounter with Mason had left her reeling, she needed to focus. Stepping on the porch, she put her sea sack down and kicked off her ballerinas, placing them next to Tammy's cowboy boots and Tim's sneakers. She missed her own boots something fierce and decided that one day soon, once everything settled down, she'd get herself a new pair.

She pushed open the screen door, being surprised at how Mason's jacket almost felt like armor, making her more brave and giving her a sense of security she clearly needed.

"Tammy! Taylor's here!" Tim bounded down the stairs squealing just as she stepped inside. He threw himself at her, and she caught him even though he was getting heavy fast. She cuddled him close; Skype talks couldn't replace the feeling of holding her baby brother.

"So happy you're home, Tay," he burst out, squeezing her tightly while her sister followed at a much slower pace. Timothy struggled, and Taylor placed him back on his feet. She kept her eyes on her sister, and her heart broke as she realized how grown up the twenty-one-year-old woman appeared. In fact, it was as if Tamara carried the weight of the world on her shoulders, and Taylor hated it. "Are you gonna have pizza with us, Tay? Tammy promised we'd celebrate with pizza since"—he made a face, wrinkling his nose—"Tammy's cooking sucks."

Taylor kept her focus on her sister while ruffling Tim's hair. "Why don't you go ahead and figure out what you want?" she suggested, and he skipped away.

Tamara's eyes glistened with tears. "I'm so sorry, Lori." She was the only one who got away with calling her that. "I prayed every day that someone would stay around long enough until Tim's going off to college, but I guess Dad got tired of everythin'! I'm so sorry!" Tamara went on, and Taylor pulled her into her arms, kissing her hair.

"Stop worrying. I'm happy to be here. And I hear you applied for college! Why didn't you tell me? I'm so proud of you, Tammy! Seriously!" Against her shoulder, her sister shook her head, bunching Mason's jacked in her fists.

"I'm not goin'. I'll get a job and help you with the farm. I..."

"Tamara, this is not a discussion. You were accepted, and you're going. I should've stepped up much earlier, and I'm sorry you had to carry that burden, but now, I am here, and I'm not ever going away again."

Tammy pulled back, scrutinizing her. "Guess what, it's not your job, either, Lori. Our parents should be here; you and Andrew should be planning a family instead of you managing one," she admonished, and Taylor closed her eyes. She and Andrew should've planned many things, but somehow, they never went further than the dating part. They told everyone they were a couple and maybe would think more about the future once everything settled down. The moment she knew she'd have to return, Andrew had been the first thing to go. Walking away from him had been too easy, and it probably should've made her pause, but he was the least of her worries.

"Hey." She smiled, brushing some tears away from

Tammy's face. "I'm still gonna manage something, only now it will be a farm and family instead of parties. Someone needs to fill that position when you leave for school."

Tammy's eyes finally shrank to slits as if only then she noticed something being off.

"This jacket smells awfully familiar, and it's a guy's jacket," she pointed out.

"Mason Stiles drove me home. He found me walking down the street." Taylor bent to retrieve her bag, careful to avoid her sister's eyes. "Did you know he and Ash had been a couple?" Tammy must've known yet never mentioned it to her. Then again, maybe she just figured Taylor didn't care anymore. After all, she had walked away. "You know, never mind." She waved it off, reconsidering the question.

"Mason, huh? I could've picked you up. I just didn't know when you'd be arriving and –"

"I wanted to walk, Tam," Taylor interrupted.

Her sister just stared at her while Taylor took off the jacket, righting it on the coat rack. She felt the gaze burning on her back, and it made letting go of that tiny piece of Mason almost impossible.

"You were afraid," her little sister guessed, and again, Taylor couldn't get around noticing that her little sister was way too serious for her age.

"I'm no longer the country bumpkin people

remember. Coming back here is like walking into everything I used to be and everything I wanted to leave behind. Besides, you have every right to hate me, and I wasn't sure you really wanted me back." She willed herself to stop talking. She wanted Tammy to stop worrying and be the young woman she should be, while Taylor would be the adult this household needed. They weren't equals when it came to that.

"I wanted you back every damn day but not like this! Oh, Lori." Tamara wrapped her arms around Taylor from behind, squeezing her before following her movements with her eyes as Taylor finally let go of the jacket.

"So Mason, of all people, found you?"

Taylor faced her sister again, arching a brow at the hidden meaning in Tammy's tone.

Her sister grinned guiltily. "You're town talk. Everyone expected you and him to be a couple, but it didn't happen. When I'm in town and he's there, too, everyone goes out of their way to mention how he really had deserved that Collins' girl to be happy," Tammy explained.

"We never were a couple. People don't know what they're talking about. Stiles and I were friends, and now, he's driving around with Ashley's pictures in his truck. All that aside, I'm not here to rekindle old love interests. I'm here for my family."

"And you have Andrew." It was a statement and not

37

a question, but Taylor felt like answering anyway.

"Andrew and I are over. Now, Tim, are you still here?" she called, trying to chicken out of the subject.

"Here, I picked!" their little brother answered. Taylor shrugged at her younger sister, and then she went in search of the starving pizza-boy. She just needed to distract Tammy long enough until said subject was forgotten.

four

Two weeks. That was how long Taylor managed to avoid errands in Sunburn. Tammy had done the shopping while Taylor had thoroughly cleaned the house – twice. The only room she had left untouched was her parents' bedroom. Tammy was sure it was where Taylor slept, but Taylor didn't have the heart to correct her. She knew it was absurd, but she felt as if her own ten-year-old self was back the moment she tried to open the door. Her parents had never allowed them to go inside, and it prompted Taylor to sleep on the living room sofa, taking care that she was up before anyone else in the house woke. Their parents had transformed her bedroom into a cramped study the moment she had turned her back on her hometown.

"Timothy Collins, get down here!" She stood waiting at the bottom of the stairs. Tammy had left for college the day before. To Taylor's relief, she hadn't brought up the topic again, stating without many words how excited she actually had been for college life. Tammy had insisted on coming home on the weekends, but Taylor pointed out that was when the parties were, and she'd move heaven and hell to get her sister to fully enjoy college life.

"Comin', Tay," Tim called as he rushed down the stairs, tumbling into her arms while falling over his own feet. He laughed in delight while his big sister tried breathing through all the horror scenarios she had created while waiting. How would people react to seeing her? She couldn't imagine and stopped herself from going crazy.

Grabbing the car keys to her dad's beat-up truck, she headed outside and hopped into the cab. Timmy took a seat next to her, buckling up while humming. It calmed her down more than she was ready to admit.

"School supplies first, and then school uniform, then grocery shopping," she listed, more for her benefit than his. "And bank. I need money, too," she added as she thought of how she'd pay for all those items.

"Tammy brought back most of my supplies anyway, so you don't have to worry about it," Tim reported, and Taylor smiled to herself. Of course, her sister would've thought of that. She still drove the truck toward Sunburn's general store. "Nope, don't need anything from here," Tim repeated, and Taylor shook her head, moving on to the bank.

"I'm the adult in the house, so let me pretend I know what I'm doing." She grinned, and he cuddled with her on the shared front seat. She parked the truck, ready to hop out, when he hugged her tight.

"I'm glad you're back. Tammy was getting too strict and too sad. She cried a lot," he confessed, and she swallowed. Her sister most likely had been overwhelmed with it all.

"Well, we'll make sure she's only happy from now on, okay?"

Tim nodded while he stared at the bank. "Can I wait inside the truck?"

She shook her head. "Come on, I'll be quick," Taylor promised and then helped her brother out of the cab. Three people had hugged and welcomed her back before she had even entered the bank. While it was clearly nice, a bigger part of her was freaking out. She barely recognized the faces, let alone remembered the names. Rushing into the bank, she was glad once the brass-framed glass door quieted all the noise from the street.

"Tay! Oh, my gosh! I was wonderin' when you'd be back in Sunburn! After all, the town has been buzzin' with news of your return. I'm sorry it had to happen the way it did, but boy, am I so glad you're here, honey!" It had taken all of two seconds before another hug engulfed Taylor, trying to match a voice she almost recognized with a woman that she wasn't sure she had ever seen.

The face looked strangely familiar, and she thought it was one she had seen in the pictures two weeks ago, only now it was covered with too much makeup and framed by dark waves instead of the soft blonde Taylor had been used to.

"Ash?" she finally asked, realizing that her friend had tears in her eyes.

"I missed you so much, but we all wanted to respect your wishes and leave you alone. You know, you asked us to stay away and not contact you? I always thought you'd be back, but then months turned into years, and I knew I should've known you'd be one of those who would actually succeed at leavin'. No one heard from you again, and while your parents were still here and hated you, we'd have preferred you to them."

Taylor could only shake her head in utter disbelief. "I never knew you were in love with Mason. I saw the pictures in his truck." Of all the things she could've said, she picked that. A stupid topic, really, but she couldn't help but wonder about the Ashley she had seen in the picture and the Ashley she now saw. In fact, barely anything was left from the best friend she remembered.

"He came by one day, and we talked. Then he came by here again and brought a flower and asked me on a date. I agreed, and we went out. Then we went out a few more times. He was just like you always imagined him to be, ya know? Sweet and fun, romantic and crazy." Taylor rubbed the spot above her heart, trying to ease the pressure beneath her ribcage. She turned away, watching the street outside, while her friend continued. "You were gone, Tay, and I found out why you had been crushing on him so hard. Sadly, even though things were amazin' for the time being, it took me until he held our baby girl to realize that while he had everythin' he wanted, I was the wrong woman for him. He looked at the girl, and I might as well have left the room. It didn't matter. I wasn't the right one."

Taylor spun back to her former friend, eyes wide. "You have a daughter together?" she choked out, not even noticing that her throat was so dry, she sounded as if she was on the verge of tears.

"I … it's his daughter. I signed away all rights soon after the birth. I thought a daughter would guarantee us a happy forever. It was the only reason I agreed to have a baby in the first place. Stupid, really, because I have never wanted children. Not once." Ashley shrugged and then walked back around the counter. Taylor followed, taking out her checkbook absent-mindedly. She remembered her friend saying once that she had not one motherly bone in her body.

"You really loved him." It came out more as a statement than the question she had intended to ask, but

Ashley nodded in confirmation nonetheless.

"In a way, I did. I love the idea of what Mason and I could've and should've been, but once he held Rebecca, I knew I was dumb. While a daughter clearly is the most special girl in a father's life, shouldn't a girlfriend have been able to put a look of utter happiness on her boyfriend's face, too? Just one moment when he looks at you and you know he's happy havin' you?"

Taylor smiled wistfully. She had read about those moments in books; in fact, she could definitely see it in her mind. It was something a couple should achieve in life.

"I knew exactly how it should've looked on his face. After all, I had seen it before, only it never was directed at me," Ash went on.

Not sure what to say, Taylor decided to stay quiet instead.

"Anyway, I'm more than happy that you're back because no one could be my best friend but you. Hey, will you come to the game tomorrow? First game of the season, baby! You need to come back and be you because, honestly, you look terrible, honey." Ashley winked at her, and Taylor grinned. She wanted to go; she really did because she used to be one of those women who'd have died for football. Only that wasn't part of her life any longer. She had seen exactly one game after leaving and that had hurt too much.

"Listen, Ash, I'd love to go, but I won't take Tim to a

game where everyone's staring at me like I'm the dog with two heads," she explained ever so quietly, but Tim came over nonetheless.

"People missed you, and Tammy never took me to a game. Max always gets to go," he whined.

"Max?" Taylor echoed.

"The Rivers' boy. I mean Kelly and John's boy," Ashley explained, and Taylor combed a hand through her hair, wondering if she'd ever catch up.

"Exactly how many people of our group are married?"

"Almost all of them," Ash dutifully reported, and Taylor whistled.

"Nice. Then again … we've never been normal." She winked and then handed the check over, waiting for her cash.

"Yeah," Ash replied, counting out the money. "I'm gonna pick ya up at six. Wear somethin' normal." She eyed Taylor up and down, making her feel self-conscious.

"Can we leave, Tay?" Timmy asked, grabbing her light sweater. He had been more patient than she had expected.

"We're going," she promised, giving Ashley an apologetic smile while accepting the money Ash handed to her.

"Six, Collins," Ashley reminded her as the two turned away.

"Call me Michigan. It makes me feel better. I barely remember the high-school me," Taylor admonished over her shoulder.

"You got it, babe," Ash assured her, blowing her a kiss before waving her off.

"Can we please hurry with the rest?" Timmy asked as they stepped out on the street. "I want to be done soon and … Mason!" The boy jumped excitedly at Mason, strong arms catching him while Taylor's heart did a flip-flop.

"Hey, buddy! Hey, Michigan!" He winked at her, making her involuntarily smile.

"Look, there's Max!" Tim, barely back on the ground, ran off, and Taylor groaned. She'd have to talk to Kelly next while she wanted nothing more than to forget about the shopping and return straight home.

"Hey, Mason." She wanted to say so much more, but she got caught up in his stormy eyes, being thrown right back to senior year, when her crush on him had been the strongest. She noticed differences between now and then, though; his smile was more serious, his eyes less carefree, and his face more man than boy. He had a scar on his upper lip that hadn't been there before. She found herself almost reaching out, wanting to touch it, when something bumped into her side.

"Tay, can I stay at Max's until Sunday?" Tim wanted to know, another time pulling on her sweater.

"That's three nights! I don't think Max's mom will be

too happy with that," she protested, the prospect of being alone terrifying her. Too many ghosts haunted those walls.

"Oh, honey! Actually, having Tim around will gimme a break. Hey, Taylor! Mason?" Kelly joined them, another high school friend hugging her without prompting, and Taylor couldn't get around noticing that her behavior toward Mason was a lot less affectionate.

"I gotta go, Michigan. Keep that pretty head of yours up. Kelly?" He politely tipped the visor of his hat and then vanished inside the bank. Taylor watched Kelly look after the cowboy, thoughtfully shaking her head before focusing back on her.

"As I was saying, it's not a bother at all. Tamara always brought him over, so he even has clothes at our place to tide him over." She then smiled.

Taylor felt like cold water had doused her. Tammy surely had tried to get Tim out of the house so she could study for finals, or because their dad and the little boy were too much to handle for a twenty-one-year-old, yet Taylor was fine with having Timmy around.

"You know, Kelly, I'm not Tamara. I can handle my baby brother just fine, so no need to take him off my hands if that's what you're thinking. Should you, though, have offered because you know it'll make them happy, I might be okay with him staying that long. I do have conditions. First, it won't happen during school weeks anymore, and second, they have a sleepover at our place next." She forced herself to finish the words with a smile to take the edge off her words as she waited for Kelly's reaction.

Surprisingly, the other woman teared up, hugging her. "It's so good to have you back," Kelly claimed. "I'm gonna take the boys and see you at the game tomorrow. If someone can handle whatever life's throwing her way, it's you. Tim's excited to be at the game with you."

Taylor glared at her brother, reminding herself that everyone shared everything right away and without hesitation in a small town.

"I've been bullied into going." She grinned. "But I'm excited to go."

"How about before I drop them off Sunday, I grab lunch, and we hang out and talk? We've missed you here," Kelly emphasized, and Taylor found herself nodding.

"Sounds like a plan. Well, I have to go." It was true; Taylor was anxious to be back home and out of the town that had eyes on her. She didn't turn to check who it was this time.

"Bye, Taylor." Timmy hugged her, making her bend down so he could kiss her cheek.

"Bye, Tay," Kelly added, and Taylor waved before walking back to her truck. She nodded at a few people who greeted her. Once inside the cab, she started the engine, intent on finishing her errands so she could get back home as soon as possible.

five

Mason had a hard time not turning back to the window to see if Taylor was still there. Even though he was in a hurry, he wouldn't mind looking at her for just a few more moments. She looked better already; two weeks of countryside putting color in her cheeks, yet it was more than obvious how tense she'd been. There was no doubt she still felt out of place.

"She's back."

Mason blinked in surprise and utter disbelief. Those were the first words Ashley had spoken to him since they had broken up. For a second, he considered playing dumb, when in truth, he was super aware of the fact that Taylor was still outside the bank, but then he decided against it.

"Good for you. I know you missed her," he remarked, meaning it. He knew how much Ashley had longed for her best friend, especially in the last year ... even with all the conflicting emotions she had most likely felt.

"I didn't think we'd ever see that day. Honestly, not ever. And now, she was forced back here and..." Ash shook her head, not looking at him, but stared at a point over his shoulder to where he guessed Taylor was.

"I don't reckon anyone can force Taylor to do anything." He was sure of that.

"She's loyal to a fault, Mason. Always has been and you know that. As long as she thought her siblings were well taken care of, she stayed away. They talked every night, and Tammy and Tim went up there regularly. Now, she knew they needed her, and she returned. I wonder what she thought about the fact her bedroom was no longer," Ashley mused, and Mason cleared his throat, trying to avoid thinking about how Taylor had felt walking back into her personal hell.

"I think she's keeping her head held high. Being upset or even cryin' would've given her parents too much power over her," he commented while getting the cash he had planned on retrieving.

"True. I never thought about it that way," his ex-girlfriend stated, and he just nodded. "I'm takin' her to the game tomorrow. She's a little too city," she continued.

"She's still Taylor. She'll love every minute of the

game," he reassured her, more than just a little irritated by this conversation simply because they were having one.

Silence met his statement, and he looked up, finding Ashley studying him.

"I suppose you're right," she finally gave in, and for the first time in a long time, she had a hint of gentleness in her voice.

"I gotta go. Shift," he mumbled, no longer wanting to talk about Taylor or better yet, talking to *Ashley* about Taylor since said girl was the reason Ash now was his ex.

"Be careful," Ashley told him, and it almost sounded like it had back when their lives were entwined.

He gave her a weak smile and then left the bank.

"You know, Stiles, I hated what happened between you and Ash, but honestly, I … I think I get it now." He inwardly groaned as he realized that Kelly had obviously waited for him while the boys played catch a few steps away. While he would've preferred Taylor, he was glad that at least with Kelly, he'd be able to leave soon.

"I always wondered what I did to you, but figured it was because of Ash, and I'm glad I was right. I'm sorry I hurt your friend, and I love that she has friends as loyal as you are. It's what a girl needs. So if you could excuse me now? I gotta get to work." He passed her, and Kelly reached out, stopping him with her fingertips on his arm.

"I'm Taylor's friend, too," she remarked, and he blinked.

"Okay?" he stated slowly, not exactly sure what that had to do with anything. Unless she thought... "No, Kelly. No. I have a four-year-old to take care of, I work in shifts, she just returned, and I don't know anythin' about her and..." Why was he even justifying himself? There was no need to, and therefore, he stopped. He knew that Ashley, Taylor, and Kelly used to be close, but making him the pariah was still wrong. Plus, if he continued his sentence the way he had started it, he'd only confirm what everyone guessed. "I used to be in love with her, but that was more than a decade ago, Kelly. All Taylor needs right now is a bunch of friends who have her back no matter what," he finished instead. Then he told her a polite good-bye and moved away before she could say more.

In his truck, he sat and paused, wishing for a beer instead of having to work. He dialed his best friend, putting the phone on speaker while guiding the truck out onto the street toward Freedom.

"What's up, man?"

"I get off at six tomorrow and will be home by seven. I'm gonna get Becca to bed and ask Mom to watch over her. Do you feel like hanging out and having a few beers with me then?" Mason inquired, hearing Brad sigh like an old man who had to get up just to switch the TV channel.

"Taylor? Or Ash? Because you haven't called me up for a fun beer date in ... forever," Brad fussed, and Mason choked out a laugh.

"Come again? I do that a lot," he protested. "Like seven weeks ago?"

"You had just heard that Taylor would be coming back. You sat on the bed of your truck next to me and stared at the stars until deciding that most likely ya wouldn't be able to handle it," Brad admonished, and Mason couldn't even argue. "You've become too serious, man. How about you come to the game after your shift tomorrow?"

Mason thought for a moment. Taylor would be there, Ash had mentioned, and it would give him some time to watch her from afar. "Ash is takin' Taylor to the game," he muttered, hoping that Brad wouldn't try to take his suggestion back.

"Taylor told you?"

"Ashley told me." The sentence hung between them for a few seconds, and then Brad burst out laughing.

"Was she drunk or on drugs? Tied down and locked up? Delirious or half-asleep? That woman refuses to speak to you, and she would keep that up even if she were dyin'." He chuckled, and Mason actually found himself smiling.

"I ran into Ash after I ran into Michigan," he declared, still wondering what had made his ex break her vow of silence toward him.

"Ah ... assuming Michigan is Taylor, I see," Brad asserted. Now, wasn't that interesting?

"Oh, you see, huh?" Mason growled, wondering why

he was still standing among fog when everyone else seemed to be seeing as clear as day.

"Come on, Mase. You probably gave Taylor the puppy-dog eyes like you used to. For twelve years, you've been salivatin' after a girl, or better, the perfect picture you created of her in your mind. Havin' her back must be hard for Ash because, let's face it, you still want Taylor. You never got over her. Ashley probably thought you wasted your time on a dream, but then she probably realized that it didn't matter because she simply wasn't it."

"The whole town is talking about it like that, but..." He briefly closed his eyes before focusing back on the road. There was no 'but' really. He'd been in knots since the moment he had heard she'd be back, and then, when she had been in his truck and pointed out who she was ... his mind had gone blank. Holding her then, he felt like he could finally breathe again. "I still love her," he concluded.

"No, dude, you love what you thought you two could be," Brad injected, and Mason pinched the bridge of his nose.

"So what do you suggest then?" he wondered.

"Game. Beer. Get to know the new girl, the Michigan one, and see where it takes you. Maybe this time around, you'll have a real chance ... and you can get into the panties you've been admirin' for so long," Brad teased, and Mason could hear him grin, being glad that a comment like that had come at the end. There had been too much seriousness going on. He wouldn't deny, though, that he liked the plan.

"Game. Beer," he concurred before he hung up. He needed some good old country to soothe his soul before another brutal twenty-four-hour shift started. And what helped a broken heart better than having people serenade you with promises of forever, nights in a truck, and fires ignited by sparks of passion?

six

The house was quiet. So far, Taylor had tried to read, then turned on the TV to watch for a few seconds, before turning it off again and bathing the house in another round of silence. She couldn't sit still long enough to relax, instead pacing the living room. She felt watched with every turn, making her even more antsy.

Eventually, she stepped out onto the porch, her heart urging her to where she used to find solace. Shaking her head, her steps brought her back inside. She straightened everything in the living room, placing the pillows in a neat row and lining up the magazines on the side table. She brushed her hands across the throw-cover of the couch, then she went to the kitchen. Sadly, that was just as clean as the other room and just as suffocating. Finally, she reached for a lighter, passing the coat rack and grabbing Mason's jacket since it was the only security blanket she really had. Without thinking, she followed the urging of her heart.

The evening air was cool even though it was a summer's night, and usually, she would've paused to enjoy the clean air, but her ballerina-covered feet had no intention of lingering. She had the way burned into her mind, and with every step she took, a weight lifted off her shoulders. She crossed the little creek that had always marked the spot where her heart would start racing in anticipation. This time, it fluttered in anxiousness.

The old barn door still opened as easily as it always had, and she took a moment to let her eyes get used to the darkness. She moved forward into the barn, climbing the ladder she knew too well. Next to the last step was the oil lamp that sat exactly where she remembered it. She lit it with a flicker of her lighter, and then she looked around.

The couch she remembered still sat to her right, covered by a sheet, and against the wall across from her sat the desk in the same condition, hidden from her eyes by white linen. She walked over and tried the desk lamp, surprised when it flickered to life, adding to the oil lamp's golden glow.

Back when things had gotten too loud or too crazy, she had found refuge here. During her finals in high school, she had practically lived in that barn, needing to escape her parents.

With a deep breath, she carefully pulled the sheet from the desk, her heart aching as she realized it was in the exact same condition as the last time she had walked out of here. Emotions overwhelmed her as she spotted all the pictures still standing there. Only one was missing, but she couldn't pinpoint what had been on it. Even though this once had been created as 'Mason's cool hangout,' he had given her the chance to feel more at home by decorating it the way she wanted.

"I was wondering when you'd be back," a voice remarked behind her, and Taylor spun around.

"I'm sorry, Mrs. Stiles. I didn't mean to trespass," she mumbled, feeling sixteen all over again.

"Oh, please! This place belongs to you probably just as much as it belongs to my son. During the summer, some days I felt like I had six kids instead of one." Mason's mother laughed, and Taylor looked back at the pictures. Kelly, John, Brad, Ashley, Mason, and she had spent so much time up there; she couldn't place them with one exact memory. As it was, everyone was beaming, and Taylor definitely remembered. They had laughed so much up here that she thought they would make the bad of the world vanish.

"You always brought us your sweet tea. Mason hated sweet tea." She grinned.

"He knew you loved it," Mrs. Stiles replied, and Taylor crossed her arms in front of her body, feeling her fingertips brush up against the cuffs of Mason's jacket.

"I did," she admitted. His mom had always prepared it fresh, extra for them, and they all had pretended it was her way of telling them that she loved each and every one of them.

"Did? You no longer like sweet tea?"

Taylor hadn't had sweet tea in a very long time. In the big city, she had once tried it, but it never came close to what she remembered it to be, so she gave up on it.

"I stopped a lot of things when I was in Michigan and the city." She sighed, and Stella walked over to the covered sofa, sitting down on it.

"You know, all the time Mason and Ashley were a couple, I never saw her wear Mason's college jacket." The topic change made Taylor grit her teeth. She rubbed her chest as her heart did a few painful thuds. As much as Taylor tried to pretend differently, she was more than a little jealous that Ashley had been with him.

"He gave it to me when he drove me home," she explained. "Probably pity on his part."

"I kinda figured that you didn't steal it, sweetness," Mason's mother winked, chuckling quietly. "Sit, little Collins girl."

Taylor shook her head at that nickname, almost tearing up. It had always made her feel protected.

"You do realize I have a little sister, right?" Taylor teased, and Mason's mom lowered her eyes to her hands.

"I do. I realize, too, that though you changed a lot, some things never change," she commented. "Did you know that cowboys only fall in love once? Either they are lucky and will end up spending their life with that lady, or they'll forever hunt the feeling, never finding true happiness. Seems the same goes for cowgirls, don't you think?"

"Mrs. Stiles –"

"Call me Stella," Mason's mother insisted, and Taylor watched her for a few seconds.

"So this is it, huh? I'm really a grown-up if you offer me first names," she joked, not being able to sit. Instead, she paced the small room, pulling Mason's jacket closer around her body.

"Mason's still everythin' that brings you comfort, just like he was over a decade ago. I always thought you'd end up being my daughter-in-law, and even now, my heart soars knowing you're back." Stella got up and reached for a frame on the desk. "Mason always smiled widest when you were around," she continued, rendering Taylor speechless. She walked over to the window, glancing over at the old farmhouse.

The porch light was on, and it illuminated the well-kept wood. The house had always looked small from the barn, but Taylor knew the long hallway inside that led to a kitchen, a living room, the pantry, and a bathroom, then having stairs that brought you upstairs. Mason's room, an office, the Stiles' bedroom, and a bathroom had been found there. Now, she could see multi-colored lights spin in what used to be his sanctuary, and she guessed it was his daughter's new room.

"On nights when Mase is at work, Becca needs those lights. It's as if she feels him being out of the house then," Stella observed next to her, joining her at the window.

"She most likely knows the sounds of Mason's truck leaving the driveway," Taylor stated drily, and Stella laughed.

"That might be true, too. I like my version better." Stella winked and then touched Taylor's arm, drawing her attention. The other woman had gone serious. "Why are you here, honey?"

Taylor rested her hands on the windowsill, lowering her head. "Tim isn't home and Tammy's away at college. The house felt empty yet too crowded. I ... I haven't felt like myself in months and thought coming here would ease my mind," she answered truthfully and then took a few fortifying breaths.

"Did it work?"

Taylor thought for a moment. "Yes and no. Not the way I'd hoped, but everything's better than being in that house and being reminded of my parents' expectations at every turn."

Mason's mother smiled at that and then turned to her with a smirk. "Have you ever considered that it wasn't the place that brought you comfort, but the knowledge that Mason was close?"

While it most likely was the truth, Taylor had a protest on the tip of her tongue. In the end, she decided to stay quiet, though.

"Anyway, how are you supposed to feel like yourself when you look like an imposter?"

Taylor looked down at herself, Mason's jacket being the only thing that didn't mark her a city girl.

"Come with me," Stella demanded in her typical mom-voice, making Taylor feel cradled again.

She turned off the lamp and then capped the flame inside the oil lantern. For a second, she wondered if she'd be able to return after Stella had led her to wherever. But she figured she needed to face the music at some point, so going home really was the only right thing to do. Frankly, her heart sank at that thought.

Stella led her from the barn toward the house, letting Taylor enter first. As much as she had hung out in the barn, she'd barely ever been inside the actual home. It was similar to hers, with the hallway all but separating the house and leading straight to the back door, yet the kitchen at the end was on the wrong side.

The stairs to her right didn't allow for a look to that side, but Taylor couldn't help but wish for a chance to sneak around. As it was, the house had a warm, comforting feeling, and she remembered racing up the stairs on one or two occasions, coming in and running right up to help Mason carry some CDs or whatnot from there to the barn.

"He has never once given you the tour, has he?" Stella wondered from behind her, pulling Taylor from her pondering.

"I never asked, and he never offered, so no," she confessed, shrugging her shoulders.

"We have a laundry room through here," she pointed, gesturing toward a door to Taylor's left. "Pantry's right next to it. There is a room below the stairs now. It used to be part of the living room, but we made that a little smaller and turned the other room into a spare bedroom. It's where I stay. Mason would prefer if I'd stay upstairs, but no." She didn't elaborate, and Taylor knew better than to poke. "So next to the bedroom is the living room, and across from it the kitchen. Between the pantry and kitchen, there's a guest bathroom." They had slowly started walking down the hallway, and Taylor had to grin at the glittering circles that adorned the walls.

"Becca loves coloring, but stayin' inside the lines is hard for her ... and so is stayin' inside a coloring book." Stella sighed, and Taylor knelt in front of the lines. They were all about the same height, and she figured the least you could do was make it look as if there was a purpose.

63

"Do you have empty pictures frames?" Stella looked at her, puzzled, but then went in search for some while Taylor's smile slipped from her lips.

If she had reacted differently that night at the bus station, would those be the drawings of her daughter? Would they be a family here, she and Mason? Was it possible to find true love at sixteen?

"A penny for your thoughts," Stella offered from somewhere behind her, and Taylor wiped away a stray tear that had escaped her eyes. She cleared her throat, looking at the floor.

"Did you find one?"

Stella leaned against the wall next to her, handing her some frames while guarding her expression.

"I didn't know which size you needed," she mumbled, her voice full of emotions that Taylor didn't want to analyze. Instead, she picked the frames she liked best, peeling away the foil and taking off the back covers. Then she held up two, framing Becca's drawings.

"In the morning, you should put those up. It'll make her feel special. Besides that, you can tell her to color only inside it. Otherwise, the frames won't fit any longer. It might not work, but it's worth a try," she explained, standing up while yawning.

"You know, my original plan was to give you one of Mason's lumberjack shirts, but now ... how about you stay for the night? We don't have a guestroom anymore, but since Mason's at work, I'm sure he won't mind you stayin' in his bed. Especially not if you won't find any sleep at home."

Involuntarily, Taylor's eyes darted up to the ceiling as if she'd be able to look straight into his bedroom. Her heart beat erratically at the thought of staying where he most likely was unguarded – and uncovered.

"I can't," she whispered even though she wanted nothing more. "It's his bed, and he's not here for us to –"

"Shut up, girl," Stella fussed softly. "He won't be home until tomorrow evenin', so let's get you to bed."

They never had finished the tour, but that didn't matter. She followed Mason's mother upstairs, reaching for the door she knew to be his, but Stella stilled her hand on the handle, making Taylor remember the colorful lights.

"That's Becca's room now, and Mason moved into the master bedroom," Stella explained. She paused in front of a hallway closet to get a towel for her, and then she led her to the bedroom, turning on the light.

It was a simple room. A king-size bed was pushed against the right side of the wall across from the window, then there were two dark dressers and anoak wood floor. Glitter paintings covered the walls, and as much as Taylor tried, she couldn't find one free spot. It couldn't be more obvious that Mason was devoted to his daughter. Next to her stood a dark chair, a gray hoodie hanging over the back while neatly folded black sweatpants laid on the seat.

Stella walked over to one dresser while Taylor brushed her fingertips over Mason's navy blue bedding, almost smiling as she realized that, like her, he didn't seem to make his bed.

"Here, it's one of his shirts. Just put it next to the washing machine in the morning." Stella handed over the towel and the shirt, before turning on the lamp above the bed.

"Thank you," Taylor whispered.

Stella nodded and then gave her a soft smile. "Thank *you* for havin' breakfast with me tomorrow." She winked, leaving the room afterward. Taylor crossed the floor aimlessly, just taking a moment to breathe. Here, in his space, she felt surprisingly close to Mason, realizing that Stella had been right about the person, not the place, bringing her comfort.

She went into the bathroom, finding his toiletries lined up next to the sink. She hesitated a moment and then reached out to sniff his cologne and his aftershave before mentally scolding herself for no longer being a teen. She rested her hand left and right of the sink, taking her own appearance in as she watched herself in the mirror. She had gained a little weight, but her cheeks were still hollow and her skin too pale due to the lack of sleep.

There was a knock on the doorframe, and Stella held out a spare toothbrush for her. "I thought you might need this. I swear, now, I'm really out of your hair. Good night." She left again, and Taylor proceeded to brush her teeth, smiling to herself. It didn't matter that she and Mason weren't a couple, but something as mundane as brushing your teeth seemed infinitely intimate if you shared a sink with a person. Shaking her head at her useless thoughts, she brushed out her hair and then walked back into the bedroom. She didn't think twice; the t-shirt lay forgotten in the bathroom as she went for Mason's hoodie. It fell mid-thigh and smelled like heaven. She crawled under the sheets, switched off the lamp, and was asleep almost the second her head hit the pillow.

seven

Mason parked his truck, yawning. It was two a.m., and he wanted nothing more than crawl into his bed, have a good few hours of sleep, and then have breakfast with his daughter. His mind was on everything and nothing. He couldn't even muster the strength to open the car door. While he was glad that he'd been sent home early, it still was gruesome up until that point.

The porch light flickered to life, and his mom stepped out in her morning gown. Forcing himself to move, he finally left his truck, wishing for a split second that someone else entirely was waiting for him at home.

"Are you okay, son?" his mother asked, hugging him tightly as soon as he was within reach. He shook his head, pushing past Stella to kick off his boots next to the door.

"We had to cut a couple out of a wreck. They were barely conscious, but they held onto each other. They didn't once let go. The woman died on the table during surgery. It was sad, yet incredibly beautiful to see how much they loved each other. It's..." He shook his head, trailing off.

"Mason..."

"Mom, please, I just want to –"

"Son," she interrupted him, and he gave her a look over his shoulder.

"Breakfast. I promise we'll talk at breakfast," he assured her and then walked up the stairs to check on his daughter. He opened Becca's door and watched her sleep for a few seconds before walking over to kiss her forehead. He left the room and closed the door behind him to find his mother had followed him up the stairs.

"Listen, Mason, you can't..." his mother started, but stopped as he pushed into his bedroom and his eyes fell on the sleeping figure in his bed. A person wearing his hoodie. "I gave her a shirt," his mother mumbled, but he barely heard anything over the thrumming in his ears.

"Her who?" he questioned, but it was unnecessary. His heart already knew, doing triple speed.

Taylor Collins was sleeping in his bed.

He moved forward involuntarily, walking around the bed and smiling in response to the curve that shaped her lips.

"I'll wait downstairs," his mother whispered from the doorway, but he barely noticed it. Carefully, making sure not to disturb her, he sat down on the bed. She was beautiful, but that wasn't anything new in his eyes. What was new was how young she looked being that utterly unguarded.

She shifted, pushing her left hand under her cheek while reaching out with the other. He couldn't resist, entwining his fingers with her. He brushed his thumb over her knuckles, wondering if the rest of her body would be as warm as her hand.

"Not creepy at all," he suddenly heard, his heart beating in his throat while he hastily tried to untangle their hands. It turned out to be a feat since she only held onto him stronger the more he pulled. "Hey, Stiles," she then added, and in the half-light, he saw she'd opened her eyes. "You were not supposed to be here, but now, I'm leaving!" She sat up and then swung her legs over the side of the bed, sitting in front of him. Her legs were long and slender, covered in cream-colored skin that ended somewhere beneath his hoodie. He wasn't sure that piece of clothing had ever looked as good on him as it did on her.

His mind finally caught up when she almost reached the door. He jumped up and threw her over his shoulder, surprised that she toned down her squeal until it was barely there. "Put me down, Stiles," she demanded, the humor evident in her voice. He gently placed her on the bed.

"I just did." *Move away from her, Mason, just move away from her*, he told himself, but instead, he stayed where he was, leaned over her and keeping her from sleep.

"It's your bed," she protested, sitting up again, only to now be eye-level with him.

"You were here first," he pointed out and then kissed her forehead. She closed her eyes, falling back into the pillows. It didn't take long, and she was asleep again, breathing regularly. He got up from the bed and closed her ... his door quietly. Downstairs, he found his mom, and she held a bottle out to him. Oh yes, he definitely needed a beer now.

"What happened?" He saw absolutely no scenario in which she showed up there, begging for a bed.

"I found her in the barn, and trust me, she looked ready to sleep on the sofa up there. I didn't expect you back and ... why in the world did that couple throw you so bad that you returned early?"

"The helicopter is broken and needed repairing. With no helicopter, there was no need for a pilot," he explained absent-mindedly.

"How long are you off?"

Mason turned to look at his mom. "Until next shift," he mumbled and then took a long swig out of his bottle. Rolling it between his palms, he sighed. "I wanna go up there and crawl in bed with her. I let her go once, and it won't happen again. But somethin's off with her just showing up in our barn like that. I wish —"

"That she'd tell you? Did you ask her how she's coping? How she feels being back?" his mom prompted, and he shook his head.

"I haven't been around her long enough to talk to her, and..." Hearing steps on the stairs, he shut up.

"I was sure you fell back asleep," he stated, his voice unnaturally hoarse as his eyes fell on her bare legs once again.

"I heard the hum of your voice, and while it's soothing, it made me realize that now *you'd* have to sleep on the sofa," she explained and then knotted her fingers together, clearly nervous.

"I'm off to bed," his mother announced, and Mason barely nodded, his eyes focused on the woman who held all his hopes and dreams in the palm of her hand and didn't even know it.

"Night, Stella," Taylor said quietly, and Mason felt how his mother kissed his cheek before leaving them alone. Taylor pulled the sleeves of his hoodie longer until they covered half her hands, reminding him of too many times she had done exactly that with his clothes.

"I'm okay with sleeping on the sofa," he finally muttered, and she shook her head, pointing over her shoulder in the direction of her house.

"I should get home and sleep there," she exclaimed, not moving, though.

"You should get to bed, you mean," he corrected.

"I don't have a ..." She seemingly caught herself and stopped whatever she had intended to say. It made Mason curious.

"You don't have a what?" he cross-examined her, stepping so close to her that she had to look up.

"I don't have any intention of occupying your bed. That's what I meant to say," she told him, and it couldn't be more obvious that she was lying.

"What is it, Michigan?" he inquired, noticing how breakable she looked as she fidgeted with his sleeve cuffs.

"Nothing," she whispered, stepping away. As much as she had changed, some things hadn't changed at all.

———

Taylor should've refused the bed when Stella had offered, but the thought of a full night of sleep had been too tempting. Now, though, looking at her beautiful nightmare, she regretted the decision to stay. Watching him, she could barely suppress the need to reach out and brush her finger over his stubble-covered jaw. To her dismay – and utter happiness – he followed her every step she took back, reaching for her wrist. The frayed endings of the cuffs looked pale against his sun-darkened skin as his eyes lowered, his thumb brushing her pulse through the material.

"Here," he whispered, drawing her eyes to his hands.

"What?" she wanted to know, and he raised her wrist until her eyes widened. A tiny hole, a spark burn, grazed the top of the cuff just where the sleeve started. She had caused it.

Her eyes snapped to his face, not wanting to miss the smallest emotion. "You kept that hoodie? The Halloween one?" That night felt as if it had happened in another life. Tay still felt the way his heart had beat beneath her palm.

"It's my favorite." He winked, and she arched a brow. He watched her as if waiting for something, and then he hid his emotions, lowering his eyes. Finally, Taylor realized that she was more or less naked under the hoodie.

Blushing, she tugged the gray cotton down. A yawn threatened to escape her, and he reached out, tugging on a blonde strand hanging down her shoulder.

"I need to get a shirt from my room, but then you can go back to sleep," he urged, wanting to pass her, but she reached for his hand, knowing that she craved the skin-to-skin contact.

"Would you mind driving me back?" she wanted to know, continuing to hold his hand even while she had his attention.

"No problem," he reassured her, "right after breakfast." He walked up the stairs, and Taylor followed, shaking her head as she realized that he was just as stubborn as ever.

eight

Taylor had forgotten how noisy football games were – or how much she had always loved them.

"It just wasn't the same without you," Ash called over the cheering, and Taylor wanted to reply when she spotted Mason and Brad, the former watching them while the latter screamed something in the direction of the field.

Focusing on the girl next to her, she smiled tight-lipped. "I'm happy to be back," she forced out.

"You don't look happy. Hey, how do you like the idea of loosenin' up, girl?" Ash wondered just as another young woman walked up to them, carrying a bottle of OJ and a can of soda. She instantly held it out to Taylor.

"It's vodka-o," she whispered conspiratorially, and

Taylor realized that she yearned for a few sips and as many hours of oblivion.

"You little vixen, you. Smuggling alcohol into a high school football game? Tsk," Ash scolded and then grinned. Taylor could see the girl grow with the hidden praise. Only then did the newcomer's eyes fall on Tay again and widen.

"You're Taylor Collins! I'm Sybil, but people call me Syb." The nickname sounded like 'zip,' and Taylor wondered if her friends had secretly been trying to hint at something. "You're the reason Ash and Mason aren't a couple any longer," she went on in a bubbly voice. "She's still talking to you. It's so cool. Real best friends."

"Shut up, Sybil," Ashley chided, all color having left her friend's face. "You don't know what you're talking about. Clearly, you've sampled the vodka way too much." The grin she forced on her lips looked fake while Taylor had to sit.

"But you said that Taylor was like the third person between you –"

"Cut it, darlin'," Ashley enforced, then looked apologetically at Taylor. "It's bullshit, and she knows it. You weren't even there. Look, Michigan..."

Taylor *did* look at her former best friend, knowing that Sybil hadn't made that up. Tay reached blindly for the bottle that looked so much like juice but burned all the way down her throat until it hit her empty stomach.

"Sit. Explain," she ordered after taking a few pulls

from the plastic bottle, refusing to allow her eyes to stray to Mason.

Ashley dutifully planted next to her, wringing her hands together in her lap. "You left a gaping hole, Tay. I felt the need to replace you. I tried bein' as smart, or as pretty as you, as funny, and as compassionate as you, but I wasn't a very good *you*. The group broke apart, and it hurt my heart. That group was my life, and I never realized that basically you were the glue keepin' us together. Everyone always loved talking to you, and they wanted your advice or your shoulder to cry on if need be. I wasn't much of a person without you. And then Mason came in and asked me out, reminding me of you and my happy years growing up. I was stupid, really, but I had faked being you for so long that I couldn't discern between what I wanted and what you wanted, or better, what I thought you wanted. Mason had always been on that list, and he was pretty damn amazin'. It wasn't until I had a child I didn't want with a man I didn't love the way I thought I did that I realized my mistake." Ashley's eyes went to where Mason sat, and while he wasn't looking at them this time around, Taylor saw the regret shining brightly in her eyes. "I up and left, hoping to find the real me, you know? Ashley. Turns out, I never was more me than when I was friends with you." While the last sentence might have been the truth, Taylor couldn't believe the rest. It sounded like one huge pile of bullshit to her, and she couldn't figure out why Ash would make up a lie like that. She took another swig of the bottle, her head spinning. She wasn't sure if it was Ashley's confession or the alcohol, though.

"You never expected me to be anythin' but a shoulder to cry on," her friend continued quietly. "I could be me all I wanted. I never needed to fake anythin' with you, and it's why I loved you like a sister back then, still love you the same, and missed you like hell."

"Why, then, would Syb expect you to be mad at me? And don't lie about not loving Mason because I can see it in your eyes and on your face." Her words were slightly slurred, and it surprised her.

"Fuck, Sybil, how much vodka is in that juice?" Ash inquired, clearly having noticed as well.

"The real question is how much juice is in that vodka," Taylor injected, smiling smugly. This was becoming kind of funny. She rose from her seat, the world tilting only slightly on its axis. She needed food before she interrogated Ashley more.

"Michigan, where the hell do you think you're goin?" Ashley called, but Tay just needed a minute. Making her way down, she took a second to breathe. There, under the stands, she felt thrown back in time. She couldn't stop a smile from forming as she remembered all the times she had snuck away to meet Eric here, exchanging hot kisses and stolen moments.

"Hey, you left me alone, Taylor. You were gone, and

I couldn't even hate you because we've all seen how things went downhill between you and your parents, but still, you left us, too. I was lonely. Do I still love Mason? Maybe, but not the way you think. He was one of my closest friends, and what I do miss is bein' part of a group. In fact, I miss bein' part of *our* group. I miss the way Mason made me feel as if I was the center of his universe, even when it wasn't true. He does everythin' with a single-minded determination we both know only too well. Problem was, Mason was never mine, and I technically knew that when I started dating him. I wanted things to work so badly that I was blind. Seriously, things were crazy for a while, and I hated Mason because seeing him hurt like hell. But I was to blame, too. God, Tay, what do you wanna hear?"

She had no idea, but it sure wasn't more half-truth and lies.

"You know, if you ever feel like you can tell me the truth, all of it, come and find me. We used to be best friends, and I think I deserve more than what you're dishing out. I know I've been gone for a while, but you were always like a sister to me." To her dismay, tears sprang to her eyes.

"Since when do sisters leave each other? Which horrible person would leave their siblings to fend for themselves?" Ashley cried, and Taylor felt the words hit her like a punch to her stomach. She had left her sister and her friends because she hadn't seen any other way.

"Yeah, who does that?" She raised the bottle back to her lips, food forgotten. She was more than glad that Timothy wasn't home. She had no idea if there'd be more alcohol at the house, but for now, she had little over half of the vodka bottle left, and she sure had enough determination to find more. Stepping back, she bit her lip. Shaking her head and deciding that this talk was over, she turned away.

"Tay! Wait! That wasn't what I meant. I ... Michigan! Where the hell you think you're going?"

"Back home, where this horrible person should've been for the last ten years," she called over her shoulder.

"It's two miles, you stubborn woman! You're halfway drunk and ... just let me tell the others that I'll take you home and will be back later," Ashley pleaded.

"Thank you, but no thank you. I need to clear my thoughts ... head. The thing on my shoulder." She tipped her temple, grinning widely. "You know, to air it all out or whatever you call it. You get the drift." She kept walking, gritting her teeth against the bitter burn of the alcohol. She couldn't remember the last time any of that poison had crossed her lips. That was unless Mason's alcohol-induced kiss counted.

God, Mason...

She longed to be close to him and have him promise her that things would be okay.

Then again, maybe she should just help her best

friend get back her own life.

"What the hell, Sybil?"

"How was I supposed to know that she had no idea?"

Even over the cheering, Mason recognized the angry voices.

"Your ex is pissed again," Brad commented, wolfing down his third hotdog.

"Yes, but I swear, I didn't do it this time." Mason laughed, ready to ignore the turmoil until Taylor's name reached his ears.

"Taylor was gone for over a decade, and you think she knew? I didn't tell her, and you can bet Mason didn't have the balls to, either. I'm gonna leave and drive her tipsy city ass home," Ash announced.

"Where is she?" Mason blurted out the question before realizing that he had gotten to his feet at Taylor's absence. Ashley paled, but then relief crossed her face.

"She walked home. Or she intends to walk home. She took the bottle and left. I'm … Jesus." Ashley was upset, and no matter what had happened between them, she was still a friend. Meeting her on the stairs, he took his time to hug her, promising her that he'd make it all right.

"Sybil mentioned that I should hate her for … coming between us. I couldn't tell her the truth, and she took one look at me, knowing I lied. Then I might have uttered some words that made her feel as if she had neglected her family. I need to go and find her, but –"

"I'm gonna get her. If she's drunk, it's better if you two calm down first." He brushed her cheek before walking down the stands.

Half drunk and on foot, Taylor couldn't have gotten far. And really, just a few minutes later, he spotted her.

Stopping the truck at the side of the road, he called out her name. At the sound of his voice, she spun around, dropping the nearly empty bottle. Her cheeks were tear-stained, yet his heart squeezed at her beauty.

"Ashley sssssstill loves you," she slurred, holding out her hand as if there'd be a wall that could steady her. Mason swallowed at those words. Despite the fact that things were strained enough between him and Ashley, Taylor would stay away from him now no matter what if she thought she could make things work again for him and her former best friend.

"Get in the car, Michigan," he mumbled and then went to her side to pick up the discarded plastic bottle. He took one sniff and was shocked that Taylor was still walking upright. The juice in that mix was probably only for color purposes.

"I'm not getting in an enclosed space with you. Especially not if it's all tight and closed."

"That's the definition of enclosed space, Michigan," he stated absent-mindedly as his heart cracked wildly inside his chest. Alcohol made people honest, and the woman in front of him was no exception. Pinching the bridge of his nose, he sighed. "And why would that be anyway?"

"Because I'm lonely and a woman?"

What. The. Fuck? Mason almost burst with anger until she uttered her next words. "I might end up begging you for cuddles and whatnot." The vulnerability in her voice nearly did him in.

"Oh, Michigan," he groaned, dumping the single bottle in the back of his truck before walking after the blonde who stubbornly moved forward.

"Don't 'Michigan' me!"

"What in the world do you want me to call you then?" he wondered, throwing up his arms in frustration.

Again, she turned back to him, her wet cheeks illuminated by his headlights. It was obvious that she had an answer on the tip of her tongue, making him wonder what tipsy Taylor would confess, but then she shook her head and lowered her eyes, continuing her walk.

"Stop or I'll throw you over my shoulder," he threatened, and she shrugged a slim shoulder, clearly not worried in any way.

"Whatever," she slurred. He cursed under his breath and marched back to his truck, only to drive and park twenty feet ahead of Taylor. She was furiously wiping at her cheeks, trying to stop the tears from falling, but she obviously failed miserably.

"What do you want me to call you?" he asked again, grabbing her wrists to keep her from running away.

"Nothing you should be calling me. Nothing I should want you to call me if I want to mend things with my best friend." She lowered her arms as new tears spilled down her cheeks. "I want you to call me things I didn't think I'd still want you to call me after more than a decade. How about you call me what you've always called me? Huh? Baby?" She didn't make sense, switching gears and emotions like others switched TV channels, but he couldn't resist.

"You want me to call you babe?" he inquired, surprised to realize that his voice had gone hoarse. Her lips parted in a small 'o' and then she swallowed.

"No."

He more guessed the word than he had heard it, but there was no heat, no conviction behind it.

"Get in the car," he ordered as she was swaying on her feet. "Jesus Christ, how did you get so drunk?"

She breathed deeply, but it didn't seem to help. Her every step got sloppier, and she still refused to get in the car with him. "Nope, not getting in that truck with you and those beefy arms and tight chest and..." Her eyes widened, and she slapped her hands over her mouth, suppressing a giggle before she sobered again. "Mason, don't you see? You and I together never worked. It wasn't meant to be back then, and I can't ... Ah!" The tirade of her words ended as he placed an arm beneath her knee and the other behind her back before picking her up princess style. He would've thrown her over her shoulder like he threatened before if he wasn't worried about her throwing up.

"You talk too much when you're drunk," he grunted, smirking over the compliments she had paid him. "You think my arms are beefy?"

She linked her hands behind his neck, her breath tickling his skin as she giggled and then probed his biceps. "You work out." She said it as if that was all the confirmation he needed, and then she leaned her head against his shoulder, taking a deep breath.

"You really are ... Thank you." She was soft and warm against him, and he had a hard time letting go as he placed her in his passenger seat.

"Can I finally take you home?" He waited for her to nod before moving around the hood of the truck, remembering the water bottle still in his gym bag. Rummaging through the backseat until he was successful in finding it, he handed the plastic bottle over. She grabbed it with a subdued thanks, emptying almost half of it as if he had told her to. He was even tempted to beg her to drink more but decided against it.

Eventually parking in front of her house, he couldn't help but think how looming and lonely it looked. Taylor seemed to struggle to get away from him, and he hurried to follow her to the door.

"I can get to sleep by myself," she promised, pressing her hands flat against his chest, trying to push him away. In the back of his mind appeared the same nagging feeling he'd had the night before.

"I'm not gonna leave you until I've tucked you into bed," he insisted, and she seemed to crumble before him, looking suddenly terrible small and breakable. "Taylor Collins," he growled, holding out his hand. She wordlessly dropped her keys into his palm, leaning against the wall next to the door, resting her head back. He unlocked her door, and she touched his arm, clearly seeing it as a last attempt.

"Drop it, Mase," she pleaded weakly, but that only spurred him on more. He went inside and up the stairs, having been in the Collins' house often because he had helped Tammy a lot. He opened door after door, looking for Taylor's room and therefore her secret. He found Timothy's room first, then Tamara's and across from that an office with barely any room to maneuver inside. The last door he opened led him into a room, stale air greeting him. Obviously, no one had been in that one for quite a while.

He found Taylor exactly where he had left her, but to his surprise, she was a lot more sober than when he had left her.

"Where do you sleep, Michigan?"

nine

Taylor wished for another juice bottle. Spiked, that was. The realization that Mason would discover the skeleton in her closet had sobered her up much more than she had wished for.

"Where. Do. You. Sleep?" His low growl accentuated every word, making her turn away from his scrutinizing gaze. She drowned her hands in her hair in frustration, wanting to hide behind the long strands instead of facing reality.

"In my parents' old bedroom." God, she was a pathetic liar, and even worse when being tipsy. The deaf would've recognized the false truth, had any been around. She couldn't look at Mason, too ashamed of her weakness.

His anger was almost palpable as he stepped so close, his chest brushed against her back. "Why do you lie to me?" His breath ruffled her hair as he gritted those words out.

She breathed deeply a few times, and then closed her eyes, shoulders slumping in defeat.

"You've always been so strong, Mase, and I thought you thought enough wrong with me that I had no intention of adding more. What woman comes home and then can't enter her parents' bedroom to clean it out? Worse, who'd be ready to admit to something like that? They sold everything that once was mine, and all pictures that included their eldest daughter are gone. Then they left my siblings to fend for themselves. I should hate them." She paused, collecting her thoughts and trying to regain control of her shaking voice. "The minute I touch that doorknob, I feel ten years old. I've been sleeping on the sofa since got I here, making sure I'm up before Tammy and Timmy are. Now, the strong, independent girl you always considered not grown up enough proved you right. She turned into a woman who's still not facing her fears," she spat as anger suddenly overtook her. Taylor moved away from him. She snuck around her siblings because she couldn't be the adult she should be, and self-hatred burned strongly through her veins.

Mason froze in his spot, his eyes turning almost black as storm clouds rolled in to hide the full moon.

"I never ... Taylor, how in the world..." His eyes finally lifted without him ever finishing his sentence. Shaking his head, he locked her front door before walking around the front of his truck, nodding toward the passenger seat. He was upset; she could tell by the taut lines on his face, and it made her embarrassment vanish.

"Mason," she whispered as she stepped in front of him instead of getting into her assigned seat.

"Get in the truck." His voice was trembling, and he couldn't even look at her.

She shook her head in refusal. She hated nothing more than making him mad. It had been that way back when, but now, it cut even deeper. "I'm sorry," she whispered, touching his arm. He still didn't look at her but focused on something above her head. To break his anger, she went on her tiptoes and threw her arms around his neck, squeezing him tight. He stiffened under her hands but didn't reciprocate her hug. "I'm sorry," she repeated against the crook of his neck. "I'm sorry for whatever I said wrong. I'm sorry." Suddenly, he gathered her into his arms, holding her warm and tight in a cocoon that made her feel safer than anything else ever could.

"I never thought anything was wrong with you, Taylor, not once. And knowing you thought... What kind of bad friend am I if I made you feel you lacked anything?" he pondered, rubbing his hands gently across her back.

She kissed his shoulder out of impulse, and then

rested her head back against it. "You were always one of my best friends, always there when I needed you, so don't worry or feel bad," she pleaded, brushing her fingers through the hair at the back of his neck.

"And because of that, you move your butt into my truck and sleep in my bed."

She stepped back, hugging herself, her fingertips digging into her upper arms as she told herself to stop standing around and go back inside. "Thank you for the offer, but I need to get up early. I need to run to our suppliers and maybe find some new ones. While Timmy's out, I figured I'd use the day," she pointed out. He groaned, but she didn't let him speak. "No, Mason, I –"

She was interrupted as yet again he picked her up and dumped her unceremoniously in his front seat, careful not to hit her head.

"You'll come along now, and tomorrow, we'll worry about the rest." He walked back around his truck and then got in next to her.

"I cannot go in there, Stiles. Everything reminds me of their disapproval. Besides, what if..." She let the thought go unfinished as Mason placed his hand on her knee, squeezing it gently.

"They are not coming back anytime soon, Tay. You need to own this house," he remarked, his eyes never once leaving the road. She started chewing her lip, contemplating her next words.

"I failed at owning that house because it's exactly what I didn't want, and still, I'm back. I mean I'm a ship sailing an ocean at night without a compass or a star to guide me. I don't know what to do or say." It was the harsh truth. She put on a brave face and pretended to be fine, hoping that one day she'd wake up, and it just would be true.

"For what it's worth, you're doing pretty well," he replied, his voice hushed.

"Of course." It had been too long since Taylor had a friend who'd look at her and instantly know that her world was in ruins. He took a few deep breaths, clearly trying to find the right things to say, only to realize there wasn't anything left to say.

His house was dark as they arrived, and he checked his watch. It seemed as if his mom wasn't home.

"Who's watching Becca?" Taylor wondered, and he rubbed his chin before pinching the bridge of his nose.

"I was supposed to. Since I was home yesterday already, Mom figured I could enjoy the evening with my daughter, giving her a Saturday off. I was supposed to be here thirty minutes ago. She probably thought I'd be in any minute, so she left and texted me that Bec was in bed." He exhaled slowly, taking out his cell, cursing low. "I shouldn't ignore my phone. Fuck."

He hit the wheel, appearing exhausted. Clearing his throat then, he raised his phone to his ear. In the silence of the truck, she could hear the dial tone.

She decided to give him some privacy, getting out of the truck and breathing in some fresh air, sobering more by the minute.

A few moments later, Mason came out of the truck as well, cursing like a sailor. "Fuck. Damn it all to hell. Shit. Fuck." He tore on his beautiful dark strands, and she moved closer, pulling his hands away from his hair to keep him from mutilating himself.

"What's wrong?"

"I gotta work, and Becca is alone. I can't get hold of my mom and..." *She doesn't have a mother who can take care of her.* She heard the words ring loud and clear even though he hadn't said them, but instead, he looked down at the hands she had yet to let go. Taylor felt his thumbs brush the back of her hands, making her swallow as well as realize that it was highly inappropriate if she followed through with her plan of making things right between Ash and him.

"I can take care of her. I'd feel better that way, too." She stepped away, hugging her elbows tightly to her body.

"She doesn't know you and you've had quite a bit to drink," he pointed out.

"Cross my heart, she will be absolutely fine. Besides, I feel a lot more sober than I did before we got out at my house," she whispered, knowing that it was true.

"She doesn't take well to female strangers. The

psychologist says..."

"She's four. She doesn't need a psychologist; she needs a woman she can trust to be there for her without it being her grandmother. Until you and Ash get back together, let me show her that not everyone is out to leave her." She saw Mason flinch, and it solidified her resolve to bring those two back together.

Indecision twisted his features until he groaned and pressed a hard kiss to her cheek, handing her the house keys then. "I'll be back as soon as I can," he promised, and she nodded.

He didn't even let her inside, so she decided to walk over before he left, tapping his window. He opened it, and she gave him a smile, leaning in ever so slightly.

"I don't have any clothes."

"Mi closet es su closet." He grinned. She smiled quickly but then got serious.

"Drive safely, Mason," she pleaded, stepping back before doing something stupid like, let's say, touching his cheek or kissing his lips.

He nodded and then put the truck in gear, leaving. Something rumbled somewhere far away, and Taylor looked up. In the distance, she could see lightning split the sky. With any luck, it would move past without them catching the worst of it.

Finally, she walked inside, changing into the clothes she had worn the night before. She added the sweatpants from the chair, then ventured into the kitchen and filled a glass of water. Her mind was crowded, her thoughts bouncing from Mason to Ash to her parents and back to Mason.

Every minute she spent around him made her realize more and more that she still could fall deeper in love with him. She probably never had stopped being in love with him in the first place, and it cut deep to register how much time had passed. She should've stayed that night he had asked her to. Maybe they'd be a couple now. How often could you wonder if life would've been different then? For her? For Tammy and Tim? For Mason?

Thunder and a yelp jolted her out of her thoughts. She placed the water glass on the counter as the pitter-patter of tiny bare feet across wooden floors reached her ears. It took a moment, and Mason's daughter appeared in the room, freezing as she spotted Taylor.

"Who are you?" the little girl instantly asked while Taylor had to swallow at how much she looked like her father. Her dark hair curled around her chubby cheeks, her blue eyes wide with fear and curiosity. The last time Tay had been there, she'd left before the girl had left her bedroom in search of her father.

"I'm a friend of your dad's," Tay answered, kneeling down to the same height as Rebecca. "He told me that I could come here, and you'd protect me from the storm."

"You 'fraid of storm?"

Taylor nodded solemnly. "Totally. My name's Tay. What's yours?"

His daughter poked her own chest right where her heart was. "Becca, Mason's daughter," she introduced herself, making Taylor smirk. Clearly, Stella introduced her granddaughter more often than her father did.

"Hey there. So will you protect me?" The girl nodded, and Taylor pointed up the stairs just as another loud crash from outside shook the house. Rain started pelting against the windows, giving the house an eerie feeling.

Becca trembled like a leaf in the wind by now, and Taylor cupped her cheek. "Wanna go back to bed?"

Rebecca swallowed; clearly not keen on the idea of going back to her room. "Well," she started, chewing her lower lip.

"Since your daddy's at work, how about you and I share his bed so you can protect me?" Becca started beaming before her face fell.

"Daddy says no strangers," she mumbled, and Taylor laughed.

"I'm in your house and in your dad's clothes. I'm not a stranger," she promised, finishing exactly as another lightning bolt lit up the room, making the tiny human squeak.

"I'll protect you," Becca stated hastily, jumping into her arms. Tay pressed her little body against her own, carrying her upstairs after turning off the kitchen light.

"Don't tell Dad I'm scared," Becca pleaded against her shoulder, and Taylor inched her feet toward the bed, not yet familiar with the layout of his bedroom, then she placed the child underneath the sheets and crawled in next to her.

"Thank you," Mason's daughter muttered sleepily as Taylor pulled her close.

"Always," she assured her, kissing the dark hair while cuddling the girl to sleep.

———————

Mason finally returned home at the first light of dawn. The storm had taken its toll on him and the team, grounding them longer than he had hoped. He was exhausted, but he was too wound up to think about sleep while his body was ready to drop. His mind was playing the pictures of last night on repeat. Blood, so much blood, he was sure he'd be washing it off his hands for the next decade to come. He needed a smile to replace those memories and quick.

As always, his first way led him into his daughter's room, only to find her bed empty. His heart rate accelerated in worry. Becca hated storms and had a tendency to hide in the weirdest places. Searching, he went to all the possible and impossible hideouts, drawing a blank. Panic had him in its tight grip. Where the hell was his daughter?

Realizing that he had left Taylor here as well, he

decided to ask her. Gently pushing open the door to his room, he stalked into the room with every intention of waking her when he spotted his little girl curled up next to Taylor, Becca's little hands wrapped around Taylor's arm.

He took out his phone and couldn't resist snapping a picture. Then he moved back to the door, his clothes brushing the doorframe with a light rustle.

"Dad?" a small voice asked, and he looked back at her.

"Hey, sweetie. Wanna go back to your bed?" he wanted to know, waiting.

"I stay with Tay now," she decided almost instantly, wiggling closer to the woman in question. Mason nodded, returning to the sofa downstairs. He grabbed a book, figuring it would keep him awake until Becca didn't want to sleep anymore. It couldn't be more than an hour or two since she never slept in and the sun was already coming up on the horizon.

Only when giggling woke him did he noticed that he had fallen asleep after all.

"Look, Daddy. I made Tay's hair!" Without a care in the world, Becca jumped into his lap, making him drop the book to catch her instead.

Following his daughter, Taylor came in, wearing his hoodie and sweatpants, showcasing a weird mix of ponytail and bird's nest on her head, presenting his daughter's non-existing design talent.

"Your daughter will be a great hairstylist one day," Taylor promised, and as quick as Becca had been in his lap, she was gone again, jumping into Taylor's waiting arms. Only then did Mason registered the carefully crafted French braid on his daughter's head. He got up, wondering why he had never thought it possible to fall even harder for Taylor, when in truth, watching her dance around the living room with his baby girl in her arms made it clear that so far what he had felt wasn't anything compared to what he could feel.

ten

"Ash, I know we haven't been on the best of terms, but this is about Tay, so please don't hang up!" Calling his ex hadn't been easy, but he had a plan, and he couldn't do it alone. A few guys were already there for the hard work, but he needed a few women who knew Taylor.

"Mason..."

"She's sleepin' on the sofa, not touching her parents' bedroom. She's out all day today. I wanna make that room hers. How is she ever going to feel like it's home if she's a visitor in her own house?"

After a long pause, Ashley finally answered. "I cannot imagine how she must feel. Everythin's the same, yet nothing is as she knew it. If she sees us together, Mase, your chances will be slimmer and slimmer. She wants to make it right for us and..."

"That's not what this is about," he interrupted, knowing that he needed to sit down with Taylor, even if it was merely to stop the wild matchmaking idea.

"What do you need me to do?" she asked in an exasperated breath.

"Blankets, sheets, decorations. Take it out of my account," he explained and then listened with relief as she promised that she knew exactly what he needed. They hung up, and he turned back to Taylor's front door, patting around the frame until he found the spare key. Entering the house, he took Brad and his two brothers upstairs. The furniture needed to go before they got some color on the walls. Ashley arrived promptly as they had stored away the last box of memorabilia in the barn. Brad had covered the wooden floor before they started to color the wall around the door in a light shade of yellow, which worked well with the light violet they'd put on the wall left of the door. The paint would complement the white walk-in closet there. Next wall, yellow again, and then, the last one violet. The lady at the store had assured him that the choice of color was exactly right for a young woman's bedroom. Now, he wondered if maybe they weren't the right ones for *this* woman.

"She won't be able to sleep in here today," Brad reported, and Mason nodded He had guessed that much, but at least they'd be able to make her imagine how it would look done and dry.

"Let's go and get the dresser, night tables, and bed." With two trucks, they'd easily be able to bring it all back without much trouble. Downstairs, they found Ashley draping a lavender quilt over the back of the sofa. It fit the color upstairs perfectly.

"You know, that's always been Taylor's favorite shade of purple. I remember back when we were in high school, she used to tell me how she imagined her bedroom if only she had the money. I don't think she knows who she is any longer, so let's remind her of who she was," Ashley whispered as if she guessed his thoughts.

"We're going to get the furniture," he explained after clearing his throat.

"I'm coming. You and I need to talk, honey," she decided, and Mason groaned, throwing a glance back it his best friend.

"Meet you at Woody's," he hinted, waiting for Brad to move.

The name of the shop was misleading, since it had everything from guns to food, and just his luck, exactly the pieces he imagined for Tay's bedroom.

"If you ain't there in thirty, I'll call the cops," Brad stated under his breath, clearly worried that Ash planned to hurt him.

"You're a true friend." Mason laughed, locking up the

house as everyone was out, and then he held the truck door open for Ash.

"Still a gentleman," she commented, and though the drive was less than thirty minutes, it sure would take forever.

"When Taylor said that you still have my pictures in the truck, I thought she was lyin'." Ashley touched their smiling faces, and Mason couldn't deny that he wanted them to go back to not talking to each other. There was just so much he didn't want to face, that he couldn't explain or apologize for, and no man liked facing that.

"I don't think she could've made somethin' like that up," he persisted, starting the truck, wondering if turning on the music would make her shut up.

"Why, Mason? You never looked at me the way you think you did, so why?"

"I wanted to remind myself not to make the same mistake again." He heard her swallow, but figured since they were being honest, he might as well continue. "Being with you was amazin' and fun, but you're right, I was in it for the wrong reasons. I hurt you so much, and I never want to do that to anyone ever again. I thought I had to move on after Taylor left, but come on, move on from what? The day you told me you were pregnant, I swore to myself that I was going to do everythin' to make you happy. No matter what, you deserved more." They both had been lying to themselves, but that wasn't going to happen again. "We should've never dated, but while you weren't Taylor, you reminded me of her so much."

"I thought I wanted it all with you, but when I held your daughter in my arms, I realized that I've never wanted kids. I didn't want the responsibility. It was always Collins' dream, and you know, people in town expected me to have that child with you, but I adopted *her* dreams because I had no idea who I was and what I wanted." Mason had to swallow, slowing down the car. He knew Ash wasn't done talking yet. "Mase, the moment we got together, we started livin' a lie. A ghost pushed us forward, and as much as I hate to admit it, I love you. I always have, only not the way I thought. I told you before that I could see it in your eyes when you looked at her, but it pales compared to the way she smiles when she sees you. I'll give you a month max, and then I sit her down and make your confession for you."

Mason parked the truck, staring at Woody's. "Well, we can't get around that anyway because unless you tell her why we aren't a couple any longer, she won't..." She wouldn't do what? Move forward? Give in? "Last night, she basically told me she has a crush on me." He smirked, and Ash turned toward him in her seat.

"She always had a loose tongue when tipsy." His ex laughed.

He had smiled before his good mood vanished again. "If, just if Taylor and I get where I hope we'll get, it'll be hell for you. She wants to be your friend, and we'll be spending time together. How can she make it right for both of us?"

"We used to be friends before, and I miss it," she admitted.

"Before I hurt you."

"I wasn't an angel, Mason. I left you with a child … an infant, really," she appeased him, and it gave Mason the opening he had longed for months ago.

"Do you want to see her? Do you sometimes miss her?"

Instead of answering, Ash got out of the truck, and Mason followed her example. "She's not my daughter, Mase. When I see her, I don't get all tingly and warm. She's a little girl, adorable, but that's all. I think I'm broken because no baby makes me want to reach out and touch it. They are annoying, and she's no exception. She was always calmest when you held her. And in case you didn't notice, she looks nothin' like me. She deserves a mother who adores her, and we both know we wish for the same girl to be just that."

Mason decided to stay quiet. How could he ever expect Taylor to raise a child that wasn't her own, and even worse, her best friend's baby?

"Let's get movin'. You and your sweetheart –"

"I'm not, Brad, and you can stop bein' an ass. Mase and I are friends again," she snapped at his best friend.

"The ex-dragon and you are friends again? You don't want Taylor anymore?" Brad asked in a hushed voice.

"We aren't back together, you idiot! But we now should get movin', or Taylor will be home before anyone manages anything!" With that, Ashley marched ahead, making the guys smile.

————

Taylor was exhausted. In addition to the late night with Mason's daughter, followed by an early morning, she had spent the day talking to a million people, debating and comparing prices, yet she felt as if she hadn't gotten anywhere. Fact: She had no idea what good prices were. Second fact: Her heart wasn't in it. Last fact: She had still gotten discounts and promises of further reductions if only she could get regular food orders in. The cows needed fodder and so did the horses. Taylor was thinking about adding a few chickens; just enough so she wouldn't have to buy eggs. She didn't know if that could work, but she would think about it. Maybe. In the future.

Fact: Taylor hated farming and everything to do with it, but maybe she could do animals and all that shebang.

She stayed in her parents' truck a little while longer, not too keen on spending a night on the sofa after spending two in Mason's bed. She hoped she'd be too exhausted to ponder that long and simply fall asleep.

Her front door opened, and Mason and Ash came out, startling her. Only then did she notice the two cars parked by the side of her house.

Pushing open the door, she scrambled out of the truck.

"Hey Collins," Ashley greeted her, kissing her cheek before wishing her well and leaving.

"Mason, what the hell have you two been doing in my house?" She shook with anger as her very imaginative brain provided a vivid picture of those two naked on her sofa. She didn't mind the sofa part. Instead, awareness slammed into her at the thought of those two back together. She absolutely wouldn't be okay with it, no matter how hard she tried to convince herself otherwise.

"Michigan, it's not what ya think," he promised, and she stalked past him into the house. The smell of fresh paint assaulted her nose, and she spun around as her head caught up with her jolting heart.

"Oh, God. You didn't clear out the bedroom. Promise me you didn't!" Fury made her tremble as tears of frustration jumped to her eyes. "Tell me you fucked her on the kitchen counter instead," she demanded, and shock warred on his features as he was trying on and dismissing words.

"Why are you so angry, Taylor? We wanted to do you a favor! I —"

"You had no right. Those were my demons to fight. Now, I'll never win! Plus you spent money I don't have! I'm indebted to you when I tried by damnedest to never be indebted to anyone again." She was screaming and didn't care.

"Look at you, Taylor Collins! You slept on a sofa, you talk about demons, and you know, I actually know that you have no control whatsoever over your life or your farm. You have a cattle farm and not once have you been in the barn, or you'd realize they are still out in the paddocks. You have three farm hands, and you don't even know it. How do I know? Because Tamara called me and asked me to check on them." He grabbed her upper arms. "You don't take the lead in your life, so someone else had to do it. Hate me all you want, but I'm not going to let you waste away!"

They were both breathing hard, and Taylor felt Mason's angry breath on her lips. They had moved so close to one another, they literally shared the same air. She knew that no one else could cause feelings as deep in her as he did, even if the current one was total fury.

"Get out, Mason Stiles! Right now!"

"And then what, Taylor? You bury yourself in here, pretending you're all right? I'm your friend, Tay, and even if you left us all, ready to forget us, we didn't forget you."

"Forget you?" she spat, venom in her voice. She hadn't once been able to forget him or her friends while she was up there. "*Forget you?* I didn't leave to *forget* you! I just wanted to be me and couldn't do that here. I..."

"You never once looked back. Did you call us? Contact us? Come to visit? No! And still, we're here, aren't we? Even though you don't deserve it, we..." His own words seem to register, but Taylor had heard enough, feeling all the color drain from her cheeks.

"I'm glad you all showed up on my doorstep and called me ten times a day. A phone works both ways, you know?" She pushed at his chest, wanting him out of the house so she could cry in peace.

He looked devastated even though he didn't move one inch. "Tay, I'm so sorry. I didn't mean that. I'm sorry!" Mason looked as pale as she felt, but she didn't care. She could barely see straight through the curtain of tears.

"Don't even try. I don't want to see you again. Ever. But then, it shouldn't be a problem since I don't deserve it anyway, right?" With all the strength she could muster, she forced him out onto the porch and slammed the door in his face.

That had escalated quickly, and while Taylor rationally knew that they both had been angry, saying things they didn't mean, she was terribly hurt.

She rested her head back against the door, feeling it vibrate with Mason's frustrated punch.

"I'm sorry, Michigan! Please, just let me back in! Just listen," he begged, and she could almost feel his heat through the door, only the wood separating them.

"I think I listened enough. Just go, Mason," she ordered, pleaded, and whispered, all wrapped in a few words when all she wanted to say was 'Hold me, Mason, make the pain go away.' "You were right. I never looked back. I never wanted to come back, either. This town... held nothing I ever wanted, so why return?" She made her voice sounds strong, but her whole body shuddered as she bit her index finger not to sob out loud.

There was a long pause on the other side of the door, and then she heard two short raps of his knuckles against the wood before his truck started and he was gone.

Taylor sank to the floor, crying so hard she couldn't catch her breath, and only after pain invaded every inch of her body did the river of tears cease to flow.

eleven

Hours later, Taylor had dragged her tired body to the sofa, finding sleep despite the restlessness of her mind. Only the buzzing of her phone interrupted her nightmare-riddled rest.

"Collins?" Loud country music burst through the speaker until the noise was muffled.

"Taylor?" Instantly, Tay was wide-awake, clutching her cell to her ear.

"Ashley? What's wrong?"

"Pick up Mason. He's drunk off his ass, and it's your fault." Her friend was mad, and it was no wonder really.

"Ash, I'm sorry. Whatever he said I said was a heat-of-the-moment thing and..."

"Get your skinny ass over to *Dooley's* and pick him up. You two need to stop hurting everyone, including each other."

"Give me ten," Taylor replied and then was about to hang up, but Ashley's voice stopped her.

"You need at least twenty. Drive careful, babe."

Careful wasn't the problem; worry was. She couldn't imagine the damage her words had done to all her fragile friendship flowers here.

The moment she stopped her parents' truck, Ashley stepped out with Mason.

"There she is, the woman with the ice heart. Prettiest girl around and no one can touch her," he slurred.

"Oh, big boy, you had better shut up," Ashley suggested, and Mason pushed her away, stumbling over to Taylor and, with surprising precision, drew her in to kiss her like there was no tomorrow.

Like once before, he tasted of cheap whiskey and undeniably Mason. Taylor knew only that she was kissing him back when his stubble tickled her palm.

"Fuck, Mason, again?" she cursed, gently pushing away from him.

"Wait, what? Again?" Ash repeated, and Taylor nodded.

"Before I left, he found me at the bus station." Her eyes went from her former best friend to the guy who held her heart. His gray eyes focused on her as if he tried hard to remember that moment. "He was totally drunk and basically ordered me to stay after kissing me."

"Even then I wasn't good enough. Never good enough for the perfect Taylor Collins," Mason interrupted, and Taylor closed her eyes, rubbing them in mental exhaustion.

"Time to take him home, Michigan. And tomorrow evenin', I'll come by with a bucket of ice cream, and we'll talk." Ash gave her a hard stare that she then softened with a smile.

"I'll heat the chocolate sauce," Taylor promised and was relieved when Ashley hugged her.

"Everyone loves Taylor! Everyone loves Ashley! No one loves Mason. Can I get an 'oh' everyone?" Mason called, but except for raised eyebrows, Mason didn't get anything.

Taylor opened the passenger door for him, and he climbed clumsily into the seat, instantly turning toward her as she climbed in the driver's side. "Damn, you're beautiful," he said, and she rested her head against the steering wheel, noticing that she had to fight a smile.

"Shut up, Mason. You can't think straight. I sure hope your mom's home," she stated, and he reached out, brushing his thumb across her chin.

"I can never think straight when you're around. I can't say the right words, or do the right things where it concerns you." His tone was subdued, thoughtful, and

Taylor wanted to believe that they could have a decent talk, but he was barely holding himself upright as it was, so silence was it for now. He made it hard, though, since his fingertips still danced across her skin, making their way from her chin to her cheek and then the back of her neck.

"My little ice queen," he whispered, and she swallowed, glad as they eventually came to a standstill in front of his house.

Getting him up the porch steps and into the house was such a feat that they woke Stella, and she came out of her room, throwing on a blue morning robe.

"Mother! Look who came into our home! The beautiful, ice-cold Taylor. The woman without a warm heart." He was giving Taylor whiplash, and she didn't like it one bit.

Maneuvering him into the kitchen, she sat him down and filled a glass with water for him.

"There, Mason. I'm out before you say even more things I won't ever be able to forget or get over."

"What's wrong with me, Taylor? Everyone gets a piece of you, yet none for me. I guess I wasn't shiny enough back then, and I'm only a country boy now that the city girl is somethin' better."

"Mason Stiles, shut your mouth," his mother ordered, a warning clear in her voice, but Taylor was frozen to the spot.

113

"Why, Mother? Taylor doesn't care. She never did. Taylor only loves herself." He rested his arms on the table and then lowered his forehead to them. "Taylor Collins can't love the right guy because the wrong guys don't threaten her independence," he yawned and then it had taken less than thirty seconds before he was snoring.

"I don't know what to say," Stella muttered in disbelief, but Taylor waved her off.

"It's not your fault, Stella. I'm..." She couldn't speak, because she didn't know what she was going to say. "When he wakes up, tell him his money will be back in his account by tomorrow. Tell him I apologize for what I said earlier to him. Everything but the part about never wanting to see him again." She took one last look at the only guy who could ever truly break her. She left the house, running past her car and the stables toward the barn, but once she had the handle on the door, she figured she had to let go of all of it, even if it was the only sanctuary she'd ever had.

———

Mason woke with a strain in his neck and an ache in his back as a cup of coffee was slammed down on the table next to his head. The noise almost made his skull explode. Why in the world was he at the table and not in his bed? His memory had a huge black hole, making him miss part of the night before. He remembered going to *Dooley's* to get a drink and talk to someone, and only now, he reminded himself that this was never a good idea.

"I see you're alive," his mother commented, and he lifted his head.

"Alive is different, but at least I'm awake," he replied and then noticed that his mother was glaring at him. "How did I get home?" he wondered, and she shrugged carelessly.

"The ice queen brought you home," she snarled, and Mason furrowed his brow. What the hell was that all about? His mother waited, but he clearly couldn't remember.

"Spill it," he demanded.

"It what you called Taylor before basically implyin' she was a whore. A heartless one at that," she explained, and Mason felt as if a truck had run him over.

"What?" His voice was small.

"Son, I think you need to have a coffee, brush your teeth, change, and then go over there. I don't know what's going on, but the two of you seem pretty broken right now. Whatever damage you did, you should try to contain it."

He got up, his headache replaced by regret. "Why did you let me talk?" he growled, and she rolled her shoulder in a shrug. He knew it wasn't his mother's fault, but he needed someone to blame.

"She told me to tell you that she's sorry for all she said … except the part about never wanting to see you again."

He had known that Taylor hadn't meant any of the words she had said, yet he had gone to look for oblivion.

115

"Fuck," he cursed and then hurried up the stairs, getting ready in record time before stepping outside and noticing that, of course, his truck wasn't in its usual spot. Not debating long, he turned toward the barn and followed the small path that led to the Collins' property. Dew still covered the ground, and fog rose from the fields. He knew Taylor would be outside. She always had loved mornings because they offered her peace. And indeed, she was sitting on the porch steps, a steaming mug of coffee cradled in her palms. He watched her for a few moments, seeing her wipe away a tear. She cleared her throat and took a sip of her coffee as he forced himself to step forward. He knew if he waited any longer, he'd most likely turn away instead of talking to her.

"Tay ... Taylor." He had to clear his throat twice in order to make his words heard, and her eyes snapped to him. She couldn't hide the pain in them even though she almost instantly focused on the ground again. He licked his lips, wondering where best to start. How do you apologize for something you didn't even remember?

"I can't..." She got up, and Mason knew that he should say something, but his mind was blank. He wanted to pull her into his arms and tell her how sorry he was, but somehow, he was missing the right words.

They looked at each other, and he knew that for this issue to be solved, someone needed to speak. Instead, it appeared as if they tried to remember each other because

116

this was going to be the last time they saw the other one.

"Remember I told you about this first kiss after high school? You said he was lucky because if he wanted to, he'd get a chance to do it right the second time around." Queasiness threatened to overcome him as a dark premonition worked its way up his spine. He almost wished she wouldn't continue. "Well, how many chances does a person need to get it right?" Her voice was breaking, and he shook his head, willing her to stop. "Well, I'll tell you. I know three times is a charm, but you aren't getting a third chance, Mason Stiles! Especially not since I'm such a terrible person in your mind." She paused as if deciding it wasn't worth it while tears rained down her cheeks.

What the hell had he said? And why weren't words coming out of his mouth?

"For weeks after that kiss, I thought and prayed that you'd remember, and you'd come and find me, or at least call me, trying to convince me I made a mistake in leaving. It never happened. And then twelve years later, *you,* of all people, find me walking down the street. I slide into the seat next to you, and all I can think is how I wish that we could have a do over, and I'd agree to stay with you, while all you think about is how I consider myself better than anyone else is. I look at you and wish I could touch you and be touched by you when all you think is that I'm selfish and not able to love anyone." She placed the mug down on the banister and then spread her arms as if showing him all he had lost. "A lot of the things you said yesterday afternoon were true, except that I never looked back. I missed you most of all, but coming back without any hope wasn't in my plan. But all you said last night ... God, Mason, what lies have I told myself about us? About the way you look at me even though I thought you were in love with Ash? I was ready to make it right for you two, but instead of being with her, you were with me. What do you think ... You know, it doesn't matter. This ice queen is done hurting you. I'm sorry for everything you think I should be sorry for."

He was talking too damn much when drunk and not enough when sober. Taylor turned away, and he leaped the three steps up her porch in one.

"Wait, Taylor! Listen up, you nerve wracking woman!" He grabbed her, twisting her around and making her back hit the wall of the house. "You drive me crazy. You always did because when I see you, my whole body goes into overdrive. I can't think straight, and clearly, when I'm drunk, I can do so even less. Fuck, Taylor, I don't know what I said, but I was clearly and obviously fully out of line, yet while my tongue was loosened up, I still didn't manage to say the damn words I should've." He drowned his hands in his dark strands, holding onto them until it almost hurt. As long as he had no idea what he had said to put so much pain and self-hatred in those beautiful hazel eyes, he couldn't say the words that were on the tip of his tongue because she wouldn't believe them.

He wanted to kiss the ever-loving hell out of her, but after two drunk kisses, she deserved more than a most likely painful and angry meeting of lips.

"There's somethin' you and I have been doing wrong ever since you came back, Michigan," he then stated, and she looked at him, her eyes wide and tear-filled. "We thought we could pick up where we left off, but we can't because nothin's the same. While it doesn't change where my heart is at, it sure changes the way I'm gonna go about this. That is after I make last night up to you. Just one more thing, Taylor Collins. You're my girl, and if you don't believe me, ask Ash why she broke up with me – the real reason. I'm done hurtin' you, too, Tay. I'll only make you happy from now on. I promise." He framed her face and pressed a kiss to her forehead before leaving the porch, not looking back.

twelve

Mason had been right about Taylor and the farm, so while he still haunted her thoughts, she figured it was time to move forward. Her steps led her toward the stables, and Mason had been spot-on. They were empty. While it wasn't exactly late in the season, she should make sure they'd be brought in soon. She knew, too, that they used to have horses, but for the last months, she couldn't see any in the books. Taylor had simply assumed it was a mistake, but clearly, it had been the truth. She had no idea what happened to them but sure intended to find out. It as well made her wonder how they dealt with the cows since trucks could do only do so much and getting cows together didn't work with them.

There was no sign of horses in the stables, either, and frankly, it made her long for one just so she could take a ride and clear her head.

She walked along the wooden doors, looking for hay, crawling up the storage space, too, but there was nothing. While the cows didn't need it during the summer, horses would've needed it. She really didn't have any on this stupid farm.

"First thing to be rectified," she whispered to herself.

"What's that, boss?" She jumped, turning toward the cowboy who now stood in the stables with her.

"Don't call me boss. I haven't been very bossy." She laughed, walking over to the guy she had never seen before. He was your typical cowboy: jeans, flannel shirt, boots, and a cowboy hat. When she came closer, she noticed a scar on his eyebrow and a slightly crooked nose, but it took nothing away from his handsome looks. Blond hair and blue eyes completed him, but while he was beautiful, his classical good looks did nothing for her.

"I'm Daniel," he introduced himself, and she shook his hand. "You have a strong grip. I like that." He grinned, and she winked.

"Country girl, despite what they say. Honestly, though, up in Michigan, I learned that it makes a hell of a difference to the men you're doing business with, so I know how to shake hands. I'm Taylor Collins," she gave back.

"Heard a lot about ya, lady." He nodded, and she groaned.

"Whatever they say, less than half is true, I'm sure. At least, I think so." She shrugged. "And I was talking about horses. I think we need some again," she explained, deciding to finally deal with her farm.

"Your horses are at the Stiles' farm," he reported, and she wondered if there was anything Mason *hadn't* done for her family.

She pursed her lips. "Well, let's get them back. I like taking care of horses, and it'll give me something to do besides the books. So, next up, I need to find out what's missing, what needs to be done, and what we need to plan money for." She arched a brow in question, and he rubbed the back of his neck.

"I sure hope you have some time, lady," he stated, and Taylor sighed.

"Let's get started. Timmy is getting back by lunch, but until then, I'm all yours," she promised.

"Best sentence I've heard all morning." He flirted with her! While Taylor felt flattered, she decided to let him down easy.

"Charming, but there's work to do, and while I have no doubt you do your job perfectly, I've been slacking at mine. I really need a rundown on all that's been happening."

He lowered his eyes, silent laughter on his lips. "Got

it. Let's go and start with the barn then," he suggested, and she nodded. His tone was no less warm but much more businesslike.

They entered the huge space, and Taylor spotted the hay. Clearly, the horses had been relocated since she had left and no longer stayed in the stables but were usually in the barn.

"There's somethin' classical about horses in a barn, so your father thought it was a better place for them. I actually agree," Daniel told her, and she nodded. The stalls had been built big enough so each animal would be able to lie down. She counted four and liked that. It was a nice number and something they sure could handle.

"Equipment?"

He pointed at a closed door in the back of the barn. "Still there. Mase picked them up with one of his own, so everythin's still in place. It might need some cleanin' and some wipin' down, but other than that, you should be fine. I do have to tell you, though, that your horse is no longer among them."

She had figured as much, but it still hurt.

"It was old, very old. Just couldn't get up anymore. It was for the best." She breathed a sigh of relief, wondering if he'd been able to read her that well or if Tammy had mentioned how she'd feel.

"Well, I guess I shouldn't have been surprised." She laughed through the tears that had come to her eyes.

"Your father bought you a new one. I know it's not my place, and I should probably not comment on it, but your father loved you. He just loved your mother more, I think. After she was gone, he was a different man."

"Damn, how long have you been working on the farm?" she asked, trying to rein in her emotions.

"I came the summer after you left. It was the first summer I worked here. I came back the summer after that and eventually was here longer. After he had left, Tammy hired me full time because she figured..." He stopped, another time rubbing the back of his neck. "So we need more hay if we get the horses back."

She didn't mind the topic change. She couldn't believe that her little sister had known her so well.

"I owned a business when I was away, and I had ten employees. I should be able to handle this here," she whispered, and he turned back to her after having started to walk toward the cattle paddocks.

"It was somethin' you loved, not somethin' you had to do. It'll take some time, but trust me, you'll come around. I'll make it easy for ya," he promised with a wink, and Taylor couldn't help but feel better.

"No doubt." She grinned, and then fell into step next to him, making a mental note to pick an especially thankful card for him for Christmas.

After everything was done, Taylor went into the house and jotted down everything she'd need to take care of, and then she dialed her sister.

"Collins?"

"Collins, too," she replied, and Tammy started squealing. The girl sounded much better than the last time Taylor had heard her. "Sounds like you have a great roommate and a lot of fun?"

Tammy giggled and whispered something toward a person who seemingly was in the room with her. Taylor kicked off her shoes and looked up the stairs, wondering if she should go and check out the room Mason had created for her. In her anger, she had refused to go in there, but now, she was curious.

"So checked out the farm yet?" Tammy finally asked.

"Just finished a list with Daniel. He's really nice. And smart around the farm."

"And handy. He knows how to repair stuff. And he's easy on the eyes," Tammy stated, making Taylor giggle.

"He is," she agreed, placing her hand on the door to what was now her room.

"While we're talkin' about bein' easy on the eyes ... how is Mason?"

Taylor turned her back to the door, sinking to the floor. "I don't know. I had a few fights with him."

"Wow, a few? One wasn't enough, huh?" her sister inquired, and Taylor paused for a long moment.

"It's either fighting or staring at each other. I don't know what to do. I can't look at him without being hurt and angry, lonely and feeling like a failure. He cleaned out Mom and Dad's old room," she whispered.

"Someone had to. I couldn't," Tammy confessed, and Taylor breathed a laugh.

"Neither could I."

"How does it look?"

"I don't know."

"Well, go and look, and tell me all about it," Tammy ordered softly, and Taylor got up, opening the door. The room was beautiful, and while she still needed to push the furniture back against the wall, it was all she could have ever wished for and more. He even had a single, long-stemmed rose placed next to the bed, only now it looked somewhat sad. Taylor went over and took it from the nightstand.

"Perfect, isn't it?" Tammy wanted to know in a hushed voice.

"Yes," Taylor brought out.

"You worry about the money, don't you?"

"I worry about the future, Tammy, and wonder if maybe all those years I never really knew him."

There was a long silence on the other end, and then her sister finally sighed. "What the hell did he say?" Taylor sat down on her new bed, wondering where she should start. "Just start somewhere and we'll take it from there," Tammy prompted as if she had asked that out loud.

Taylor laughed and then fell in the tale of Mason and

her, part ... whatever. She already had lost count and didn't really care.

thirteen

A week after seeing Taylor last, Mason spent another sleepless night wandering the house as if he was its personal ghost. Lightning suddenly lit up the room, closely followed by thunder and screaming upstairs. Becca's door flew open, and he met his daughter on the top of the stairs. The girl had her pink PJs on and a black sweater in her hand.

"Taylor!" The cry went through Mason's bones, and Becca didn't stop repeating the name, even after Mason had picked her up.

"What's going on?" His mother came up the stairs, clutching her morning robe closed in front of her chest. Talking over the little girl seemed nearly impossible, so

Mason simply shrugged in answer.

"Tay's scared! Need to 'tect Tay!"

He sighed, and instead of leaving the house, he went into his daughter's bedroom. She started kicking her small legs, screaming even louder, if that was possible. Mason's head threatened to split open with the noise.

He checked the clock on the little girl's nightstand. It was one a.m.; an impossible time to bring someone to the house of the girl you loved yet turned against you.

"Taylor hates storms!" Becca was protesting more and more, tears falling rapidly.

"Maybe you should take her over," Stella suggested. "You want to see her, Mase, and this is the perfect excuse."

Yes, Mason was dying to see her, but she was angry enough without him showing up in the middle of the night. The problem was that the girl in his arms was wailing more and more, no matter how often he shushed and whispered to her. Nothing helped, not even offering chocolates. He assumed that the thunder rattling the windows didn't exactly help, either. Hesitating just a few seconds longer, he finally grabbed the car keys his mother offered.

Becca instantly calmed down with nothing but small sobs coming from her. She still winced each time she heard thunder, but she'd stopped screaming.

"You don't need to be scared, baby," he reasoned, but she just looked at him, her face tear-stained.

"Tay is scared. I'm worried for Tay," Becca admonished him, and he took a deep breath. With each mile he got closer to the Collins' farm, his heart beat louder until it was all but drowning out the noise from the rain. He parked as close to the porch as he could, then he grabbed his daughter and ran for the front door. He hesitated, but a warm light spilled through the milk glass in the wood, and that made the decision for him.

He knocked; knowing that while a person downstairs would definitely hear it, he knew it wouldn't necessarily wake up anyone else who was asleep in the house. It took only a few seconds until Taylor pulled the door open. She was wrapped in a blanket. God, Mason's heart ached. He wanted to hold her so bad, but he had to tell himself not to reach out.

"Tay! I'm a 'tect you!" The moment Becca had spotted Taylor, she threw her little body forward, and Michigan instantly reached out, taking the girl from him.

"A thunderstorm came, and she didn't stop cryin' until I promised to bring her over so she could protect you."

Footsteps echoed from the stairs, and Timothy appeared with a baseball bat raised and ready to be used. "Everything okay, Taylor?" he inquired, and Mason felt pride swell in his chest. The little guy was ready to protect his sister, even though she was older, and he most likely wouldn't ever stand a chance.

"It's Mason and Becca," Taylor whispered gently. "Go back to bed."

Timmy came closer, lowering the bat yet shooting daggers at Mason with his ice-cold stare. Fury dripped from every pore of the boy's body, and it caught Mason off guard. He'd always gotten along well with the Collins-boy.

"If you came here to make her cry again, you can leave right now, buddy!"

Mason's eyes flew to Taylor's face, but she looked as shocked as he felt.

"Tim!" she reprimanded, but he just squared his shoulders, trying to look bigger, more intimidating.

"I hear how you cry yourself to sleep each night, Tay, and I hear you and Ash say his name whenever she's here. I'm not dumb, you know?" her brother pointed out, and while Mason was glad that Taylor and Ashley were mending their friendship, he hated that it happened at his expense.

Anger reared its ugly head. "What?"

Instead of reacting to him, Taylor knelt and placed Becca on her own two feet. "Timmy, can you take Becca to my bed? I'll be right up," she promised, and though reluctant, Timmy gripped Rebecca's hand and led her up the stairs.

Finally, Taylor turned to him again, and Mason was curious for that explanation. "You asked me to go to Ashley for the whole story, Mason, and I did. Despite what you might think, it's emotional and long. I think it's the first time Ash really worked through her own issues," she then explained. She hugged her elbows close, grasping them so tight her knuckles turned white.

"It wasn't supposed to make you cry. It was supposed to enlighten you," he growled, and she nodded, her skin pale.

"I realized how much you two have been lying to each other and yourselves. How in the world could you have let it get that far?" She shook her head.

He didn't know. "We were lost," he rasped out, and she took a deep breath. It couldn't be more clear that despite him almost saying the 'l-word' and the statement that she was his, they weren't any closer to being a couple. She was hurt and still mad at him.

"Why are you cryin' yourself to sleep, Taylor?" he then wanted to know, noticing how her lower lip trembled slightly until she bit it softly.

Slowly, as if worrying that he'd bite, she reached out and cupped his cheek. Mason instantly turned into her touch until she all but ripped out his heart.

"I used to be in love with you for a very long time, Mason," she whispered, and his head started spinning. "You were right the other day. You and I aren't who we used to be," she went on and then pulled her hand away from his face, closing it into a fist as if she tried to hold into something that could not be held.

132

Mason shook his head, panic seizing every cell in his body. "But that ... I mean..."

She stopped him, raising her hand with her palm facing him.

"You were right, Mason," she repeated.

"You're still mad at me. I get it, but –"

"We're okay, Mase. Besides, that bedroom is a dream. Thank you. It's perfect." He had noticed that his money was back in his account, plus a little something that supposedly had been for his hard work. He didn't want the money. He just wanted her to be happy.

"Taylor..."

"Everything's okay between us," she promised another time.

Shit was okay between them, but his daughter's call for Taylor reminded him that it was the middle of the night.

"I'm turning a year older next Saturday. If things are okay with us, you'll come, right?" Even before she answered, the 'no' was clear on her face. He didn't want to hear it, so he shook his head and then took his eyes off her face. "Forget it. Stella's gonna drive her to pre-school. I'm gonna be at work. Just have her ready by –"

"I can drive her, Mason. It's pre-school. They have clothes for her there," she interrupted. Needing to get away as soon as possible, he just nodded in agreement. God, he needed to leave so he could piece himself back together. Glancing at the ground, he quickly checked for blood. Somehow, he worried that he was bleeding all over the porch from where she had torn his heart out.

Nope, everything was clear because she knew how not to leave a trace.

"Bye, Michigan," he forced out, still remembering his manners.

"Mason?" she called, but he didn't turn back as he stiffly walked back to his truck. He couldn't stand to look at her another second without breaking down completely.

fourteen

It was rather quiet at the station the next morning, and Mason hated it. It gave him too much time to replay Taylor's words, trying to find anything that could hint at things not yet being too late for them. He stared at the faded photo in his hand; Taylor was no older than sixteen, blowing hair, eyes closed. Seth, a long-time colleague, joined him.

"God, that woman *again*?" He groaned, and Mason put the photo back in his wallet.

"She's back and ... my daughter adores her, my mother hopes for her, and each time I see her, it's wedding bells for me. It looked promising, too, and then, last night, she said she used to be in love with me. What if there aren't second chances in life? I keep messin' up with her, we end up fightin', and she cries herself to sleep. I don't think there is a chance at anythin' for us," he whispered.

Before Seth even managed to comment, Mason's cell went off.

"Stiles?"

"Your daughter never made it to school this morning," a woman stated drily, skipping introductions and greetings.

"What?" Mason wanted to know, brow furrowed. "She should be there. I –"

"Nope, never made it. Mr. Stiles, other kids would love and appreciate the spot in our pre-school, so either your daughter shows up tomorrow, or we'll fill her place. Have a good day." The line clicked, and Mason stared at his phone, cursing under his breath until dialing a number, waiting impatiently.

"Collins residence?" Taylor sounded cheery, and Mason gritted his teeth.

"Did your house catch fire?"

"Morning to you, too. And no."

"Did your truck break down?"

"No." Annoyance crept into her voice.

"You're sick, right? Close to dying?"

"No on both accounts," she replied a lot more sober.

"Why the hell isn't my daughter in school then?"

"She had a tummy ache," Taylor explained.

"Of course, she did! She didn't want to leave your house!" He was all but screaming, but too many pent-up emotions just crashed down on him like a wave, making him actually tremble from anger.

"I figured, but since I'm just gonna check fences today, I thought we'd be fine. You'll get her back tonight. I promise." Her calm demeanor only pissed him off more, especially because his initial worry about his daughter evaporated into thin air, leaving even more room for the fury to fill.

"She can lose her spot over missing a day without them being informed. Plus, you're currently teaching her that lyin' gets rewarded!" He heard doors slam and then birds singing. Taylor must have left the house.

"I'm currently teaching her what it feels like to have a mother," she snapped.

"You aren't her mother, Taylor Collins! In fact, you aren't a mother at all or you'd have considered the consequences. Take her over to Stella right now."

Her voice was colder than ice once she answered. "I will. Tonight. Bye, Mason." She hung up without giving him a chance to say more, and he released a string of curse words a sailor would be proud to know.

"You know, that second chance thing you asked me about? Yeah, not gonna happen after that," Seth pointed out. "What happened?"

"She kept Becca at home because the little girl

pretended to have a tummy ache. Taylor stated she was teaching her how it felt to have a mother," Mason gritted out.

"Hate to break it to you, man. Jacklyn used to do it with Lina all the time. They'd wait until everyone was out of the house and then they'd cuddle up on the sofa and watch Disney movies or braid each other's hair. To this day, Lina swears those were the best days of her life. To be honest, I still think Jacklyn keeps Lina home sometimes. She's ten by now." Seth grinned happily, his eyes having that far-off look a guy only wore when being absolutely in love.

"She's not her mother."

"As you made *very* clear. I hate to tell you, but shouldn't you be dancin' with joy right now? Becca doesn't have a mother who cares about her, and the woman you love wants to spend time with your daughter, ready to fill the spot that so far is a gaping hole. The only thing wrong about this whole thing is how you treated her. I wouldn't talk to you ever again if I were in her shoes." Seth shrugged and then got up.

"Maybe you should stop hanging out with women," Mason grumbled.

"Maybe you should start. And while you're at it, think about a proper apology for that stunt," Seth suggested.

"I'm still trying to come up with somethin' to apologize for the last stunt I pulled," Mason admitted, worrying his lip with his teeth.

"Clearly, you've been an idiot," his colleague commented, and Mason got up from the chair he had sat on.

"I told her she's mine, and that I think we need to get to know each other again. She has been gone for so long, and I don't ... I thought we had time, but then, last night she told me she *used* to be in love with me. I think –"

"You did everythin' right and still keep going wrong," Seth finished for him, just arching a brow in a much-saying gesture.

Maybe Seth was right. Mason grabbed his phone again.

"No need to call her back. You'll end up straight at voicemail," the other man predicted, and Mason hated that he was actually right. A robotic voice instructed the caller to leave a message after the beep.

"What do I do?"

"Prove to her that she still loves you as much as you love her," Seth hinted as if that actually was the easiest thing on the planet.

———

Taylor dropped Becca off just as she had promised. Tim was at home, playing computer games, and while she usually preferred to limit his computer hours, she figured that for once, he deserved the time, and she needed a quick break from life anyway.

As it was, she started missing Becca the moment the door fell closed behind her little body. It was true that she wasn't Becca's mother, but for a few precious hours, she almost had been able to pretend otherwise.

She turned on the country station she and Mason had always loved. She knew the song playing by heart because even though she had stayed away from any country up in Michigan, Keith Urban's *Tonight I Wanna Cry* had slipped through her armor and entertained her on more than one lonely night. As usual, it was exactly how she felt. She wanted to break down but told herself that it wasn't going to happen anymore. She was taking care of her own life. She and Ashley had started mending their friendship, and she noticed more than a few cracks in her former best friend's carefully crafted exterior. Together, they had cried and finally started healing again.

She came to her driveway and checked the clock on the dash. She could leave Timmy alone for a few more minutes, and she wanted to feel a breeze in her face, so she kept driving instead of turning.

She steered the truck toward the lake they used to go to on Halloween or bonfire nights. On her left was a field and a tractor plowing the last strip of earth, heading straight for the side road she was now on. Her station suddenly started to act up, interrupting the songs, and Taylor fiddled with it while keeping one eye on the tractor. They both had almost reached the intersection, and while he came from a side road, she suddenly wasn't sure he had seen her. In fact, he was supposed to stop, but she saw that he was texting on his cell, the heavy farming machine not slowing down one bit.

Taylor shifted gears to cut back on her own speed, cautiously inching toward the crossroad before intending to fully stop. The next thing she knew, her truck was pushed forward and then hit from the side before everything went black around her.

"Mason, get your ass in gear! There's need for the helicopter. A car crash occurred somewhere close to your hometown. A tractor and two trucks. One driver is stuck inside the vehicle and unresponsive as well as badly injured, and so far, they can't get the person out. The fire engine brought equipment, so I think they'll have that solved in a second."

Mason was already running toward his helicopter, adrenaline surging through his body. He loved knowing that, as a helicopter pilot for the emergency crew, he saved lives just by arriving at an accident site quicker than any emergency vehicle. He hopped into his seat, putting his helmet on while starting the engine with the other hand and hitting the switches he could hit blind.

One doctor and two EMTs, Seth included, joined him, and in no time, they were up in the air.

"What street?" he asked over the speaker, leading the

helicopter in the general direction of home.

"It's a side road between fields. One is a corn field, and one is empty," came the instant reply.

Mason cursed under his breath. More than enough streets fit that description and most lay in opposing directions.

"Ask for more info," the doctor suggested, but Mason just shook his head.

"Did the firefighter say empty or something different?" he inquired. He knew that people from around the farms would make that distinction because it was natural for them. He had one in mind that he at least could rule out if that weren't the case. He remembered passing a field with a tractor yesterday, and by the field's acreage, he guessed they'd still be busy.

"Actually, the dude said plowed," Seth recalled over the speaker, and Mason just hoped there wouldn't be more fields freshly plowed across from a cornfield. He knew where to go now, and it didn't take long until Mason spotted the bright red fire engine, a tractor, and...

"That's Tay's truck! Oh, my God, that's her!" Describing that piece of junk as a truck was like calling a whale a flounder. As if his worries weren't enough, Mason's mind had the courtesy to replay all the things he had said to Taylor; all the ways he had hurt her.

"Fuck, Mase, focus until we are down!" Seth called over the speaker, and Mason took a few calming breaths, and then cleared his throat.

"Right side of the crash. I'm going down on the field, and I will *not* stay behind this time." Usually, he stayed near the helicopter to make sure they were ready at any given time, but with Taylor being in the accident, he wouldn't stay by the heli until he'd seen her. Shutting down all emotions, he landed the helicopter, touching down as gently as ever and turning off the engine before everyone jumped out. Mason followed, his whole body numb with worry.

"Taylor? Please, Taylor, answer." His call echoed across the accident site, and he didn't care what people thought of him. He didn't see her blond head anywhere, and it made his lungs seize.

A firefighter stepped to his side. "Sir, you need to calm down. The driver's still in the truck and is unconscious. Is there someone we can contact to meet us at the hospital once the injured is out?"

Mason's head was swimming. He stared at the guy, but every word was hard to comprehend. He didn't want to call Tammy with news like that, especially since Taylor would hate to have worried her sister. That was if Tay was still alive. God, he couldn't even think that.

"Miss, you need to ..."

"I need to do fuck! Let me go."

Mason's knees almost gave in as he heard Taylor's voice just behind the fire engine inside the open ambulance doors. He reached for the truck, the relief so great he wasn't sure his racing heart would ever calm down again.

"Mase, it's not her," Seth screamed the moment he got close enough to the second truck. He threw a glance at Mason, checking, and Mason gave him a thumbs-up.

He turned and looked for the doctor, spotting him checking on the driver still stuck.

"You gotta live with an EMT for now," the firefighter announced, reading his questioning gaze. Mason nodded and then moved over to where Taylor was.

A bloody handprint covered her blonde French braid, clearly a spot where she had checked for a head injury. Her red hands waved frantically through the air as she tried to avoid the exasperated EMT.

"Let me go, John, and don't act as if you've never seen me before! Timothy's alone at home!" She turned to the side, enough for Mason to see what John actually was reaching for: Taylor's brow was cut and bleeding heavily. The whole right side of her face was swollen.

"I need to see ..." John's eyes fell on Mason, relief flooding his features. "There's a second EMT taking you over now."

"I'll take it from here," Mason agreed in a hoarse voice, and Taylor stiffened, hugging herself.

"Take what you need," John replied as he pointed toward his bag before walking away a little too hastily to let Mason fend for himself. The moment he stepped around Taylor, his body went into EMT mode, needing to take care of her. He sat down on the steps leading up to the ambulance, the open doors looking rather inviting. Left of him was the health kit and he tucked Taylor closer until she stood between his knees. He avoided her eyes, knowing he wouldn't be able to function if he saw her expression. Blood was running down her cheek like rain, and his stomach dropped. Technically, he knew that head wounds tended to bleed more than most, but seeing hers, he worried she was losing too much blood.

"Dizzy?" His tone was clipped. Anything else and he'd pull her into his arms before assuring himself that she was fine.

Her lips pressed together as she shook her head.

"Pain?" She gritted her teeth. He felt it against his fingertips as he prodded her cheek gently to see if anything was broken. She had another cut right below her eye on her cheekbone. That one wasn't bleeding any longer, making him release a breath. The pain question had been redundant, he knew that, but he needed to know if she was in agony.

"No pain," she lied, most likely knowing that she couldn't convince him.

"You need stitches. Let me bandage you up and then we'll take you to the hospital. I-"

"Thank you, but no. I'm fine. I just need to go home."

145

She glanced back at her broken truck; rapidly blinking as well as her swollen eye let her. "Tim's home, and while I'm not his mother, I'm his legal guardian. Therefore, I need to take care of him." She was hurt, angry, and Mason couldn't blame her.

The problem was he shook so hard that he didn't trust himself to do more than bandage her up. He wrapped the white dressing around her head, applying just enough pressure to hopefully stop the bleeding, and then he pushed her gently away from him. No way could he ensure she didn't have broken bones or internal bleeding, so while he wanted to close her in his arms, he wouldn't for fear of hurting her further. Instead, he fisted his fingers until his knuckles turned white, trying to keep his hands occupied and gritting his teeth so hard he worried they'd crack under the pressure.

"Sit," he finally ordered, but to his dismay, she just stood there, head lowered as silent tears rolled down her mutilated cheeks.

———

Mason was so mad at her; he couldn't even meet her eyes. Taylor clenched her hands, trying to regain control of her whirlwind emotions, but it was impossible. Instead of focusing on him, she took stock of her body. Her feet hurt but worked fine. Her legs carried her, though they were shaky. Arms and upper body? She moved the left side slightly, then the right, flexing her fingers, too. Worked well as well. Needless to say, everything hurt, reminding her with even the tiniest movement that she'd just been in a crash, but it seemed as if nothing was worse than bruises and swelling. Head? She softly shook it, instantly wincing as the world started to spin. She reached for something to hold onto and found warm skin. Her fingers wrapped around Mason's biceps, and it was only then that she noticed his short-sleeved uniform.

"Michigan," he whispered, steadying her against his side. It felt good to absorb his warmth. In the back of her mind, she knew there was no reason for her to freeze, especially because October had brought warm weather with it. Still, her teeth clattered together, giving off a weird staccato sound.

"Taylor!" Suddenly, she was pulled against Mason's chest. She felt the weight of his arms settle around her, yet the touch was barely there as if he feared he'd finish what neither truck nor tractor had been able to do.

"He was texting," she stuttered. "It wasn't my fault." She grabbed his shirt, holding on as if her life depended on it. "The second truck pushed me from behind. I wanted to stop. I saw the guy, but he was busy with his phone, too. Shouldn't you be at least ... I don't know, looking at the street with one eye?" She all but sobbed now. "He was speeding, too. On a country road! I didn't do it. I wasn't being irresponsible. I swear it wasn't my fault." Her breath hitched. "I'm just so glad I had returned Becca already. I would've never forgiven myself if she'd been hurt. That beautiful little girl. God!" She felt his arms tighten around her at that.

She raised her face to his, but he just leaned in closer. "I wasn't irresponsible," she promised again as he stayed silent, his cheek gently pressed against her uninjured one. They were almost breathing the same air as he whispered nonsense to calm her down and stop her sobs, but she couldn't relax.

A guy she didn't know stepped toward them, and Mason pulled back, making Taylor ready to protest.

"Status?" the other guy asked, obviously being a doctor.

"Shock, heavily bleeding cut across the brow, definitely needs stitches. Swelling to the left side of her face, eye seems to be okay, maybe broken bones in her cheek. I couldn't feel anything without hurting her. Possible concussion; has dizzy spells when moving her head too fast. No other obvious injuries, but we can't be sure until we've done an ultrasound and x-rays," Mason reported, his tone somber and professional, as if she was just any other patient to him.

Only then it registered with her that they wanted to take her to a hospital.

"Okay. Get her in the heli, we're taking her," the other guy decided.

"Yes, Doc," Mason said, confirming her suspicion

about the other man. That moment she didn't care, though, starting to shake her head until she remembered the effect it had on her. Swaying on her feet again, she forced herself to speak.

"Home. I'm going home," she gritted out, but Mason pulled his cell from his pocket, dialing before lifting it to his ear.

"Mom, get Timmy from the Collins' farm. Tell him he's having a sleepover and that you'll drive him to school afterward. Make something up, but be sure he doesn't start worrying. I'm taking Michigan's stubborn ass to the hospital. I'll call you later with updates and everything that happened," he promised the person on the other end of the line.

"How am I ever going to prove to you that I can do that parent –"

She was interrupted when Mason picked her up, careful yet without hesitation. "What the hell are you doing, Stiles? I'm not exactly…" He placed her inside the helicopter and then strapped her in, all the while noticing that he still couldn't look at her.

She took a deep breath. "I'm so incredibly sorry," she stated and then was surprised when his stormy eyes finally lifted to hers and made her swallow. They were swimming with emotions.

"*You* are sorry? God, Michigan, no. I am sorry. I was wrong to scream at you the way I did. I was wrong to accuse you of not being a mother. Mostly, though, I'm sorry about not being able to press you against me to make sure you forgive me. As it is, it takes everythin' in me to refrain from doing that. You're fucking injured, and I could break a bone that so far was only fractured."

She stared at him, noticing the way his hands shook, and his whole body trembled. "You're scared," she whispered in surprise. "Why?"

He paused his movements, resting his forehead against her bandage ever so lightly. "Why? Because I thought you were badly injured or dead. After everythin' I said to you. My last words to you would've been hateful and my chances at making it okay were..."

Guilty. He was feeling guilty. Disappointment settled in the pit of her stomach. He probably thought his screaming at her had distracted her so much that she hadn't paid attention.

"It wasn't your words crashing into me, Stiles, so you don't have to feel guilty. This wasn't your fault. I'm fine," she assured him, her voice shaking.

"Stupid, stubborn girl," he cursed, brushing his lips over her uninjured ones in the softest way, more a peck than anything else. He moved to the front and jumped into the seat while next to her, doors were closed and orders shouted. Someone took the seat to her right, holding out her handbag to her.

"The phone's busted, but everything else looks okay.

I'm Seth. Good to see you sitting upright," the EMT explained, and she reached out to shake his hand. Her fingers shook so hard, she pulled them back instead.

Her teeth hit together even harder, and black dots entered her vision.

"I nearly died," she whispered.

"The lady's going into shock!" were the last words she had heard before her whole body became blissfully numb.

———

Hours passed before Mason could finally break free from work to go and check on Taylor. He had written up the demanded report, wondering since when those couldn't wait until the next shift, and then they had been called to another accident with a drunken driver and a tree. The tree was fine, but the driver needed a cast and some stitches. In fact, he was much better than anticipated or they'd never have called the helicopter in the first place.

"Stiles, you need me to come along and kick your shin when you start saying somethin' stupid?" Seth offered, stepping to his side.

Mason just glared at him before his anger melted. "I thought it was her. I saw the truck, and I freaked. I could've gotten us all in trouble," he mumbled, and Seth patted his shoulder.

"Dude, we'd have never involved you if we'd have known her truck was in the accident. No one expected you to think straight, but above all, you still managed to get us down safe and back here the same way. You did great," Seth assured him.

"I didn't even tell her I'm sorry until I realized that she thought I was still mad at her. I wasn't. How can she even think that? She stood in front of me, bleeding, and she thought I was mad at her." He shook his head. "I almost went crazy with worry about her. Seth, what the hell am I supposed to say to her when I see her? If they let me see her? She thought the only reason I apologized was because I felt guilty..." Set rested his hand on Mason's arm, stopping his tirade.

"All you need to say is you're sorry and that she's your world. Everything else, the two of you can figure out once she's left the hospital," Seth promised.

They walked along the white halls, and people greeted them with smiles. Mason and Seth were the reason many lives had been saved in here. Reaching the intensive care unit, a nurse stepped toward them, telling the guys that Taylor already had been transferred to a normal room since she was just being kept overnight for observation.

Out of relief, Mason hugged Seth, smiling widely. "I guess I'm okay to go alone." He grinned, almost light-headed. Taylor would be perfectly okay in no time at all.

"Fine. Just remember not to say anythin' stupid. As soon as you open your mouth, monitor your words carefully. If it sounds like an accusation, don't say it," Seth instructed, and Mason punched him playfully in the side.

"Jerk. Just move." Laughing, Seth walked back to where they had come from while Mason made his way to Taylor's door. It was open, and he just wanted to rap his knuckles against the doorframe when a sob reached his ears.

"Stop, Michigan. Jesus," a different voice reacted. Clearly, Stella had called Ashley, and Taylor's former best friend had made her way up here. Instead of running, which was his first impulse, he knocked and then went into the room.

"Hey." His voice was subdued since he had no idea what mood he'd find the girls in. His caution proved right when Ash shot daggers at him with her eyes. Taylor just closed hers, turning her battered face away from him.

Ash leaned over, giving her friend a gentle kiss on the top of her head. "I'll go and score some chocolate and coffee. I'll be back in a little bit." The smile she gave Taylor was tender, yet as she pushed past Mason, she bumped her shoulder into him. It was clearly done on purpose.

"Taylor." Mason couldn't care less about the woman who had just left; his whole focus was on the one in the bed. He forced his feet to walk over to her, and he took a clipboard from its holder at the foot of her bed.

"Just a minor concussion, stitches, contusions, and bruises," she reported, her voice hushed. He nodded. Her ribs and shoulders were fine, which was all he needed to know for now. Mason moved around until he stood next to her, sitting down before leaning in to hug her tight.

"God, Michigan, I was so worried that my last words to you were hateful instead of everythin' I should've said like, for example, thank you for lovin' Becca exactly the way you do." Taylor was stiff under his hands, but he held her, burying his nose in the crook of her neck. "I'm sorry, Taylor, so sorry. There's no way I could live happily in a world without you and seeing your truck –"

"I'm fine, Mason, and you're hurting me," she stated, and he leaned back. Of course, he was since his head pressed against her cut cheek. He wondered what went on in her head, but she seemed to have reached a decision that he was not yet prior to.

"I'm sorry," he just repeated and then searched her eyes. It was hard to ignore the different hues of purple and yellow on her face. In fact, it was impossible for him because he could imagine how much pain she had to be in. "Why don't I go and find somethin' to take the pain away?"

She shrugged wordlessly, and he left her alone to hunt down a cooling pack and a towel. It definitely would help with the swelling, and it gave him something to do.

"Mason, do you ever stop to think before you talk?" Ash rounded the corner, almost running into him.

"My brain shuts off when she's around. I don't know how to change that. It's like my body goes into survival mode. Breathe and just don't appear stupid. There's no time to think."

154

Ashley didn't seem appeased. She still glared at him, and he wished he could read her better.

"Could you make her more unhappy?"

"Not my goal," he retorted, and she crossed her arms in front of her chest.

"What is your goal then? Because I thought you wanted to win her for you, and unless you changed your mind about that, you have a pretty weird way of going about it. Have you ever considered *those* words? The three magical ones?"

He watched her for a long moment and then decided to just throw a question out that bounced around his skull every time he heard that Ash and Tay hung out together again. "You're really okay with this, Ash? Because Taylor won't do anythin' that could potentially –"

Ashley rolled her eyes. "She and I solved that already when you started to insult her, and she couldn't stop cryin'. I want her to be happy, and frankly, I want you to be happy, too, even though right now I think you don't want that!" It wasn't exactly what he wanted to hear, but it was enough for now.

"You never deserved to be in that weird triangle that was me, you, and the ghost of her. You never should've gotten that baby. It was more a desperate move on my part than real hope. I thought you wanted it, and maybe that could fix us. I should've never allowed it," he blurted out. "I would never give her up, but you didn't deserve that.

Any of it."

He watched as she wiped away a tear, the hostility long gone from her face. "I fell in love with the way you loved her. It was stupid, but let's face it, you can never love two people the same way. You'll never love anyone the way you love her. I wasn't okay with the way you loved me. I was jealous. I wanted *her* way. I thought giving you a child would get me that. Instead, you found a new, amazin' way to love another human being, while I realized I wasn't a mother and would never be. Good news, though. There's a perfect mother just down the hall, and if you're ever ready to pull your head from your ass, you might manage to say more than the bullshit you're spitting out." The fire was back in Ashley's eyes, but he still noticed the teasing curve of her lip.

"What woman will raise her best friend's daughter like her own?" That was his biggest worry and all it came down to really.

Ash smiled. "A woman like Taylor Collins."

———

Returning after this shift was brutal. He no longer had any idea what to do or say to Taylor to make things right. Stella waited for him when he stepped out of his truck. It was the middle of the night, yet she sat outside on a rocking chair, sipping a glass of white wine.

She got up the moment she spotted him. "What happened today? Is Taylor okay? Will she be out soon? Are you okay?" She fired questions in such a rapid succession; Mason didn't get a chance to answer any at all.

"Mom..."

"What am I going to tell Tim? Are you goin' back tomorrow?"

"Mom!"

"Does she need anything? Clothes? Food? I could –"

"Mom, stop! I'm not gonna go back there, and no, she won't stay long. She wanted you to know that she's grateful you picked up Timmy. She doesn't want Tamara informed, either." He rattled off all she had instructed him to say. Even though that wasn't really the right word. He'd asked her if she wanted Stella or Timmy to know anything. Manners, again, because his body didn't really function anymore.

"Why?"

He couldn't remember why. It was something about Tamara having grown up too fast. His mind was so crowded; it might as well be blank.

Maybe it's best if we don't see each other for a while. Taylor had uttered those words in a tone that made his bones freeze. There was no room left for debates or pleas, no room left for doubts. He'd been right about her having reached a decision.

You and I need to stop hurting each other. I need to stop being a disappointment to you and hating myself for it, and you need to take care of your daughter instead of

157

me.

How often would his mind have to replay those words until his heart would finally go back to beating normal in his chest?

"Mason?" He focused on his mother again, seeing her brows arched in question.

"What?"

"What happened?" Her tone had an edge of annoyance, hinting that she had asked that exact same question a few times already.

He recounted the events from the moment they were alerted of the accident up to the moment he had left Taylor's hospital room the second time.

"She was in an accident that could've easily killed her." His mother collected her thoughts and then lowered her eyes. "You know, maybe it *is* a good idea for the two of you to take a break from each other. I'm not saying you should give up. I'm not saying she's been right and you've been wrong, or the other way around. I adore Taylor, and you know that. All I'm saying is that maybe for once, let her come to you. You tried everythin' and put your heart on the line more than once." She smiled softly. "Maybe you haven't handled some situations right or the way you should have, but is there a better compliment for a woman than you stopping to think when bein' around her?" She hugged him tight.

"I thought if I just say the right words, the ones I

thought she'd been longing to hear, we'd be happy, but instead, I put pressure on her to be what she thinks I want her to be. I, of all people, should've known how she'd react!"

His mother led him inside, sitting him down on the kitchen table. "She runs."

He nodded, hiding his face in his hands. "Only now, she can't run. She's trapped, so she lashes out instead." His palms muffled his words, but then he lowered them again. Stella pushed a steaming mug into his hands, and Mason took a deep pull from the hot coffee. He was glad his mother had prepared him one.

"Exactly, which is why I'm sayin' let her come to ya. I know you hurt, and you worry, but son, sometimes you need to let go of somethin' you love, knowin' that if it returns, it's truly yours."

He moved the cup out of the way and then crossed his arms on the table, resting his head on them. "She nearly died, and I couldn't look at her and just tell her I love her. It's all I should've done. Mom, it's Taylor. I don't know if I can stay away from her."

His mother gently kissed his head. "Go upstairs, pick up your daughter, and hold her close. Taylor will come around. I'm sure she won't be able to stay away too long. If there's one thing I know, it's that."

Mason raised his head, staring at his mother for a long time before slowly nodding.

"Good idea," he decided, getting up to kiss his mother's cheek goodnight and find his daughter.

After all, next to Taylor, Becca was his light in the darkness.

fifteen

Taylor had trouble moving without hurting. She was sore all over, but since she had seen the pictures of her truck, she was more than glad about the fact that she was *only* sore. It could've been much worse.

As much as she was pissed at the second driver for having destroyed the only transportation she had on hand, she had sighed a breath of relief upon hearing that he had been conscious throughout the night. Ashley had picked her up from the hospital and dropped her off at home, where she currently tried to get her head together enough to prepare a late lunch for her and Tim. The bus had passed their house just a minute ago, and she knew that he'd be inside the house at any second.

He burst into the kitchen, dropping everything by the door and then hugged her tight around the hips. She hugged him back while gritting her teeth against the pain.

"I'm so glad you're home! The teacher at school told me you'd been in an accident. Why didn't Stella tell me? I would've come and visited you in the hospital," he sobbed against her stomach, and she bent softly to kiss the top of his head.

"It was just one night as a precaution, baby, and I had no intention of worrying you until I knew what was going on. And then it was clear I'd be out soon. Look, I'm home already, and I figured we could –"

The door flew open, interrupting them.

"Taylor Collins!" Tay winced. Tamara wasn't supposed to know or be home.

"Who told her?" she asked in a hushed voice toward her brother, and Timmy shrugged. "No one was supposed to tell her and..."

"Ashley called. Hell, Tay, it should've been you calling me, not her! I'm your sister! I need to make sure you're all right and takin' it slow the way you deserve," her sister announced, waltzing into the kitchen.

"My best friend's a traitor," she said in the same hushed voice to Timmy and the little boy giggled. Taylor winked at him and then looked up at her sister.

Tamara had pulled her blonde hair up into a messy bun, and her hazel eyes were swimming with tears. It was exactly the reason why Taylor hadn't wanted her informed. There was no use in anyone worrying about her. She'd be fine in no time again.

"Your stubborn ass -"

"Tamara Collins! Clean up your language around Tim," Taylor scolded, and Tamara rolled her eyes before leaning in to kiss Tim's cheek.

"Go and get the burgers that I brought from the car and set up in the living room, okay?" Their brother nodded at Tamara and then left. Tammy straightened, placing her hands on her sweats-covered hips. "Your stubborn ass needs to get used to the fact that you have family around again. You don't have to take care of yourself alone anymore. And you had better get that through your head quickly. Otherwise, you and I will have a problem! If Mason wants to buy you a whole damn bedroom, you say 'why, thank you, mister' and hug him tight. If Kelly Rivers wants to take Tim off your hands so you can settle in, be grateful and accept it. If I wanna come and spoil you rotten because you have been in a fucking car accident, you hug me tight, assure me that you're fine, and then you move to the sofa while I take care of you! That's how country works, honey. That's how Sunburn works. So, hug, please?" Tam's tirade ended in tears, and Taylor moved in, hugging her little sister.

"I just want to prove to people that I can do it, you know? It's hard being back, but I'm capable of being

Timothy's guardian. I get him to school on time, and I make sure he's fed. That bedroom ... it was Mom and Dad's, and they ... I just couldn't go in there!"

"And now, it's your safe haven. Mason did amazing," Tamara pointed out, and Taylor decided to change the topic. Mason was just not something she wanted to talk about with her sister.

"Thank you for coming home, Tam," she whispered into her sister's hair. "And thank you for bringing food. I don't think I could've been on my feet long enough to cook well," she admitted.

Tam pulled back and winked at her. "I figured that, Lori."

"Come on, you two! I'm hungry," Timmy called, and together, the sisters left the kitchen, following the call of the food.

————————

Later that night, the two sisters sat on the sofa and watched movies together. They had decided on *Divergent*, but Tamara was constantly looking toward the door, making Tay nervous. Their brother was in bed already, and she was glad about that.

"Don't you just love Four?" Tammy sighed, and Taylor smiled. No doubt, the actor was handsome, but he had nothing on Mason, which in return made Taylor's heart squeeze. Another time, her sister snuck a glance at the door, and Taylor had had enough.

"Who the hell are you waiting for?" she wondered, and Tamara furrowed her brow.

"Isn't that obvious? Is Mason on shift or why doesn't he show?"

Taylor untangled herself from her sister's arms and got up, pulling her knitted jacket tighter around her body.

"Mason and I agreed that we shouldn't ... see each other for a while." She swallowed, the lie burning like acid in her throat.

"Taylor," her sister growled, a warning clear in that one word. "What did you do? What did you tell him? What the fuck happened? I thought by now you two would be all cuddly and perfect and happy!"

Oh God, how Taylor wished it were true. "I thought maybe he'd want to be with me when I showed him how much I loved his daughter, and that was wrong, too. You should've heard him fussing at me and telling me that I'm not a mother." Tears sprang to her eyes as the words cut just as deep as it had the first time. "He pointed out that Becca's not my daughter, either. I know she isn't. It couldn't be more obvious, but..."

"You'd be ready, right? You'd be okay with it, too? Raisin' your best friend's child? Everyone knows, Tay. Everyone in town knows who the mother is, and one day, Becca will know that, too. Are you seriously okay with that?"

Taylor arched a brow in question. "What? Are you

telling me I shouldn't love her like my own when her father is the only man I've ever wanted?"

"I'm tellin' you that it'll be hard and complicated," Tamara replied, and Taylor nodded slowly.

"I don't care what the town thinks. I care what Ashley thinks, what Mason thinks, and what's best for Becca. Let them talk. I know Ashley wants her to have an amazing mother. I know Becca needs one, and I know that I love her. Mothers are made from the heart, Tamara. It's about loving a child unconditionally. That's what it means to be a mother. I'm ready to fight for her, to dry her tears, and to show her that she is wanted, no matter who gave birth to her." If there was one thing she was sure of, it was that.

"You're pretty amazin'. You know that, right?" her sister wanted to know, and Taylor shrugged a shoulder. To her, it was nothing great. After all, loving Becca was no feat at all.

"It doesn't matter, though. Right now, I won't see her, mainly because I can't face Mason. I can't be what he wants me to be and…"

"You mean you can't be you?" Tamara inquired, and Taylor shook her head. That wasn't what she meant.

"I mean I can't be who I was back then, and I can't be who he hoped I would turn into if I had stayed. We fight or we get drunk and confess to each other how much we like the other one … only to hurt each other *more*. I can't do it anymore," she whispered, and Tamara got up as well, hugging her tight. She winced, making her sister jump back instantly.

"I'm so sorry! Seriously, so sorry," she mumbled, patting Taylor down as if she'd be able to feel each and every bruise. Of course, she couldn't, but that didn't matter. Tay swatted her hands away, giving her a smile to calm her down.

"You know if I had stayed..." Her phone interrupted her, and she stared down at it, cursing low. "I wish Ash hadn't replaced that stupid thing." She hit 'ignore,' but it didn't take long until the screen lit up again.

"Who is that?" Tamara asked, clearly not recognizing the number Taylor hadn't bothered to save on the phone.

"Andrew." He was pretty much the last person she wanted to talk to, even though he had never done anything but be the wrong guy. And that really wasn't his fault.

"How often has he been calling?" Tamara sounded everything but happy, and Taylor sighed.

"Too often. Just ignore him. He'll take the hint at some point," she assured her sister. "We aren't a couple any longer, and we certainly aren't friends. There's nothing he can tell me anyway. So yeah."

"He bought your business, Taylor," Tamara gently reminded her, and Taylor gritted her teeth. God, she missed planning parties, especially the high-class stuff. She wanted to have elegant decorations, low-playing classical music, long-stemmed sparkling glasses, and as much money as she wanted at her disposal. She missed feeling as if she was in control. Right now, almost none of her savings was left, and she needed a new truck - yes, it would have to be a truck again, not a small car - and having paid back Mason had put a dent in the finances she had considered her backup for the farm.

"So?"

"Maybe somethin's wrong with it."

Taylor took a deep breath and then turned away from her sister. "It's no longer my business. Whatever is wrong with it, he has to figure it out alone." Staring out the window, she gritted her teeth not to cry again. She hadn't even thought about how much she missed it, but now, it bubbled up with all the other emotions that were just too much right now.

"Once I'm back and done with college, you can think about opening a new event management business. You'd be surprised how many people down here would book you," Tamara whispered, but Taylor didn't react. As nice as the idea sounded, she couldn't. No one here needed what she had offered in Michigan, and hope was a treacherous thing. No, for now, Taylor was done hoping for anything. All she'd do was live one day at a time, and maybe, someday, she'd find a path that would be just right for her.

sixteen

Mason watched from Becca's bedroom window as his friends hung strings of sparkling lights everywhere. The barn and every damn fence leading to it shone in a soft, warm glow. It was romantic, no doubt, but romance wasn't what he wanted. Taylor wouldn't come, and in fact, he was not ready to be among all those people, celebrating his special day.

"Daddy, I'ma princess," Becca announced, dancing circles around him. She had tried to replicate the braid Taylor had once done on her head, and it was a mess, but the little girl refused to let him touch her hair.

"Tay will make it right when she's here," she had told him, being so sure of the fact that his heart was breaking.

No doubt, Taylor would come over if Stella called her, just because Taylor would never neglect the little girl, but she'd try like hell to avoid Mason, and that was probably why he hadn't asked his mother to get Taylor over.

He missed her like crazy, and his mood had taken a turn for the worse. It killed him not to know how she was doing, or if she needed anything. He longed to take her in his arms and hold her tight. He wanted to whisper words of love into her hair and make her forget how bad they had fought in the last weeks. He wanted her to say that she was his. Instead, he currently faced the need to force a smile and thank each and everyone who'd be dropping by that night. A local band would be playing, everyone and their mother had prepared food, and there certainly would be more than enough beer to go around.

Before Taylor had returned, he'd been excited and happy to celebrate his birthday at all, even had gotten excited about doing it big eventually, but now, he regretted that decision.

"Daddy, dance with me?" Becca inquired, holding out her little hands. So far, no music was playing, but she began to hum the moment he grabbed her little fingers and started to sway his hips. The door opened behind them, and his mother leaned into the doorframe, watching them for a moment. He could tell by her expression that she had something on her mind. Sadness tinged the smile on her lips.

"Rebecca, why don't you go and dress your dolls in princess dresses so we can have a ball later on?" she suggested, and his daughter dashed off without saying a word.

"Usually, Becca manages to make you smile, son, but today, not even that worked. Are you that sure Taylor won't show? She knows it's your birthday, and I'm sure even if she had forgotten about it, Ashley most likely reminded her. By the way, it was a good gesture to invite her."

Mason grinned sheepishly, and his mother's eyes lit up. "You only invited her because you figured and hoped she'd drag Taylor along. You're terrible!" She had to laugh, and he nodded.

"Besides that, though, I can't believe how things have changed between us since Taylor came back. It's as if Taylor's return finally started gluing back who we were before everything broke apart. Ash's pain slowly subsided, and I think we finally know that we both were at fault. Why did it take until Taylor for us to face the music?"

Stella shrugged and then walked into the room, sitting down on Becca's bed while pulling a teddy bear into her lap. "Because she was the root of all evil, so to say. Now, all that's left to fix is the way the two of you talk to each other. Did I mention I'm sure she'll show today?"

No, she hadn't, but it didn't make a difference anyway. Mason was sure she wouldn't turn up at his party, especially considering that her bruises would still be all too visible. Everyone would stare at her, and Taylor hated nothing more.

"If she comes, I'm gonna tell her I love her. Nothing else. It's the only thing she needs to know."

"Good plan," his mother agreed, and Mason walked back to the window. "Is that Ashley?" he asked in disbelief, and his mother stepped to his side.

Even though from above they couldn't hear the words exchanged down there, it was clear Brad was pushing all of Ashley's buttons. The woman more than once reached for him, but he avoided her touch, laughing.

"She's blonde again," his mother commented. Mason very well remembered her blonde hair even though she had changed it literally an hour after they had split up. It was growing out again, too, and the new, or better said former, color seemed to be a sign that Ashley was slowly finding who she was again. At least, he hoped that was the reason and not the fact that she tried to copy Taylor.

"It looked better on her. Gave her a softer edge," Mason mumbled, watching how his ex got into a car. Her truck was at Taylor's, that much he already knew. Brad came over to the house, and it took only a few seconds until Becca told his best friend where to find him after Brad refused to dress dolls with her.

"Your ex-dragon ... oh, you saw. She turned her hair back blonde. I asked if she was going for Taylor Two, and she instantly got mad." Brad grinned, clearly proud of himself.

"Ex-dragon. Shame on you, Bradley," his mother scolded, and Brad had the decency to blush.

"Sorry, Mrs. S." He pushed his hands into his pockets, and Mason leaned back against the windowsill.

"Well, what was her answer?" He couldn't help his curiosity.

"She said she had changed it because blonde didn't feel like her anymore back then. She wasn't that girl. Now, she changed it back because she never had felt better than when she'd been blonde, no matter what had happened between you and her. She said, too, that Taylor had suggested the change and actually been right about it. And she added some words to describe me that I'd rather not repeat in front of your mother." Brad winked at Stella, and Mason's mother actually blushed, laughing.

"Then I'm gonna leave you boys alone. I need to check on my grandchild anyway," she told them and walked to the door.

"You should; she's glittering the carpet, saying it's prettier now." With a groan, Stella hurried outside, and Brad turned serious.

"Everything's prepared, your Royal Highness. All we have left to do is get the elusive princess to show, being enchanted by the fairy lights and the soft melodies that'll be playing tonight."

Mason glared at him, and Brad started to grin. "If all else fails, I already hired a group to kidnap her, tie her up, and bring her over. Some women need it caveman style," he added, and Mason rubbed his hands over his face, groaning.

He sure hoped it wouldn't come to that because he knew Brad would definitely go through with it.

———————

"Michigan, move your ass!"

Taylor didn't want to. She had enjoyed the weekend with her sister and then the quiet week at home, hiding out and hanging with Timmy after he came home from school. They had done homework together, and it was probably the first time she realized how smart he really was and how great he had turned out even though his childhood had been everything but easy so far.

Focusing her eyes on the mirror and the task at hand, she took stock of her body. Ashley had brought her a dress and cowboy boots. While she was in love with the boots, the dress showed too much of her legs and arms. Bruises had turned her skin from black over purple to the nicest yellow-green colors. She looked hideous and knew it, yet Ashley was adamant when it came to her outfit.

Looking the way she did, like a badly worked canvas, Taylor had no intention to show at Mason's party, no matter what Ashley insisted. If she wanted to fix things between Mason and her, it was best to remind him as little as possible about what had happened and where they last had seen each other.

She reached for a denim jacket, hoping that this way, at least, most of her would be covered. Damn, that dress was short. She pulled on the hem, hoping to maybe get it down to her knee at least, but no such luck. The soft white cotton reached down to the middle of her thigh. If she'd be fully healthy, this would actually blow her away, but as it was, she wanted to cry.

"Want me to put makeup on your face?" Ash asked, showing up next to her and placing her chin on Taylor's shoulder. Tay's eyes went to Ashley's blonde hair, and she smiled.

"You look much better with that color. Less aggressive," she mumbled, hoping to distract Ashley enough so maybe she could change into jeans without Ash noticing it and wear them under the dress.

"I never thought that could really influence me that much, but I feel calmer, too. Better with who I am. Thank you for convincing me," Ash whispered, hugging her. Luckily, most of her aches had passed, and hugging wasn't any longer uncomfortable. "So makeup?"

Taylor shook her head. All she'd put on was mascara and some lip-gloss. As she thought about that, she shook her head. She wanted to stay home, now more than ever. Mason would take one look at her and pity her again. "I think I'll stay home."

"I think you should go. You miss Mason. And it's his birthday. You know, there is nothing sadder than when no one shows to your birthday," Timmy explained, standing in the door. Taylor turned to him, furrowing her brow.

"Besides the fact that I doubt no one will show to Mason's party, shouldn't you be gone already?" She checked the watch on Ashley's wrist and then gave Tim a questioning look. As much as Taylor had hated the idea of Tim sleeping somewhere else overnight again, she couldn't fight Ashley and her brother on this. Ash had talked to Kelly, and they'd agreed to take Timmy in, and her brother had been excited about it.

"Max called. He's sick. I'm gonna stay home," Timothy replied, and it was exactly the excuse Tay had needed to chicken out of this evening.

Her brother walked over to where Ash now sat on Taylor's bed and plopped down next to her. "Sorry, Ash, you can see I can't –"

"I'm grown up, Tay," Tim announced and warmth spread in Taylor's body. Jesus, she loved that boy.

"She smiles; that's a good sign," Ash grinned, bumping Tim with her shoulder.

"She's smiling because he'll always stay little in her eyes," Taylor protested, resting her hands on her hips. "He's not staying home alone. I'm sorry, Ash, I can't go." Oh, wasn't that just awesome? Taylor had a hard time containing her smug smile.

Ashley rolled her eyes, mirroring her little brother's gesture exactly. "Lucky me that I had already asked Stella earlier to make sure I had a plan B. Tim can go over and spend the evening with Becca and Stel; and the moment you're ready to go, you can take him with you."

Taylor suppressed a groan, walking over to her brother to kneel in front of him. "It's your choice," she stated softly, brushing a hand across his head. "You stayed there quite a lot during the last time."

Timothy reached out and hugged her. She ignored the stab of pain as his head came against the cut on her eyebrow because she wanted to enjoy those precious seconds when he was so close.

"I want you happy, and you are always happiest when Mason or Ashley are around. Go to the party and tomorrow make me pancakes?"

Taylor leaned in closer. "I don't want to go," she whispered conspiratorially, and Tim gave her a grin.

"I know," he replied, making her gape at him. "I love being over there. Becca is like a tiny sister. And Stella makes awesome food. Go, Taylor. I'll have fun," he reassured her, and Taylor sat back on her heels, staring at the two who had teamed up against her.

"Look at me." Her voice broke.

"You're pretty," Ashley voiced, and as much as Taylor wished she could detect a lie, she heard nothing but sincerity in her best friend's voice. "Tim, leave. We'll be right down," Ash instructed. She took Taylor's hands in hers the moment he was gone. "You'll still be the most beautiful girl in Mason's eyes, and that's what matters. He nearly died with worry when he saw the accident, and I know you two agreed not to see each other for a while, but honestly? Jump over your shadow and kiss him. What better day is there than his birthday?"

'They' wasn't right; she knew that, but Ash didn't.

"You know, maybe I should mention that *we* didn't agree on it, but that *I* couldn't handle any more pain. Being in a room with Mason clearly hasn't worked out for us the way I had expected and ..."

"Stop it, Michigan. How did you feel not seeing Mason? And don't try to lie to me," Ash needled.

It had been horrible. She had missed his voice, his smile, and the casual touches and hugs even more. Actually, she missed just being around him and taking comfort in his presence. The answer must've been clear on her face because Ashley framed it carefully.

"Now, get on the bed so I can put makeup on you."

"Mascara, eyeliner, and something for the lips. No powder or foundation, Ash," she insisted, and Ash nodded, getting to work quickly.

Later, Taylor's stomach dropped the closer they got to Mason's barn. She promised to drive, especially since Ashley had given her the truck. Tim chatted away, entertaining Ashley until her best friend suddenly reached out and touched her knee.

"Find him first and solve this thing or you'll shatter," Ashley pleaded, and Taylor parked the truck among a row of similar vehicles. Lights were strung up everywhere, and Taylor loved the decorations. Music reached her ears, and she realized that Tim had called out a good-bye and left to hurry inside the house.

"Tim!" She wanted to hug him and promise him that they'd leave if he didn't feel like staying any longer. He had been her perfect excuse for a delay, but that had quickly gone down the drain.

Reluctantly, she got out, too, watching her best friend before turning her attention to the twinkling lights adorning the fences. Someone really had done a fabulous job.

"Oh, the ex-dragon and the fair princess," Brad greeted them, earning a playful slap from Ashley. "You're fashionably late," he then added, scowling.

"Best comes last. Which, of course, means you were here first," Ash jeered, and Brad made a face. Taylor's stomach somersaulted, and she figured she needed to get going.

"Where is he?" she inquired, impatiently stepping from one foot to the other. She didn't care the least about the banter between her friends.

"Actually, he vanished up the stairs to your little escape and our hangout within minutes of coming out here."

She just nodded, touching Ash's arm before moving forward with just one goal in mind. Only, when she placed her hand on the wooden banister to walk up to the changed hayloft, her steps faltered.

She was so close to everything she had ever longed for, yet she worried that it was too late now. Step by step, she climbed the ladder like it were a mountain. She reached the top and spotted Mason at the window. His back was to her, and her heart jumped into her throat. Her lips almost automatically split into a wide smile. This was her and Mason. It just *had* to work.

———

Mason lowered his head as he heard steps on the floor behind him, feeling the wooden planks vibrate with each step closer.

"I'll be right down," he promised without turning.

The steps didn't stop until they were so close that he thought he felt the person exhaling.

"Ashley kept talking about your wallet, so now, I'm curious."

His heart did a double take, and he spun around to face the only person he wanted to see on his birthday. Her eyes were on the photo of her he carried, and she stared at it so long, he thought she had gone into shock. Finally, her eyes lifted to his. The emotions in her gaze were unidentifiable, but still, his heart swelled because the smile that accompanied them said so much more.

"That is ... Mason!" She shook her head, collecting her thoughts. "I didn't bring you a gift, and I look like hell, but you wanna know something? If one person takes me as I am, it's you." She pressed her lips together before exhaling. He smelled strawberry chewing gum, and it made him bite his cheek to stop himself from grinning. "Only you can drive me batshit crazy, and it's a good thing. What I'm trying to say ..."

"I love you, too," he interrupted, and her eyes widened slightly.

"Too many words, huh?" she wondered, a blush creeping up her cheeks. It was the cutest thing ever.

"I'm sorry for everythin' I said, and I ..." Her tiny smirk prompted him to stop, and he rested his forehead against hers. "How about we try that first real sober kiss?" She bit her lip in response, letting her arms come around his neck.

"You had better impress me this time, cowboy," she teased, and he groaned, deciding to step away.

"That kiss you talked about in the truck was ours. I hadn't realized it, or I would've kissed you then and there. Everythin' I said between that day and today hurt you or pushed you away."

She placed her hands on her hips, cocking her head and causing blonde waves to tumble over her shoulder. "You were about to kiss me, and *now,* you wanna talk?"

Her brow furrowed, and he spread his arms in a gesture of innocence. He wanted to reply, but before he could, her lips were on his, her arms wrapped around him, and her fingers in his hair.

He couldn't believe that he had forgotten the way she tasted or felt against him. He nudged her to jump, and she wrapped her legs around his hips without breaking the kiss. Her lips were soft against his, yet the kiss was anything but.

"Man, you can do that so much better when you're sober," she whispered against his mouth, and he claimed her lips another time. Once he had his first fill of her, he put her back on her own two feet and brushed his thumb over her bottom lip, releasing a deep breath.

"Hi." He grinned, making her laugh.

"I think you have a party going on downstairs. Happy birthday, by the way. We should –"

"Collins," he interrupted, pulling her back against him as she attempted to walk back down. The way her eyes lifted and her lips slightly parted in awe made his throat go dry.

"You called me Collins," Taylor whispered, and Mason nodded, making her spin on the tip of her toes. She was exactly like she used to be yet more mature, and even with bruises in the colors of the rainbow covering her; she was the most beautiful woman in his eyes.

"Well, you look like yourself again. All boots, denim

jacket, and an attitude," he stated, making her beam.

She reached out and cupped his cheek, and Mason kissed her palm. "You've always been the best part of me … and a big part of what makes *me* me." She gently touched her nose to his and then brushed a quick kiss on his lips. "I wanted to be someone better for you, and I can't remember one day since meeting you that I haven't loved you. You hear me, Mason Stiles? I love you. And now, let's go. Everyone's waiting for the birthday boy who was sulking upstairs in the hay loft," she told him and then tried tugging him along.

"Hey, one last thing." She groaned, making him chuckle before he turned serious again. "I cannot have Becca's heart broken," he mumbled. She turned back around, cocking an eyebrow.

"Listen up, cowboy." She tapped his chest with her fingertip, making his heart do crazy things. "For over ten years, I have wanted you, and I'd only ever leave your ass again for one reason: cheating. So you can avoid breaking her heart by not breaking mine. It isn't about the sunshine. It's about dancing in the rain and weathering the storm. Through fights, screams, and tears, Mason, that's what you wanted, and you had better not have changed your mind by now," she pointed out, and he gaped at her.

"You remember that?"

She nodded. "Back then, I thought you were talking

183

about us. I thought you'd be marrying me, so of course, I remembered." She walked over to the stairs, clearly deciding that someone had to start going down, or it wouldn't ever happen.

"I will marry you," he called after her, and she threw him a look over her shoulder.

"Not without a pretty ring, you won't," she replied, her tone sassy as she made her way back to their friends. Mason grabbed the wallet and the photo from the ground where she had dropped it before kissing him. He followed her, smiling as if he owned the world. And, in his mind, he finally did.

seventeen

"Tim, wake up!" Her brother turned, but then just grunted something incoherent. Taylor contemplated picking him up, but he'd be heavy, and she'd have to climb down the stairs. "Timmy, let's go home," she pleaded, but again, he just grunted in response. She lowered her head. While her body was energized, she just wanted to go to sleep. Somehow, somewhere, during this almost perfect night, she had started to worry that she'd wake up and everything would be a dream and nothing more.

"Just stay," came a warm voice from the door, and she turned in the darkness, seeing Mason framed by light. "I want to wake up and finally know you're mine." His voice was hushed, almost pleading. It made her realize that he was just as disbelieving as she was. Hesitating before kissing Tim's cheek, she got up from the bed and walked over to Mason, stepping out into the hall with him. She closed the door behind her back before leaning against it. She watched his face in the dimly lit hallway, and her heart ached. God, he was beautiful. His unruly dark curls beckoned her to touch them and his lips, shining from when he licked them out of nervousness, begged her to kiss them.

There, in the small space of the hallway, they were suddenly teenagers again. Taylor had hated all the insecurities back then, and even more the fact that Mason hadn't been hers.

"So much wasted time," he mumbled, his tone rough as he voiced the thought that had just sprung to her mind. He nodded her over, and she went willingly, letting him close her in his arms. It was strange how something so utterly familiar could suddenly be new and exciting.

She never wanted to be anywhere else again.

"Yeah, I was just your friend, remember?" She only half joked as jealousy burned its way through her body. She hadn't forgotten the Halloween she'd been close to telling him what she felt. He instantly reacted by gently pinching her side, making her yelp.

"You little minx," he accused, and then grabbed her as she tried to escape his arms. She stifled her laughter as her back hit his chest. The next second, he kissed her neck, making her want to purr.

"It's our first real date, Mr. Stiles. This lady here should be going home to follow the proper Southern way," she teased. She could hear him gasp, looking for words that clearly evaded him. It made her grin.

Mason should be doing exactly what she had said, but years had been wasted, and he wouldn't ever get them back.

"Hey, Mase," she called softly, getting him back from his wayward thoughts. "I was joking. Let's go." She took the initiative and walked to his room. Inside, he watched how she moved around his space, clearly feeling at home. He liked that more than he cared to admit. She opened drawers and got out sweatpants and a shirt for herself.

"You can always sleep in a bra and panties," he offered graciously, biting his cheeks as she glowered at him before arching a brow.

"I could, you know, if I was wearing any." With that, she vanished in his bathroom. He stared at the door for a few seconds, wondering if she'd been serious. He lit a few candles around the room before pulling his own sweatpants on. His hand hovered over a shirt, but then he decided against it. It wouldn't hurt anyone if he teased Tay a ...

His thought trailed off as she came out of the bathroom, holding the black sweats in her hand while his shirt barely reached over her butt. Clearly, she, too, had decided to tease him. He surely didn't mind, especially not as her gaze settled on him, prompting her to lick her lips.

"Cowboy," she whispered, and he laughed, realizing that being with Taylor was easy, albeit a little like a first ever relationship.

"Come here," he instructed, and she dropped his pants on the floor before walking over. Her eyes never left his chest, her gaze following her fingertips as she let them wander over it without really touching him. It appeared as if she was afraid of coming too close.

"You know, you won't feel anything unless you get skin to skin," he pointed out, realizing that she was trembling. He grabbed her hand and then kissed her fingertips.

"I ... this is unreal. I've longed to get my hands on your chest for years, and now, I'm suddenly worried it won't be as good as I always imagined." Mason stared at her in outrage. For a second, he expected her to start laughing, but she kept a straight face.

"You ... I ... what?" he stuttered, and finally, she broke into a round of giggles. She wanted to walk away from him, but he just pulled her toward him again, kissing the back of her neck while she laughed softly. His heart did flip-flops, and it probably was the best thing he'd ever felt.

"Jesus, Collins, I love you," he whispered, and she stilled, leaning her head to the side to give him better access to her neck. He rubbed his nose along her skin, before letting his lips follow. Her sweet scent clouded his senses, and he'd never tire of that feeling.

Slowly, she shifted in his arms, and he loved the way she looked in the soft light of the candles. "Oh my, Mister Stiles, you look at me as if it's something serious." She grinned. He brushed a stray blonde strand out of her face, wondering how in the world it couldn't be serious when for more than a decade he had longed for this.

Framing her face, he drew her in. He met her lips in a gentle, unhurried kiss, slipping his tongue inside her mouth the moment she went onto her tiptoes to silently demand more. He picked her up and then put her down on the mattress without breaking the kiss. She placed her hand directly above his heart, and it made him smile. Eventually, he broke the kiss, pressing his lips to her forehead before pulling the blanket up to cover her.

"Where the hell do you think you're going?" she wanted to know, wearing the cutest pout on her face.

"Just gonna blow out the candles," he promised, smiling as she touched her fingertips to his lips.

"Okay," she slowly agreed, and Mason moved around the room, extinguishing the few candles before padding back to the bed and crawling in by her side. Feeling her so close was maddening, yet he was set on just enjoying her by his side. After all, it was more than he had imagined that morning. Additionally, they had all the time in the world to get intimate since he wouldn't ever let her go again.

———

Taylor woke from the sounds of little feet hurrying across the cold wooden floor. Mason's left arm was draped over her middle while his right one pillowed her head.

"Daddy?" Becca asked; the words barely loud enough to cross the distance between her and the bed.

"Bec?" Tay replied just as quietly.

"Tay!" Becca squealed as hushed as possible, and finally, Taylor's eyes had gotten used to the darkness, making it possible to see the girl's outline where she stood. Wordlessly, Taylor lifted the blanket, prompting Becca to join her. Mason's daughter sure didn't hesitate, snuggling close while pressing her ice-cold feet against Taylor's warms thighs. She shivered, pulling Becca even closer.

"Missed you," the child whispered, and Taylor felt her breath tickle her lips. She, too, had missed the little girl something fierce.

"Missed you, too, babe," she answered and then kissed Becca's forehead, breathing in the mix of chocolate and baby powder that always seemed to surround Becca.

"Can I stay?"

Taylor had no doubt that Mason forbid it usually, but nothing was usual about this night.

"Of course." Taylor laughed quietly. "I absolutely want to cuddle with you."

The child sighed in contentment and then yawned. Taylor listened until Becca's breathing evened out, then she reached out to kiss Mason's palm after taking his hand.

"This is an exception," Mason mumbled sleepily, and Taylor melted at the huskiness of his voice.

"Of course," she gave back, biting her cheeks. She already knew that she wouldn't turn away the girl half as often as Mason probably hoped.

"You're incorrigible," he fussed gently.

"Incredible, you mean," she teased. "Incredibly happy."

eighteen

For a few weeks, everything was chaotic between two farms, a tiny girl, and Taylor's brother, but eventually, Mason and Tay settled into a routine that allowed them to spend as much time together as they could without neglecting anyone else. Tim actually loved the big brother role, and therefore, never minded when Becca was around. The girl followed him everywhere and looked at him as if he'd hung the moon. So some days, they stayed at the Collins' farm, and sometimes, they spent their evenings at the Stiles' home. To Mason, it didn't matter. He loved knowing that Taylor brought his baby girl to school, and he could pick her up.

It was a nice routine. He didn't mind knowing that

his mother finally had time for her own life, and – surprise, surprise – she was busier than ever, catching up with friends and looking for a job she could do a few hours a week, something like working in a café or diner. Mason's guilt about having taken up her time for so long finally eased.

Pulling up in front of the pre-school, he was ready to collect his little girl and head home. He knew she had a lot to tell him since it was the day before Halloween and they'd dressed up for school. As it was, he hadn't seen Becca in costume yet since Taylor had taken care of it, and now, he was curious.

It took him a moment, but then he noticed that Miss Lavera, Becca's teacher, actually stood by the door, clearly waiting for him. It made his stomach churn. Usually, she'd just wave at him and he'd find his daughter.

"Mr. Stiles," she greeted him, and he paused next to her, all hope of simply slipping by being gone.

"Miss Lavera," he replied, deciding to go for another attempt at leaving, but she ever so softly touched his arm, commanding his attention. Her face didn't look promising, so he sighed. "What did she do now?"

Becca's teacher laughed softly, before sobering considerably. "You know how kids are, right? Rebecca is still so young. She doesn't know about relationships and rights and wrongs, or what the difference is between a biological parent and new partner in one parent's life," she started, and Mason forced his hands into his pockets so he wouldn't reach for the first child he could and just get away.

"Okay?"

"When your girlfriend drops Becca off, she hugs her, kisses her, and tells her she loves her."

Mason smiled as he could all but see that in his mind. He saw how Taylor would bend down just so she'd be at eye-level with Becca. It warmed his heart. Unfortunately, he couldn't see anything wrong with that. "So?"

"You know how kids are. We teachers know that Miss Collins is just your girlfriend ..." She was so much more to Mason, but people who hadn't grown up with Tay and him couldn't know that. "... and not Becca's mother, but Rebecca was repeatedly told that everything Miss Collins does is what moms do. To make a long story short, children don't see the difference. All they see is the treatment and not the role that person is playing. All I want is to warn you that Becca now refers to Miss Collins as her mom. She explicitly told everyone her mom would take her trick or treating. We tried to tell her otherwise, but she refuses to listen. "

Mason nodded slowly. Taylor indeed had promised to take Becca and Tim trick or treating before her sister would watch the two while Mason and Taylor would take part in something Ash called 'Halloween Friends Revival.' "Okay, you are saying that basically it's likely that Becca will call Taylor 'Mom'? Did I get that right?" he wanted to know.

Miss Lavera nodded. "They are young, and really aren't to blame. It wouldn't be the first time that this breaks up a couple. We've had everything, from guys being called 'Dad' too early to women having the same problem. It's something about them not being ready to take on the responsibilities. May I be frank?"

He just nodded.

"With the way Miss Collins treats Becca, it's hard not to call her a mother. You know, mothers aren't necessarily created with a blood bond."

Mason felt pride swell in his chest. "She's amazing, no doubt."

"Many partners run," the teacher added.

"Thank you for the warning." He meant it, even though there was no way to say how Taylor would react. Or he, for that matter.

"Daddy! Tomorrow is Halloween!" A cloud of glitter, white fairy wings, and a tulle dress came running forward, and he caught Becca in his arms. Taylor had gone all out. Becca's hair was braided like a crown around her head, and she was covered in glitter hairspray. His daughter's eyes were sparkling, being no competition to the fake glitter stones that adorned her cheek. She was beautiful and clearly happy. Mason's throat clogged with emotions.

"She is beautiful. And today, she even was on time."

Miss Lavera winked. Taylor had a tendency to run late with Becca, but she clearly had enough charm that no one was ever mad at her. "She really is incredible, that woman of yours."

Mason already knew that, and he definitely couldn't agree more. Thanking the teacher, he grabbed Becca's backpack and then strapped the little girl into her seat in the backseat of his truck. She instantly reached for a doll, occupying herself with the toy while Mason started the truck, homeward bound.

He waited for Becca's usual chatter, but instead, the girl was humming quietly, not keeping his thoughts as occupied as he wished.

Ashley's truck sat parked in his driveway when they pulled up, and suddenly, he was presented with a totally new problem.

"We're home, babe," he announced, and the doll dropped from her lap, lying forgotten on the seat. She unbuckled herself and then waited until Mason helped her out of the truck. She hurried up the porch steps, and Mason followed, not caring that the truck doors stayed open since he feared what she'd say once she met ...

"Ashy!" Becca hadn't been able to pronounce the name right since the first time she had heard it.

"Hey, fairy." Ashley grinned.

"Where's Mom?" Becca asked, and Mason's heart dropped. Ash's eyes flew up to him, a smirk playing over her lips.

"Let's go and find out." She winked, taking Becca's hand to lead her to the kitchen.

"Mom! I won!" The little girl scrambled over the moment she spotted Taylor. If Tay was surprised, she didn't let on. Instead, she picked Becca up to set her down on the counter before resuming her task of cutting vegetables.

"You did? Did you get a certificate?"

"Yes because you made my hair pretty! Thank you, Mom!"

"You're very welcome, baby." Taylor laughed, leaning in to kiss Becca's nose. Afterward, she brushed the cut pieces of vegetables in a pan.

"Everyone wanted to be me. The other girls liked my hair ..."

Mason tuned them out, just watching. It was impossible for him to say a word. His heart was simply too full.

"It's okay to tear up. I wanna tear up. This is ..." Ashley shook her head next to him, and Mason cleared his throat.

"Her teacher warned me that Becca might call her that. It's something that the kids –"

"Mason, does it matter why she calls her that? Honestly? No, because fate has finally righted all the wrongs. Anyway, I'm out. Tomorrow at the bonfire?"

Having Ashley constantly around was weird, but Mason was okay with ignoring the feeling as long as Taylor was happy, and that definitely was the case whenever her best friend was there.

"Tomorrow at the bonfire," he confirmed.

"Bye, *Mom*," Ash called, winking at Taylor. Tay blew her a kiss, and Becca waved at her, then the two focused on each other again.

As much as Mason had to do, or should organize, he couldn't get his feet to move, so instead, he just stayed back and watched.

———

Taylor couldn't ignore the shadow in the door. In fact, she was more than conscious of his eyes on her, and her skin prickled with awareness, but since she had no idea how he'd react to the fact that Becca had started calling her mom, she wasn't ready to face or deal with him.

"... and everyone wanted to touch my wings," the little girl went on, making Taylor smile. She cut the chicken and then placed it with the vegetables in the pan. Her heart was racing in her throat, tying it close with worry.

Things had been finally going smooth for her and Mason, and she was more than glad that they spent as much time together as they did. Now, though, she feared dark clouds on the horizon. It was crazy that one tiny girl was all the protection she needed.

"Timmy?" Becca suddenly called, listening intently.

"Living room," her brother called back. He was bent over his homework, Taylor knew that, but he'd most likely let Becca join him. The two were like siblings - only they didn't share the same blood.

"Coming!" Becca answered, wiggling her feet until Taylor swept her off the counter and set her down on the ground. Instantly, Mason's daughter hurried away, taking away all excuses Taylor had not to look at Mason.

She reached for another tomato even though she already had enough in the pan. All she wanted was another reason not to look up.

"Hey, Mase," she whispered ever so quietly. He'd been on shift the night before, and while she had missed him like crazy and wished she could be in his arms, she didn't want him to be angry with her.

He came closer, stepping behind her and trapping her between the counter and the heat of his body.

"Taylor," he growled; his voice was so low, she wasn't sure he had really spoken. Warm hands stilled hers on the cutting board, and then one turned off the stove before he turned her around with his hands on her hips.

She swallowed, hoping he didn't notice that she was already close to tears. Correcting Becca hadn't been on her mind until he'd walked in. Taylor didn't mind the girl calling her mom, especially not since that was what she wanted to be, but she hadn't exactly forgotten what Mason had told her before. It didn't matter that everything was forgiven. Her heart couldn't forget.

"Taylor," he repeated again as she still hadn't looked at him. When she finally lifted her eyes, a heated gaze met hers. His hand cupped the back of her neck, holding her in place as he leaned in to claim her lips in a wild kiss. The passion he conveyed with every stroke of his tongue almost made her incinerate on the spot. His fingers left her neck and his arms wrapped around her as he moved even closer to her, clearly intent on wiping every thought she'd ever had straight from her brain. She could feel his arousal pressing into her thigh and then against her core as he picked her up and pushed her onto the counter.

She crossed her ankles behind his back, moving as close to him as she could while finally participating in the kiss, hoping to drive him as crazy as he was driving her. His stubble scratched her skin, and it just heightened the sensations. God, she wanted him, and if there weren't two kids in the next room, she probably wouldn't even mind getting what she wanted right there and then.

Mason's hands pushed under her top, seeking and finding skin as he bit her lower lip, making her moan softly. He swallowed the sound by slanting his lips over hers again.

Tay squeezed her hands between them, finding the waistband of his jeans and pushing her hands inside. Just a few tiny movements and she'd feel his ...

"Hi, guys ... whoa, I'm blind!"

Tay pulled her hands free, wishing the ground would open up to swallow her whole. She had totally forgotten that Tamara was bound to be home soon. Mason pulled her shirt down and then rested his hands left and right of her on the counter, exhaling slowly.

"Hi, Tam," Taylor greeted her, clearing her throat as she realized how raspy she sounded. This really was the worst timing ever.

"Give us one second," Mason demanded, not even looking at Tamara, but making Taylor meet his eyes.

"You got it," her sister replied, and Taylor could see from the corner of her eye that she didn't move.

"I love you, Taylor. And I never thought I could love you more, but it turns out, every day I can, just a little more. You're my sun, my moon, and my stars. You're the very air I breathe. Thank you," he whispered. No matter what Taylor had expected after their make-out session just then, it certainly wasn't that.

Tears came to her eyes, and she bit her lip while trying to find the right words to say. "Forever and for always," she promised. He gave her the sweetest of smiles, winking.

"I think it's safe to step back now." He grinned, and Taylor couldn't help herself, reaching between them to brush her hand across the former erection.

"Agreed," she stated.

Mason groaned, stepping away. She knew exactly why because in his eyes lay a dark promise. They'd finish what they had just started, and it was obvious that next time nothing would interrupt him. It made need pool in her stomach as she hopped off the counter and resumed her cooking.

Mason playfully slapped her ass before kissing her cheek and telling her that he still had to water the horses before he and the kids could carve pumpkins. She knew they were a little late with it, but time was limited.

Mason hugged Tamara at the door; her sister walked over, sitting on the other side of the kitchen counter.

"You know, I'd totally kiss you hello, but not after that." Her eyes drifted to the door Mason had just vanished through, then returned to her. "So things seem to be working out pretty well."

Taylor blushed, nodding slowly. Things were perfect as far as she was concerned. "Yes." What more was there left to say?

"So what did he thank you for?"

Before Taylor could answer, Becca burst into the kitchen. "Tammy! Hello!" She wrapped her arms around Tamara's legs, hugging her tight.

"Look at you, little fairy!" Tamara hopped off the counter to spin the little girl around until she broke into giggle fits because she couldn't stand right anymore.

"That's what he thanked me for," Tay mouthed, and

Tamara arched a brow.

"I'm the most pretty fairy," Becca pointed out, and Tamara nodded in agreement.

"So how about you go and find the jeans and shirt I put on your bed? Can you go and change like a big girl?" Taylor asked.

"But I like the fairy costume," Becca pouted, making a half-circle with her toe across the tiles.

"You cannot cut up pumpkins in that dress." Taylor gave her a stern look.

"Okay." Becca sighed, drawing out the last letter until she sounded like a broken tire. She stalked off, clearly not at all enthusiastic.

"Wow," Tamara stated, and Taylor turned back to her sister, a question on her face.

"You got that mom-thing down, don't you? It's incredible to watch," Tammy mentioned, and Taylor blushed.

"I ... well ..." She wasn't sure how to react to that. Being a mom to Becca was as easy as easy came. She couldn't say why, but it was fun, and everything she'd ever wished for. Frankly, she sometimes needed to remind herself she was Timmy's guardian and sister and not his mother, too.

"You?" Tammy asked, moving behind the kitchen counter to taste what Tay was cooking.

"Becca started calling me ..."

"Mommy, Mommy, it doesn't work!" The girl in question came down the stairs, almost falling, but Mason came in on time, catching her before she stumbled. She had gotten her head stuck in a sleeve of her sweater, and he laughed, putting her down before untangling her.

"Thank you, Daddy. Can we cave now?" she wanted to know, and Mason grinned at Taylor over Becca's head.

"Carve, babe. It's called carve," Taylor mumbled, feeling self-conscious because she knew everyone was watching her as she took Becca's jacket off the hook, making the girl dress properly before going out into the cold.

"Be careful and let ... Daddy help you, okay? Don't take a knife in your hand unless he's with you," she urged.

"Promise," the little girl stated and hugged her tight before slipping into her rubber boots and then pulled the door open.

"You –"

"I'm gonna make sure she and Tim are fine. Stop worryin' and make some hot chocolate, okay?" Taylor cocked her head, and Mason leaned in to kiss her. "You're pretty perfect. Enjoy some time with Tamara. Will you stay here tonight or go home?"

She sighed and already knew he wouldn't like the answer. "I'll take Tim home. Tammy is alone with the kids tomorrow, and we have a whole night then, so you'll have to live without me tonight," she mumbled, pressing her hands flat against his chest. She loved the feel of his beating heart under her hands and was sure he knew it. It was as if then she was reassured he was real and there.

"Okay, you had better know that I don't like that answer at all," he growled. She didn't like it, either, but her sister deserved more than just a 'hi' and 'bye' when she was home.

"Mason ..." she warned, and he kissed her again before Tim came, wearing a jacket just like she'd have instructed if gotten the chance.

"Can we go, Mason? Please?" He tugged on Mason's hand, and Mason groaned, acting more annoyed than he really was.

Taylor lazily strolled back into the kitchen, getting the cream from the fridge before pushing her sister out of the way. It looked like Tamara wasn't ready to wait until dinner was done.

"It works. It works very well. And Taylor, you look so much better," her sister pointed out, and Taylor couldn't help but beam at her.

"Now that you're here, I have everything I need," she whispered, kissing her cheek before focusing on the cooking again. It was true—with her sister here, her family was finally complete again.

————

Mason stared at his ceiling, constantly touching the right side of the bed that unofficially belonged to Taylor now and which reminded him with coldness that she wasn't there. Whenever he was on shift, he missed her something fierce, but he usually didn't have to sleep without her. He shook his head, sitting up. They had left around nine, and it was half-past eleven now. He already longed for her as if he hadn't seen her in forever.

Leaving the bed, he pulled on a sweater and padded outside into the hall, finding a light glow coming from beneath his daughter's door. He already knew what he'd find, mainly because Becca had gotten even more used to having her around than he had.

Opening the door carefully, not wanting to wake her in case she had simply fallen asleep with the light on, he snuck a glance inside. Becca stood on her bed, her elbows resting on the windowsill while she stared outside.

"Hey, Dad," she mumbled, and he arched a brow before realizing that his image reflected in the glass of the window.

"Hey, sweetie. What are you looking at?" he wanted to know, sitting down on his daughter's bed.

"The stars. Mom showed me Owen's belt."

"Orion's belt," Mason corrected quietly. He had been curious what went on during those nights he was on shift, but it shouldn't have surprised him that Taylor took the time to show his daughter things.

"Yes, that one," she replied, her voice subdued.

"What's up, babe?" He placed his hand on her back,

realizing how small she was still. Rubbing gentle circles, he watched how she crossed her arms on the sill, resting her cheek on them without ever stopping to watch the twinkling lights in the sky.

"She said that if I miss her and look at the stars, I'm really close to her. And Tim said he's always looking at the stars, so when I look, he looks, too. He says it's a family thing, but Dad?"

He cleared his throat. "Yes?"

"They aren't family until you have a wedding with her, right?"

"Of course, they are, Rebecca. Taylor loves you, and for Timmy, you're the little sister he never had."

"Why do they have a second home then? I don't like it when they're not here. I don't like sleeping when I'm alone in a room."

Mason glanced at the makeshift bed in the corner Timmy slept on when they stayed here.

"You want to share your bedroom with Tim?" he asked, and she finally looked back at him, her stormy eyes wide with unshed tears.

"I want them home."

God, Mason wanted that, too. Without thinking any longer, he grabbed Becca's jacket out of the closet, putting it in her, and then he wrapped her in her blanket. The end of October had come with a wave of cold, hinting at the winter to come.

"Where are we going?" Becca asked as Mason carried her down the stairs, slipping into his trainers before grabbing his truck keys and walking outside.

"We're going to go and sneak into Tay's home." He grinned, kissing the top of Becca's head, and then he strapped her into the seat.

The drive didn't seem to pass, especially because he couldn't wait to cuddle up next to Taylor. When they arrived, the light was still shining through the glass door. Mason didn't have to wait or knock because he had a key, just like Taylor had one to his house.

To his surprise, Tamara greeted them right behind the door. "Hey, you two." She laughed, clearly not at all surprised. On the stairs, bare feet came down, and a halfway asleep Tim came, his face lighting up as he spotted Becca.

"Oh, hey," he beamed. "Come on, it's late, and your bed is still prepared," he announced, waiting until Mason put Becca down. His daughter dropped her blanket, and Tim helped her out of her jacket before going upstairs with her. She didn't once look back.

"Whoa, this is weird," Mason mumbled while Tamara watched him.

"Storms again?" She winked, and Mason shook his head, scratching it in embarrassment.

"We just missed her. It took me forever to get her, so having her away from me isn't really an option," he admitted, and Tamara nodded. "So what are you doing still up?" He nodded toward the books he spotted on the dining room table, and Tamara pulled up her shoulders.

"I feared Taylor let the books slide, or didn't really have any idea what she's doin', but wow, she might not be out on the farm that much, but the books are clean and well kept, and she found a lot of potential to save some shiny coins. Seems like she doesn't need me anymore," Tammy whispered, and Mason blinked.

"You think that's the only reason your sister needs you? For the books? To keep the farm running? Did she ask you to check on the books?"

As he expected, Tamara shook her head.

"She wants you to be the young adult she knows you deserve to be. Carefree, happy, wild. *That's* what she needs you to be. I can't believe both of you run around here feeling guilty. Her for not havin' been here earlier, and you for not being here at all. Tammy, you're barely twenty. Live your life, enjoy college, and then come back here and take over the farm if you want to. And if not –"

"I want to. Contrary to Taylor, I love this whole thing. I love the cows, the fieldwork, I love the horses and the smell, I love talkin' about the feed for the animals, and I even don't mind the bookkeeping. I just wish Taylor would let me do it without the whole college thing," she fussed, and Mason couldn't help but lean in to kiss her forehead.

"She's smart to make you go. What if you ever decide

you don't want to do the farm anymore? Havin' a college degree will help you big time."

"I shouldn't be surprised that you side with her," Tamara scowled, and he laughed. "She went up a while ago to get her Kindle. I think she might have fallen asleep," she then added with a soft smile.

"I'll see you in the morning." He gently touched her chin, knowing she most likely felt like a little girl now, but for him, she was almost like a little sister.

He climbed the stairs and decided against knocking, opening the door slightly and freezing in the frame.

Taylor was lying on her stomach on her bed, wearing nothing but a black satin bra and underwear while clearly having gotten lost in her reading. Her feet were crossed at her ankles up in the air, swinging softly. God, she was beautiful.

He closed the door quietly, but she was so submerged in her fictional world that she didn't react until after he had dropped his sweatpants, sweater, and shirt and lay down on top of her. She was cold against his heated skin, but the Kindle instantly hit the mattress.

"Mason!" She wiggled under him, clearly trying to turn, but he didn't let her. Instead, he kissed her shoulder, and she finally relented, resting her head on her pillow while giving him access to her neck.

"Hey. Babe. I. Missed. You," he whispered between peppering tiny kisses across her skin. Slowly, taking his time to enjoy the closeness of her, he licked down her spine, seeing goose bumps spread across her body.

She made an appreciative sound in the back of her throat, and he opened her bra, pushing the straps down her arms until her back lie freely before him. Sitting up, he started to gently massage each muscle, beginning with her shoulders until eventually reaching the muscles in her lower back. She purred, making him laugh. With a quick wink over her shoulder, she grinned, and then she rested her head back down, enjoying his treatment. He wished he could give it to her each and every night. She'd probably be the most relaxed woman out there.

Brushing his hands under the waistband of her panties, he felt her tense in a whole new way. His body followed suit, making his boxers tighten. Leaning up enough so he could free her from the material, he moved down with the panties, dropping them to the floor before he kissed his way up, hoping and praying that his daughter was definitely fast asleep down the hall.

"Mase," Taylor breathed, her voice hitching as his hands got ahead of his mouth, gently parting her legs to better accommodate his body. She moved against his hands as he brushed one finger down her center, making her gasp quietly.

This wasn't the first time they'd slept together. No, they had done that about a week after finally admitting their feelings to each other. Yet each time with her felt like the first time all over again.

Caressing her wet core with one hand, he tried to get rid of his boxers with the other. He leaned over her until he lined up with her, his hands resting left and right of her hips.

"Taylor," he whispered, slowly lifting her ass before pushing into her in one fluid movement. She was willing and ready against him, wiggling her hips and making him hiss. He stilled her movements, kissing her back before pulling out and pushing back in, trying to find a rhythm that would make them both last longer yet not frustrate them.

Taylor bowed her back, pushing up onto her hands and taking him in deeper, throwing her head back while biting her lip. She wasn't a screamer, but all the sexy moans she made could definitely penetrate through doors and walls and be amplified in a silent home.

"Jesus," she gasped as he covered her body with his, biting her shoulder to keep himself from groaning out too loud. Her movements got quicker, and she reached between them, cupping his balls in the palm of her hand.

"Fuck, Tay," he rasped out, and she chuckled, a throaty sound that made him lean back, his hand on her hips as he met her hip thrusts.

She definitely didn't want him to go slow on her, and as much as he wished he could savor being with her, he knew why she was hurrying him along.

No matter how late it was, Becca had a tendency to come in at least once to earn a hug and a kiss. Having her walk in was the last thing he wanted. Not that he could hold back much longer with the way Taylor massaged his balls, sending shots of arousal and the need for release through him.

"Girl, stop or you won't ... Tay," he growled, and she laughed quietly, not relenting the grip she had on him.

"Won't what?" she teased, and he stilled his hips, thinking that this would change anything really, but it didn't. Instead, she was grinding against him until he thought he'd have to lose his mind. Pulling out, he turned her and made her back hit the mattress, then he was back on her, feeling how she wrapped her legs around him, drawing him closer. He captured her lips in a kiss, holding her close as he thrust strongly into her a few times, making sure his pubic bone rubbed her exactly the right way. Her back bowed off the sheets, a low moan making its way past her lips. He captured them; letting his tongue taste all of her while meeting the movement of her hips harder, feeling her tremble under his hands.

Taylor's nails dug into his back, spurring him on until she shattered beneath him, coming apart with a long, drawn-out shiver. Only after she had come down from her high, which he lengthened with deliberately slow movements, did he allow himself to come, taking nothing more than three quick jerks of his hip.

"I love you," he mumbled against her shoulder, kissing the skin there until their breathing had evened out again.

"Right back at ya, cowboy." She smiled, and he got up, vanishing in her en-suite bathroom to clean himself up before getting a washcloth, wetting it with warm water and then going back to her. He cleaned her up before discarding the cloth in the sink again to join Taylor in her bed. She had pulled on her panties and a shirt. He followed her example and pulled on his boxers, not ready to deny Taylor the feel of his skin under her hands. He knew she loved to roam her palms across his chest.

"Are you excited for tomorrow?" he asked as he cuddled her close. She brushed her fingertips across his heart, drawing lazy circles.

"Walking with the kids to get candy? Yes. Having a high school memorial bonfire? Hell yes. It's going to be fun. Well, for us that is, since we're a couple and so are Kelly and John. We'll have to make sure Brad and Ash don't feel left out."

Mason nodded against the top of her head before kissing it. "There'll be more people, but it'll still be nice. Like old times."

"We should get to sleep. I have a feeling it'll be a short night tomorrow. Plus, your daughter is up at the crack of dawn." She laughed, and Mason went onto his elbows until he could look at her in the light of the night table

214

lamp.

"Our daughter," he corrected, and then leaned into kiss her long and sweet. She sighed against his lips, a sound of contentment, and he turned off the light before falling asleep with her in his arms. It really was the only thing he knew he wanted forever. She should never again be sleeping away from him, and he'd make sure that she knew that soon, too.

nineteen

Taylor leaned back in Mason's truck, wondering if she'd ever been happier. The trick-or-treat run with Tim and Becca had been successful and so much fun; the little girl had a hard time stopping. After two hours, though, Taylor had insisted they finally went home. Besides the fact that it was getting late, she was impatient to have a carefree evening with their friends and the man she loved.

Rubbing her palm across his thigh, she saw how he gave her a strained smile. Something was off with him. She'd already noticed how tense and absent he'd been once his daughter had started telling him all about her evening. Where he usually was attentive and amazing, he had been distracted, barely nodding when prompted to.

Taylor had tried asking him about what was wrong, but he'd only given her an irritated shrug, asking her what she meant.

"We'll be late," he stated, and she giggled.

"Late? We can be late for something that has no starting time?"

"We were supposed to meet Ash at eight," he growled, and she turned in the seat until she could see his face, watching him.

"So? It'll be half past when we're there. Breathe."

"I hate bein' late," he only replied, and she placed her hand on his arm.

"Stop the truck, Mason," she instructed, and he glanced at the clock. "Right now," she enforced, and he sighed in defeat, parking it on the side of the little road. She unbuckled herself and then him, moving until she straddled his lap, framing his face. As much as she was not going to have hot truck sex with him, she was ready to kiss him until his tension melted from his shoulders, giving her the feeling that he'd enjoy this evening as much as she would.

"What are you doing, Tay? I –"

She interrupted him with a kiss, feeling how he tried to gently push her back until he suddenly relaxed into her touch, drawing her closer to kiss her deeper. She felt how his fingers cupped the back of her neck while the second hand squeezed her hip.

"Feeling better?" she asked, resting her forehead against his as they had kissed each other breathless.

"I'm feeling fine," he replied, and she gently bit his bottom lip.

"Liar. You've always been the worst at that. It's you and me, Mase, no matter what's coming. You and I will be weathering the storm and dancing in the rain, no matter," she promised, and it was only then that his whole body seemed to go lax, all tension finally drawn out of his muscles.

"I should've kissed you twelve years ago when I drove you home, and you told me I could be anythin' I want," he groaned, and she laughed. As much as she regretted the time they had wasted, she wasn't sure they had needed it to realize they belonged together forever, ready to live through everything life would be throwing at them.

"You became a helicopter pilot in the emergency team," she whispered, remembering that she had wanted to comment on that.

"You wanted to be a nurse. I figured if you'd ever be back here, we'd be working together somewhat, so yeah, I became and EMT in the heli. Best job ever. As much as I love the farm, this is the better part of me, and it's only because of you. Otherwise, I would've stayed on the farm and nothin' more. Thank you for encouraging me when I didn't know I needed it."

He softly brushed his lips over hers again, and she

cupped his cheek, kissing his nose before going back for another taste of him.

"I'll always be there to tell you how amazing you are," she promised, and a smile broke across his face. Satisfied with her handiwork, she moved back into her seat, letting him take her down to the lake.

Ash was waiting for them in the parking lot, not even giving Mason a look. "You were supposed to be here an eternity ago," she fussed, pulling Taylor along before she could protest. She threw a glance back over her shoulder at her boyfriend, but Mason just gave her a helpless shrug before throwing his college jacket at her. She caught it, glad that at least one of them had thought about bringing more along than just a sweater and a scarf, but she'd been so excited and overheated, it simply had slipped her mind.

"Why in the world are you in such a hurry? And where are we goin'?"

"I wanted some time with you before everyone's gathering at the bonfire!" Her best friend tagged her along until they stood by a keg. Ash filled a cup for herself before handing Taylor a can of lemonade.

"Umm ... you know, I'd be totally fine with a beer," she stated, crossing her arms in front of her chest.

"You ain't getting drunk today," Ash replied, and Taylor snorted.

"I said one beer, not I'm going to get drunk off my ass," she retorted. Ash watched her face for a long time, making Taylor arch a brow in question before she went forward and got herself a cup while a grumbling best friend put the can back into the cooler.

"Fine," Ash conceded, and Taylor shook her head.

"What is wrong with everyone? You seriously act weird," she fussed and then took a sip from the red cup. She didn't often drink beer, but some occasions like bonfires or football games just called for the bitter tasting liquid.

"So where to next?" she asked as Ash contemplated something, her brow furrowed and her eyes focused somewhere far off.

"Can we walk the corn maze?" she wanted to know, and Taylor gaped at her. For real?

"Yeah, because I love that so much?" she stated, shaking her head in disbelief.

"For old times' sake," Ash pushed, and Taylor gritted her teeth. How bad could it really be? She was older now, knowing that the things inside that maze were fake. Then again, she had known that back then. Glancing around, she hoped to find Mason, seeing as he had saved her all those years back. Maybe she could get lucky this time around, too.

"Fine," she gave in, and Ash clapped in excitement, grabbing her hands and conveniently producing two tickets from her pocket as if she had known Taylor would go with her anyway.

"Leave the cup. We don't want ya to spill anythin' when you get scared," Ash explained and then tugged on her hand as if she were on a deadline.

The guy manning the entrance nodded at them, giving Ashley a look that made Taylor wonder what she was missing.

"Don't start screaming, ladies, it'll only spur on the people more." He grinned, and Taylor absolutely didn't like the smug way he looked at her.

It took less than ten steps into the maze to remind Taylor why she hated the cornfield horror. Around the first bend, there was a guy with a chainsaw, and Taylor started to walk faster, not caring where she went as long as she got away. Ash still clung to her hand, pulling her toward another bend without giving Taylor a chance to protest.

"I hate you. Ashley, I hate you forever," she fussed as they ran into an artificial spider web. She hated those things, and nothing had changed. Ash just pulled her along until she suddenly froze, turning three hundred sixty degrees on her heel.

"Shit, we're lost," Ash fussed, and Taylor stared at her, feeling that something was up.

"Of course. That's why it's a maze."

"No, I ... I mean, yes, but I don't mean it like that." She nodded, and her smile couldn't be more plastered on.

A woman came around the bend, wearing white

clothes, but that wasn't what made Taylor's skin crawl. She backed up before the longhaired woman could get any closer to her. She remembered that woman from a long time ago, and she still had huge spiders covering her body, one slowly crawling across her hand.

"Right isn't always right," the woman mumbled, coming slowly closer even.

"Got it. Thanks," Ash called out, grabbing Taylor's hand again as a cacophony of screams and sounds of horror welcomed them just two more turns into the maze.

"How far in are we?" Taylor wanted to know, and Ash grinned.

"Not yet far enough, but wait … I think … stay put. I'll just check out which way to go before the huge spider comes," Ash explained and then she was gone. Taylor stared after her. Together, she had been halfway okay, but alone? No way would she move any further until –

The sound of a fiddle reached her ears and while everything was possible, she knew that this didn't belong to the Halloween sounds. Curious, she moved forward, suddenly finding strung up lights and rose petals leading her way. A nervous tremble overcame her as if her body knew something she hadn't realized yet, and her throat got dry.

She knew by the closeness of the bends that she was nearing the center of the maze. She pushed up the arms of Mason's jacket, smiling to herself at the comfort it provided, even though Mason was God-knew-where.

The music grew louder, being nice and slow, something romantic. More rose petals covered the ground, and finally, she rounded one more corner, her hands flying up to her mouth as tears instantly sprung to her eyes. Mason stood in front of a plywood panel covered in pictures of her. She recognized a few, knowing Ashley had taken them back in high school. Some were newer, and she hadn't seen those before. As much as she wanted to explore that more, the man in the middle holding a single red rose drew her eyes. Candles were burning to the left and right of him, and the fiddle music changed to a Ben Rue song. It was something about not being able to wait until someone became his wife.

A tear slipped down her cheek, and she bit her lip, stepping closer until he could reach out to take her hands in his.

"Don't cry before it gets serious," he joked, but she heard the tremor in his voice.

"I feel played," she fussed softly, wiping away the tears before placing her hands in his again.

"You were. Anyway, Taylor," Mason started, and she felt her heart ready to beat out of her chest.

He was going to ask her to marry him, and while they hadn't been an official couple for long, Taylor felt as if she'd been working toward this moment her entire life.

"Taylor, when I first fell in love with you, it was the

way you smiled no matter what life threw at you. I fell in love with the way you made a rainy evening in my truck the most amazin' evening ever. I fell in love with the way you made it possible for everyone to feel as if they were just right. Everyone loved you because you just gave them the feeling that no matter who they were, they were great. When you returned, I fell in love with the way you devoted your life to your brother and the way you wanted only the best for Tamara without thinking about yourself. Every day, somethin' new makes me fall for you. I never had a doubt in my mind that you were the one for me. Not when you threw me out for cleaning up your mess, or when you screamed at me just because I've been an ass." She laughed through her tears, and he gave her a heartwarming smile.

"I'm glad I have no makeup on," she sniffed, and he framed her face, kissing her softly.

"It's another thing I love about you because you're the most beautiful woman I've ever met. I could probably name a million things that made me fall in love with you, but Taylor, seeing you with Becca, the way you love her unconditionally, is probably what sealed the deal for me. I never want to lose you again. Last night, knowing that you weren't with me, sucked. I couldn't and wouldn't sleep without you by my side. And I plan to never again be without you unless I'm on shift. So," he whispered and then went down to his knee, holding her hand.

"Taylor Collins, I always knew you were going to be my wife, and I would do anythin' to fulfill this wish. I want to spend the rest of my life with you, and you've been my girl since this night twelve years back, even if you didn't know it. Make it official. Become mine." He swallowed while she was crying harder by the second. "Will you marry me and my daughter, Taylor Collins?"

He opened a black box, presenting her with a deep brown-pink, heart-shaped diamond ring, framed by tiny clear diamonds. It was breathtaking, but Taylor would've married him even if had he presented her a plastic ring shot at the local fair.

"Yes! Oh my God, yes!" She didn't wait until he placed the ring on her finger. Instead, she fell to her knees and threw her arms around his neck, kissing him. This was better than anything she could've ever dreamed.

———

Mason was shaking from head to toe, kissing her another time before he pulled back. "Let me at least put this on your finger," he demanded, and she laughed, holding out her hand while standing up again. Her slim fingers were trembling, and he kissed her fingertips before pushing the ring down her finger, feeling as if finally he could breathe again.

She was his, forever and longer. Resting his forehead on her hand in relief, she kissed the top of his head.

"You didn't think I'd say no, right?" she asked in

disbelief.

"Of course, he did! You have a tendency not to do what people expect of you," Tamara announced, stepping forward from behind the plywood board. She was crying, carrying Becca and holding hands with Tim. Ashley, Kelly, and Brad stepped forward, too, all looking emotional.

"You traitor," Taylor sobbed, hugging her best friend tight before taking Becca from her sister's arms.

"You deserved it. So much."

"And now, I'll take the babies back, and you all go and enjoy the bonfire. I simply couldn't miss this," Tamara announced. Only then did Taylor seemed to realize the whole extent through which he had gone. Mason could see it on her face as it dawned on her.

"How long have you planned this?" she wanted to know as Mason led her out of the maze. His friends had promised that they'd clean up all evidence and make the maze scary again while he could take care of his now fiancée.

He led her over to the bonfire, the diamond on her hand sparkling in the warm glow, but nothing compared to the beaming expression Taylor wore. He could see wayward tears clinging to her lashes, her hair falling freely around her face and down the back of his jacket. It was amazing seeing his name on her back, knowing that soon she would be a real Stiles.

"Spring," he mumbled as they sat down and she

turned to him.

"Spring?" she asked.

"Spring," he repeated. "I want a spring wedding. It'll be warm enough not to be muddy, but still not too hot so you can wear whatever dress you feel like. The fresh green of the leaves will look good on wedding pictures. Spring brings everythin' into bloom, and if we marry then, it'll be an eternal spring for us," he rushed out, worrying that she'd call him sentimental.

"Well, whatever, Mason. I'm yours, and as long as you'll wait at the end, I'll walk down the aisle, not caring when or what I wear," she assured him. Mason beamed at her, kissing her deeply before pulling her into his arms, knowing this evening would turn out better than anyone had anticipated.

Especially now that he no longer had any reason to be nervous.

twenty

Thanksgiving came and went, and snow started to cover everything around. Tim had begged Taylor to celebrate over at the Stiles' farm, and Tamara had readily agreed. Space was limited, but Stella had offered her bedroom up to Tamara and Timmy, sleeping on the makeshift bed in Becca's room. The little girl was excited about having everyone around, and while by now no one was thrown off by her being called mom, Timmy had picked up calling Stella grandma.

As much as Mason's mother tried to hide it, Taylor could see the pleasure on her face each and every time Timothy said that. It was as if Mason's mom finally had what she had wished for for Mason, her, and Becca. Taylor didn't mind. Stella seemed to complete the hole that had been in her own family for way too long.

"Anything else you need out of town?" Mason called from the door, and Taylor leaned back until she could see him tie his shoes on the bottom of the stairs.

"Yes, you," she answered, and he laughed, finishing his shoes before coming over to her side, leaving wet tracks on the floor. She eyed them, arching a brow at him.

"Sorry," he apologized, sheepishly looking at her.

"You aren't. And now, get moving so you will be back to help me cook," she instructed, and he grinned, leaning in to kiss her. Her phone buzzed next to them on the counter, but Taylor ignored it.

The weekend after her accident, Andrew had called for the first time, and while she had ignored it back then, sure it was a one-time thing, he now called at more regular intervals, being more persistent the longer she ignored him.

"Who is it?" Mase asked, and Taylor sighed.

"Andrew. My ex. He bought my business, and while I never again wanted to talk to him, he keeps calling. I have nothing to say to him."

"Want me to answer?" Taylor blinked. Mason's tone was calm, but she worried that was just what he wanted her to see. Still, she nodded. If someone could get rid of Andrew, it probably was Mason.

"Stiles?" he stated after swiping right on the touch

screen.

He turned on the speaker, and she looked at him.

"This is Andrew Cane. Mason Stiles ... never thought I'd talk to you one day," her ex stated, and Taylor swallowed hard while Mason was clearly shocked.

"Why's that?" he asked, his voice filled with disbelief.

"For Taylor, you were the perfect dream. You were like a god to her. I don't think anyone could reach up to the way you sing, the way you care, the way you are. It's hard for a city boy to stand up against a cowboy ghost," Andrew explained, and Taylor shook her head. She had tried everything to keep Mason out of her thoughts, but she had clearly failed.

"What?" she whispered, regretting the next moment that Andrew now knew she was listening.

"It was little things like a comment, or a look, or the way you carried his picture in your wallet. I knew, Taylor, that you'd never love me, but you were still good to me. And you were a remarkable businesswoman, which is the main reason I'm calling. I sold it."

The floor threatened to drop out from under her feet. She knew it hadn't been her baby in months, but somehow, her mind had been eased knowing that it still belonged to someone she knew.

"You what?" She placed her hands on the counter, trying not to collapse. Mason drew her into his arms, holding her tight.

"I'm going to leave the city. People loved what you turned this into, and someone paid a lot of money for it. I don't want it. Any of it. I sent the check to your local bank. That's all I meant to tell you. I figured you'd call me once you picked it up, but you never did."

"Ash never said anything," Taylor mumbled, and Mason kissed the side of her head.

"Who's Ash?" Andrew wanted to know.

"My best friend," she answered absent-mindedly, and Andrew laughed shortly. He sounded tired, but not like he hadn't slept in days. More as if he was tired to his bones.

"Yeah, it was my name on the envelope, so I'm not surprised. She probably wanted to make sure I don't get between you and Stiles," he mused, and Taylor turned in Mason's arms, kissing his shoulder. She was done talking to Andrew, still trying to get over the fact that he had sold her business.

"Dude, if that was all, thank you for sending her money, and fuck you for selling," Mason growled, clearly catching on to her pain.

"I cannot stay here any longer. I need to see what is so tempting about the countryside," Andrew replied.

"Good luck then," Mason replied and then ended the call. "You okay?" he wanted to know, and Taylor shook her head, burying her nose in the crook of his neck. It was terrible how quickly a day could go down the drain.

Mason held onto his fiancée, sighing heavily. It was incredible how much the selling of her firm affected her. He had no idea what she'd done exactly in Michigan, and he had to admit that he never had cared because it reminded him of a time when she wasn't his.

Then again, the way her ex had talked, she maybe *always* had been his. And she carried his picture in her wallet? Maybe they'd been more connected than he'd thought.

"I wanted to ... it was my baby. It was everything I wanted, and even though I never wanted to go back, it's terrible knowing that it's no longer there." She sniffed, her body shaken by silent sobs. Suddenly, she pulled back, reaching for her phone. "Ash. I need to call Ash."

She fumbled with the device until nearly dropping it with shaking hands, so Mason took over, dialing his ex's number. She answered after a few short rings even though she was at work.

"Hey babe," she chirped into the phone.

"Open the letter from Andrew," Taylor demanded, her voice thick with tears.

"I didn't say anythin' because I figured nothing good ever comes from exes," Ash replied truthfully, and Mason was surprised that she knew exactly which letter they were referring to since obviously it had been there months.

"Just open it," Tay pleaded and then moved until her

hands were resting left and right of the phone on the counter. They heard the tearing of the envelope, and then a gasp.

"Fuck, I gotta sit down," Ash mumbled. "Holy shit, Taylor. Do you know what's in here?"

Mason snorted. Of course, she didn't, or Ash wouldn't have to open the letter.

"Oh, while talking about ex," Ash fussed, but by now the heat was missing in her voice with those statements. Clearly, she finally came to terms with being friends with him again.

"What does it say?" Taylor wanted to know, getting the focus back to the topic at hand.

"Note or check?" Ash asked back.

"Note first."

"'I don't want any of it, Taylor Collins. It was your baby and every damn day reminded me of the fact that I am not you, and that you aren't with me anymore. I can't woo people the way you do. So bye business. Bye Taylor. Bye sucky memories,'" Ash reported, and Mason wanted to get in the car and drive until he found the douche.

"How much?" his fiancée prompted.

"For how much did you sell it to him?"

"Ten grand," Taylor whispered. Mason almost whistled. That was a lot of money.

"Well, I assume he took that out of the final sum," Ashley mused, and Mason felt as if he needed to take a seat before hearing the sum. Ash was stalling, so it was either a lot of money or nothing at all.

"How much?" Taylor repeated, and Ashley sighed.

"Two hundred forty thousand."

Two hundred forty thousand... Mason was floored while Taylor didn't seem surprised in the least.

"Turn the note," she ordered.

"'I sold our client list for one hundred and fifty thousand. It could've been more, but I knew you were going to be pissed. Have a great life, TyCo. I loved you,'" Ash read the rest of the note.

"How high-class were your clients, Taylor?" Mason wanted to know, and Taylor swallowed, not looking at him.

"Tay, you're rich," Ashley pointed out the obvious, but it still looked as if Taylor couldn't comprehend that.

"Open a bank account for each Tim, Tamara, and Becca. Put seventy thousand in each account and the rest in Mason's," Taylor instructed. "I'll come and sign the permission slip tomorrow." His fiancée looked up, meeting his eyes. Mason didn't know what to say.

"Are you sure? Maybe you should think about this, Collins," Ashley urged gently, but Mason could see it on Taylor's face. There was nothing to think about. She didn't want the money.

"I am sure," she assured her best friend.

"You won't have any of the money, Tay," Ash tried

again, and finally, a first smile broke over Taylor's face.

"I'll be a Stiles soon enough, so he'll have to share the account anyway. We don't do things only halfway." They hadn't talked about it, yet Mason couldn't deny that they were on the same page nonetheless.

"We'll invest the money to make the house bigger," he decided, and Taylor's eyes widened slightly.

"You two make me sick and jealous. Have dirty sex for me, too," Ash groaned. "See you at the bank tomorrow. Love ya, Tay."

"Love you, too," Taylor replied, grinning while ending the call.

"That's a whole bunch of money, baby," Mason whispered, and she sighed.

"It was pretty exclusive clientele. I was good at what I did, and Andrew was good at investing our money. I never lived the rich life, which is why our debts were paid off pretty quickly. I didn't keep much of it. It was a good job, but that's no longer my life. I prefer boots to heels, and jeans to pencil skirts," she admitted, walking closer to where he had sat down. He pulled her on his lap, seeing something else in her eyes.

"You're worried about him, aren't you?"

She lowered her eyes. "You worry about Ash, don't you? It doesn't matter that he could've never held my heart the way you do. He was still a friend I shared a few years of my life with. Of course, I worry, and it won't ever change. What bothers me, though, is that Andrew loved money. Seriously, he lived and breathed wealth. He could've sold the business, and I would've been none-the-wiser. Why didn't he? Instead, he gave it all to me, but the little bit that I got from him for my part of the business."

"Which, by the way, is ridiculously little, considering what it clearly was worth," he scolded, and she shrugged.

"I didn't want it. I just needed money to tide the farm over in the beginning if I messed up. Nothing else." God, she was too damn perfect.

"Did you mean that with the shared account?" He cupped her cheek, making sure she met his eyes.

"Of course. Someone needs to spend all your money on books and decorations." She grinned but then sobered. "Mason, with us, it's all in or nothing at all. If we get married, we share a house, a bank account, and a family. If that's not what you want, you might as well make me leave right now," she demanded, her jaw set.

"I want at least two children with you. A boy and a girl." He named his conditions, and she beamed.

"Family," she repeated, and he leaned in, kissing her hard on her mouth. Never, in all his years, had he expected that a relationship could feel as this one did.

"So I need to get into town, and you need to finish cooking." He grinned, getting up with her on his arm before putting her down on her own two feet.

"Deal," she agreed, giving him one of those smiles

that would forever warm him, no matter what would come their way.

twenty-one

Mason hated Christmas shopping. It wasn't because he never found what he wanted, but because everyone thought they had to stop and talk to you, making sure you knew how much they appreciated and loved you. Sunburn took 'love your neighbor' to a whole new level during the holidays. Mason rarely was hugged as much as he was on that day. One more day to go until Christmas Eve; he was excited to bring home gifts and make everyone happy.

He had forbid Taylor to buy anything for anyone because her money would pay some of Becca's college education if not all of it. He had a feeling, though, his stubborn fiancée wouldn't really listen.

Making his way to the grocery store, he pulled out the

list Taylor and his mom had compiled. He nearly groaned as he realized that he'd probably need two carts to get everything he saw on it. The store was filled to the brim with patrons, and while he didn't mind, it just meant more small talk and hugs.

"Mason Stiles. One of the best guys I ever got the chance to teach." Mrs. Crook, an old lady with white hair and a friendly smile, approached him. She had been his teacher throughout high school, always pushing him to do better. Only it hadn't been her initiative that had gotten him where he was now. That had been Taylor.

"Mrs. Crook, hey," he greeted, giving her a beaming smile. She still had been his favorite teacher ever, and only during her class had he bothered to really listen. "How are you doing?"

She patted his chest, clearly happy to see him. "I'm peachy, boy. My daughter and her family came to town, and she'll be cookin'. In fact, she already invaded my kitchen, so I needed to get out of the house. My son and family will be here tonight, and so will my second daughter. The house will be stuffed with people like we stuff the turkey on Thanksgiving." She shook her head, looking as if she regretted having them all over, but Mason could see that this wasn't true. She was clearly excited, her cheeks flushed and her eyes shining.

"How many people are we talking?" he asked, taking the time to talk to her even though he wanted to go home and just be with his family.

"Fifteen so far. Suzy's been trying to get my sister and my brother to come, too. And then they'd probably bring their grandchildren. Of course, at some point, not everyone could stay at my house anymore. And you, Mason? Celebrating with that beautiful fiancée of yours?"

Mason nodded, feeling a blush creep up his cheeks as he realized that the whole damn town probably knew every little bit of their story. "Yes, Ma'am. She's bringing her sister and her brother over and we'll just mix the families," he told her, and she nodded slowly, her expression going soft.

"The Collins kids need a family. It's a shame what Bonnie and Wayne Collins did to their kids. Pressuring a young girl so much that she doesn't see any other choice than to leave her hometown and never return." She shook her head in regret. "I had Taylor in class, and then her sister, Tamara. Bright kids. Taylor was such a nice and outgoing person. Everyone wanted to be better for her. Tamara was the total contrary of her sister, though, always quiet, somewhat subdued. Not having her sister around hurt her bad," Mrs. Crook mused, and Mason had no doubt about that.

"Taylor is back to correct that mistake," Mason whispered, and the old teacher's head snapped up.

"Mistake? If she hadn't left, nothing would be saving the family now. Bonnie and Wayne never were meant to stay together. If Taylor had stayed back, letting her father and mother push her into a role she didn't want, you wouldn't have a fiancée now, boy. There'd be nothing left of the girl you fell in love with. Destiny is what it is. You wouldn't be here now if Taylor had stayed. She would've destroyed herself over her family, and you probably would've left town because you wouldn't be able to see that. No. Taylor and Tamara came out stronger on the other side, and that's what matters. So how is Taylor doing with your daughter?"

Mason wasn't the least bit surprised that people were curious about that. "What do you think?"

"Is she already calling her mom?" The old lady winked, and Mason took a deep breath.

"She is. It didn't take that long, and I don't think it bothers Taylor is at all. She's doing everythin' a mother should be doing. Sometimes, I think Becca loves her more than she loves me." He grinned and Mrs. Crook chuckled.

"No wonder. People always preferred her to you," she teased, and he couldn't help but laugh.

"She always has been amazin'," he agreed and then checked his watch. "Okay, I gotta run, or said woman is gonna hurt me when I get home." He winked, and his old teacher reached up and patted his cheeks.

"You're a good man, Mason. Take care of the Collins kids. They deserve a happy life," she mumbled, and he nodded, promising that he had no other intentions.

His phone buzzed in his pocket, and he sighed. It was most likely Taylor, wondering where he got lost, so instead of answering, he filled his cart and hurried to the checkout. Once finished, he pushed his cart toward his truck, patting down his pockets to find his car keys. It took a moment until he spotted Brad. His smartass greeting died on his lips as he saw the pale face of his best friend.

"What's wrong?" he asked, starting to load the truck with the shopping bags.

"Your Christmas is going to take a turn for the worse," Brad predicted, and Mason snorted.

"Taylor doesn't cook that bad," he replied, and Brad grabbed his arm, halting his movements.

"How about you take me serious for a second, Mase?"

"How about you tell me what got your panties in a twist, and I might actually be able to?" he snapped, feeling how the tension rolling off Brad infected him, too.

"Dude, this isn't exactly ... I had hoped someone else might have informed you already. I don't wanna be the ass to deliver bad news," Brad confessed, and Mason swallowed, uneasiness settling in his stomach.

"Bad news?"

"What could possibly ruin Christmas for you?"

As much as Mason wasn't ready to play games, he sighed, putting serious thought into it. "If Taylor wasn't there," he finally replied.

"Or cryin' the whole time?" his best friend suggested.

242

"I don't like where this is going," he admitted, and Brad closed his eyes before gritting his teeth.

"Mason, oh my God, I'm so glad I caught you before you went back home." Ashley joined them, being out of breath from hurrying over. "Have you told him?" she asked toward Brad, her brows raised in annoyance.

"I was working up to. This isn't easy to say," his best friend defended himself.

"You just don't have the balls to," Ashley snapped. "Bonnie Collins has been seen back in town. Down at the gas station, she told the other patrons she was here to reclaim her family."

Clearly, Ash had no problem holding back, making Mason feel as if the breath had been knocked out of him.

"When?"

Ash shrugged. "I just heard. Probably this mornin' or late last night. I couldn't get a hold of Taylor, but then I don't know how she'll react. I'm ... Jesus, Mason, what are we going to do?"

He shook his head, not having an answer. "Maybe she's amicable."

"She cleared out her daughter's whole room two days after she left town. She left her family. Mason, no matter what she thinks she is, do you honestly expect Taylor to be happy? Tamara? Tim?"

No, Mason didn't. This spelled disaster more clearly than anything else ever could.

"I gotta go. I at least wanna be there in case she shows up. Lucky break that we decided to celebrate on our farm," he decided, hoping it was true. Maybe, just maybe, it would give him enough time to prepare Taylor and her siblings for what was waiting for them soon.

Taylor heard the doorbell ring and saw Stella move, but Tim was quicker, already reaching for the doorknob.

"I got it, Grandma," he called while pulling open the door. Taylor didn't see him anymore, but she heard the snarl that answered his statement.

"She's not your grandma, son. But hi, big boy!"

Taylor moved up against the wall, seeing from across the room how Stella all but flew off the couch and then briskly walked toward where Taylor's little brother stood, most likely paralyzed.

"Hey, Timmy, why don't you go and let me handle that?" Stella asked gently, and it didn't take long before Timmy came around the corner, throwing himself into Taylor's waiting arms. She hugged the boy while listening intently to what transpired at the front door.

"Bonnie Collins. Never thought I'd see you again," Stella chided.

"Just here because I cannot get into my own house. Since my son is here, I have no doubt at least one of my daughters is too. May I speak to either of them?"

"I'm babysitting your son since Tamara is away at

college, and Taylor actually has stuff to do, no matter what you think."

Tim still sobbed into her shoulder, and Taylor wondered if she should be stepping forward.

"It's interesting how you speak about my kids. As if they aren't mine, but yours in fact," Bonnie pointed out.

"I'd ask you in, but we are gearing up for Christmas, and while we used to be somethin' akin to friends, you lost that privilege when you treated your daughter as if she was the pariah for wanting her own life."

"I'm not sure you're in a position to judge me and my family. Just because your boy never was smart enough to have any bigger dreams than this, you don't need to attack me," Bonnie replied. Taylor didn't care when she was the one put down, but attacking Mason? That was out of the question.

"Go and get yourself some ice cream," she whispered to her brother before straightening herself and marching over to the front door.

"Mother," she greeted her, deliberately putting a sharp edge into the word. "It's funny how you judge me for leaving and Mason for staying. In case you didn't realize, he's EMT and a helicopter pilot while taking care of the family farm. The only real disappointment here is you since I had an amazing business I had to sell in order to return to take care of the family you clearly never wanted."

"A family you left."

"I didn't leave the family, Mother. I left *you*. You were the one telling me that either I take care of the farm, or you never wanted to see me again." Taylor was surprised that she actually managed to keep her voice calm.

"You never returned when I left, so I guess it couldn't only have been me," her mother goaded, but Taylor lazily leaned against the doorframe, watching her mother. She was acting less affected than she felt, and to her surprise, it seemed to work, too.

"Tamara and Timothy were taken care of, and I had a business to run. Besides, I returned to them the moment they needed me. And now, if you wouldn't mind –"

"Did he finally take you, Taylor? The boy you've been so smitten with since high school? Were you finally good enough?"

Taylor knew it was a low blow, and her mother tried to get a reaction out of her, but she told herself not to react.

"Mommy!" Taylor closed her eyes as Becca called from the top of the stairs, coming down with a naked, glittering doll and a beaming smile on her face. No matter what her mother would now say or think, Taylor refused to ignore the little girl.

"Hey sweetie," she whispered, kissing Becca. She picked her up as Mason's daughter stretched her arms.

"Betsy and Loony aren't friends anymore. Can Betsy sleep with Daddy and you?" It was incredible how children could be oblivious to tension inside a room.

"I'd ask you inside, Mother, but it's not my house, and you're clearly not welcome." Taylor arched a brow at Stella, who stood rigidly behind her, arms crossed in front of her chest and a hostile expression on her face. "And while we're at it, the other house is mine, and you aren't welcome there, either. It's what happens when you neglect your family, Mother. Things change owners out of necessity. How about you go to a bed and breakfast and maybe, if you're really nice, we'll talk to you when we see you on the street?"

She gave her mother a super sweet smile, and then wanted to close the door, but her mother pushed her foot in before it was fully closed.

"That's why you're back! He got you pregnant, and now, you didn't have any other chance," her mother taunted, and Taylor kissed Becca's hair, putting the girl back on her feet.

"Go and play with Tim, okay?" she whispered, and Becca stumbled away, humming softly.

"I'm not sure how this is any more your business than the rest, but Mason was always another reason for me to stay. Fleeing from you was no longer necessary, so being here, Mason and I finally got where we wanted to be since forever. Now, can you please ..."

She trailed off as Mason's truck parked next to Stella's car and her seething fiancé stormed toward her.

Things just got a lot more uncomfortable.

Mason saw the defensive posture of his mother, noticed Taylor's pale skin, and he knew he'd do anything to get Bonnie Collins off his family's farm.

"Mase," Taylor mumbled, a clear warning in her voice. She didn't want him to interfere, but he sure as hell didn't give a fuck what she wanted. He had meant to have a talk with her mother since the day Taylor had gotten on the bus and left him.

"The guy that can't keep it in his pants," Bonnie taunted, and Mason froze, caught off guard by the comment. Was she referring to Becca? Mason was positive that Taylor would've never told her mother about the conception of his daughter, so maybe someone in town had talked.

"Mother, leave him alone. Just go, and maybe I'll meet you in town someday soon," Taylor tried to pacify the woman who looked so much like her, it scared Mason. Bonnie's cheeks were hollow, somewhat like Taylor's had been when she'd returned. Her mother's blonde hair hung longer than her daughter's did, but the braided length still reminded him of his fiancée. Her face was older, clearly marked by years of stress and, Mason wanted to believe, self-hatred, too, had something to do with it, but he doubted that.

"I don't remember you as so mean," he finally forced out, and Taylor's mother laughed. In fact, Mason remembered her as a soft woman, loving her daughter without reservations. How wrong had he been. It had taken until Taylor's senior year for him to see the true evil inside that woman, but now, it was hard to unsee.

"I don't remember you having to get girls pregnant to keep them. They usually threw themselves at you, and my little Taylor had no chance against all the sluts you slept with," Taylor's mother stated, shaking her head in regret. Taylor's gasp drew Mason's eyes to his fiancée's face. What the hell was he missing?

"Bonnie Collins, move your impertinent ass off my grounds and don't ever think about insulting my son or my soon-to-be daughter-in-law ever again. I promise this lady here will show you how much she can still kick someone's ass, honey," Stella threatened, stepping forward, but Taylor's expression worried Mason.

"Stop it," she whispered, holding her hand up before her mother had even drawn in a breath, ready to protest. "Let me get my car keys."

"Take mine," Mason ordered, and Taylor looked at him, desolation shining from her eyes.

"Thank you," she muttered, stepping forward as she was with no jacket on and no scarf, just a light sweater, jeans, and sneakers on her feet. He knew for a fact that her home would be ice cold. They hadn't spent one day there in more than a week.

"Tay." He held her back, but she just kissed his palm

before dropping his hand from her arm. "What's your plan?"

"Get her away from where she can hurt you, Stella, or Timmy. Tell Tammy I'll be fine," she pleaded, and Mason wasn't sure he could do that. Her sister would move heaven and hell to make things better, while Taylor would do the same to keep Tamara away. "Get in the car, Mother," Taylor ordered.

"Don't boss me around," Bonnie snapped, but Taylor just arched a brow.

"Get in the car or have the police escort you off this land. Your choice." She waited, clearly giving her mother the chance to figure out her best course of action, but then the elder Collins woman moved over to his truck, pouting after she had crawled into the passenger seat.

Mason drew Taylor in, holding her freezing body tight. "What now?"

Taylor shook her head against his shoulder, mumbling something unintelligible, so he drew back far enough to understand her.

"She has to have an ulterior motive, and I want to know what it is. And then I'll set her up in the living room and lock myself in my bedroom. Tomorrow morning, I'll have breakfast with her, and we'll figured out what her fucking deal is until then or she'll have to leave. Everything is in my name, the luck of having a minor neglected by his parents. The lawyer worked wonders. I just don't know how it'll be if she claims Timmy."

"She can put a claim in, but honestly, she won't get him back. Not after having left. And people here will be ready to vouch for you and tell everyone how bad she is for the family. Just don't let her get to you."

Taylor showed him a tiny smile, wordlessly assuring him that she'd be fine. "You should get inside and take care of our daughter. I kinda didn't correct her when she assumed you got me pregnant, and I returned because of that. First, I would've, and second, I don't owe her any explanations. Enjoy your evening with the family, and tomorrow, we'll prepare for Christmas, okay? Maybe you can get Timmy and Becca to help decorate the tree with you." She pointed at the fir still standing next to the porch. "I love you."

He kissed her, conveying everything he felt with it: the need to protect her, the fight to trust her, the regret of not spending the night with her. "Call me, sweetie. Always," he urged, and she nodded. She finally got in the car with her mother; she was not the least bit excited, that much was clear.

Mason watched until they had left, and then he turned and walked up to his mother.

"She never used to be like that. I remember when Bonnie and I were in high school. God, I wonder what happened to her ... besides her leaving the family when they needed her the most." Stella shook her head, and

Mason sat down on the stairs, rubbing his face in his hands. His mother sat down next to him, squeezing his arm. "She'll be okay."

Mason shook his head. "She was okay. This? This is a disaster."

"Maybe you should just put some faith in her," Stella pointed out, and Mason slowly nodded. He had all the faith in the world in her. That didn't change the fact that Bonnie might be the devil in disguise, and his angel sure as hell wasn't prepared for it.

twenty-two

Taylor opened the door to her home wordlessly. It couldn't be more obvious that it was hers now than the moment her mother had realized she had no key and no idea where to find it. Even though her house was cold, the smell of cookies lingered in the air from when she and Tim had spent an entire afternoon baking and joking around, flour ending up everywhere. Taylor had cleaned for hours yet couldn't get herself to regret it.

She hit the light switch, cringing at the pale shine. Normally, she would prefer turning on all small lamps around the room, but somehow, she didn't think her mother deserved the comfort those lights would bring.

While the woman in question slowly walked around

the room, Taylor went ahead into the kitchen, feeling the need to have some tea. She put on the kettle, smiling at it. It was a gift from Stella, who had told her that some days comfort lay in the tin can. It made Taylor smile when she had to agree. Getting another tin box from the cupboard, she opened the top and inhaled deeply. Mason had bought her a Caribbean tea that smelled and tasted of pineapples and bananas. She loved it. Carefully spooning the loose leaves into a tea bag, she waited until the kettle whistled.

"Are you gonna prepare me one, too?" her mother asked, finally following her, and Taylor lifted her eyes, gritting her teeth to calm herself down.

"I didn't think you were going to stay that long," she stated, and Bonnie Collins folded her hands on the top of the kitchen counter.

"You've become a hostile little thing," her mother noted, and Taylor took the kettle from the heat, pouring the steaming water into her mug. She wrapped her fingers around it, holding on tight.

"What do you want, Mother? Why are you back in Sunburn?"

She kept her eyes on her mother's face, trying to remember how it had been back when she hadn't hated her mother. Back when her mother had still been her best friend and had always wore a beaming smile.

"Back when you started high school, you were the prettiest, nicest, and most compliant girl anyone could wish for. You had amazin' grades, and everyone was so jealous of me. But then you suddenly had new friends, and while your grades still were amazin' and everyone still loved you, they didn't know about all your crazy ideas. They didn't know that you snuck out at night to see boys, and I worried."

Boys... Taylor had never snuck out to see boys. She had met Ash and Kelly, and they had taken pictures: of stars, of fireflies, and each other. They had been girls, and yes, sometimes, they had come across Mason and his friends, but he had never been her main reason to leave the house. None of them had. All she wanted was freedom and fun, and to prove that you could run wild and still be a good girl.

"You worried? About what? I showed up to every damn fundraiser you asked me to; I was a cheerleader the way you wanted it. I was the perfect daughter, yet it wasn't enough."

"We had a farm to take care of. You loved the horses, but that was all you cared about. Your father wasn't going to be able to manage it forever. It was a family thing, and you never wanted it."

Taylor shook her head. "Mother, I wanted in, but I wanted to find myself first. I wanted to go away and see the other states, maybe even the world. I wanted to know I had a home to return to, stories to tell, and parents to love me. You decided that I couldn't have what I wanted, but that I had to take what you needed me to take!" She lowered her voice as she realized that she was starting to scream. "Choices—that's all I wanted."

Her mother stayed silent, starting to walk around the kitchen. Taylor lifted her mug to her lips and slowly sipped the hot liquid. She should've known that this wouldn't get them anywhere, but somewhere, deep inside her heart, she had hoped that maybe her mother would see reason.

"I always thought that if you'd just stayed long enough, you'd see that this is exactly what you wanted. You know, I never really wanted this life, but after enough time with your father here, I didn't think I needed anythin' else. And there was Mason for you. He definitely wanted to stay around, and that could've been your chance. You wanted him back then just as you want him now. The way he looks at you, or the way you look at him; it hasn't changed one bit. Only you never saw it before, and I never commented on it because I felt that through him maybe I'd lose you, too. After all, he had his own farm that his mother hoped he'd take over. Mason Stiles was everythin' I feared yet hoped for ... even though you deserved more. So much more."

Taylor doubted that she could've found anyone better than Mason, but she didn't say that. "I got so much more, and you didn't like it, either."

"Andrew what's-his-name? No, he wasn't more. You settled for him. Each and every time you've been out with him, it was clear something was missing," her mother replied thoughtfully, and Taylor had to put down her mug so she didn't drop it.

"How in the world would you know?"

"Where else should I have gone, but to the city my daughter deemed better than her hometown? What else was there to do, but watch her trample over everythin' that she held dear back home? You were no longer my daughter the moment you walked out. I've never seen such a heartless sight before, the way your hazel eyes looked at me, void of any emotion..." Her mother shook her head as Taylor hugged herself.

"Void of emotion?" She had felt so much that day; her heart had barely been able to react to the different feelings of heartbreak, excitement, and numbness, slowing down and racing in equal parts. "I was torn apart by having to leave because you wouldn't see reason. I was heartbroken because all Dad did was stand back and watch me walk away instead of telling you that your last words shouldn't have been for me to never return, but that I'd always have a room in your house, no matter what. That's what parents do, Mother! I wouldn't have left if you'd have said those words!" she accused and knew in her heart that it was true. While she hadn't been ready to take over the farm, she would've stayed if her mother only had shown her how much she loved her and was ready to put aside their problems.

"You would've taken over the farm then?"

Nope, never, Taylor was sure of that. "I would've been around to help and gone to a community college to get the nursing degree I hoped for. But ... if you came and saw me in Michigan, why didn't you talk to me?"

"I had nothing left to say." Bonnie Collins crossed her arms in front of her chest, now looking every bit the cold-hearted bitch she was where it concerned her daughter.

"Surprised that this changed now. Or do you really think you can get your family back? How long are you going to stay around? Until Tim's tired of you? Or Tamara? Because then there's no reason to wait."

"You and your high horse. You've been somethin' better after you left, and now, you come back here, throwing around your city-girl attitude? You're nothin' more than a struggling cowgirl here, depending on your sister to manage the farm and your boyfriend to take care of you and your wayward daughter. Don't think you have any right to judge me when you're way below me." Her once beautiful mother snarled, and Taylor wondered what had happened, what she had done to deserve that much hatred.

"What did I ever do to you, Mother? What?"

The tired features contorted in rage. "You had all the chances in the world. You could've gone anywhere, and you wanted to, too! And then you left your family behind to go to the big city and become rich and a snob. You turned stuck-up with all your fancy dinners and pencil skirts, and -"

Finally, it dawned on Taylor. "You're jealous. That's all. I had the life you wanted, and you couldn't have. It was okay as long as everyone was stuck like you, huh? But then I decided there was more than the farm life, and you thought you could bully me into staying. Then you thought replacing me with another child would make you content again, but it didn't work. Instead, you left them high and dry without a word or a note. I bet you never looked back, did you? You don't care what became of them. You came here to most likely accuse me of ruining your life when the only person who really ruined it was you. You, because you didn't open your mouth and ask Dad to leave. You, because you didn't tell him you wanted more. You, because the only daughter who could've offered you an escape on regular intervals was estranged. My father loved you so much; he would've made everything possible for you, and you? You ran." She rubbed her temples as a brewing headache made itself known. She finally wasn't angry anymore. She was just tired. Her mother had ruined her own life and tried to get everyone down as well, just because she was miserable. "You ruined Tim's childhood and Tammy's teenage years. Nothing is left for you here, Mother."

"You had so much money, and we struggled to get by. We made last-minute payments most of the time, while you were sipping champagne and eating caviar."

Taylor pinched the bridge of her nose, deciding to stay quiet.

"Have you ever wondered how Dad managed to pay at the last minute, Mom? Where did he get the money from when he hadn't had it the week prior? The day prior to paying?"

Taylor's head snapped up while her mother swiveled around. Tamara stood in the shadows of the hallway, and Taylor's heart was breaking. Her little sister didn't deserve to be there. As much as she wanted to, Taylor bit her tongue to keep from declaring this was an adult talk.

"Tam," Taylor warned quietly.

Tammy didn't look at her, though. Her eyes focused on Bonnie. Why the hell had Mason let her go?

"You didn't wonder because you didn't care. Well, I'll tell you. Taylor paid all of that."

"Tamara Collins," Taylor repeated, and finally, her sister's eyes swung to her.

"How long were you going to stand there and let her accuse you of everything? How long were you ready to let her make you feel bad? Well, you're done taking the blame for everything, Taylor! It wasn't your fault our fucking parents weren't decent enough to raise Tim and me. It wasn't your fault you left and never returned. And it's most certainly not your fault that our precious, amazing, selfless mother didn't get what she wanted out of life. If you don't defend yourself, someone has to do it," her little sister snapped, and Taylor squared her shoulders. While Tammy's Southern slang should've been more pronounced in her anger, college clearly started to clean up her language. It almost made Taylor smile.

"How about you go upstairs while I prepare the sofa for Bonnie, and then we'll talk?" she instructed, her voice leaving no room for discussion, but of course, Tammy ignored that.

"I'm not -"

"Now." This time, Tammy just huffed her cheeks and then stormed up the stairs, exactly like the young woman she was supposed to be.

Her mother was staring at her, just like earlier when she didn't think she had to justify her actions.

"I'm gonna get you a blanket and a pillow. You can stay for the night, but tomorrow, you need to leave this house. *My* house," she emphasized.

"You're cruel," her mother snarled, but Taylor only smiled.

"Cruel because I take in you after you insulted me? Or cruel because I deny my fiancé the right to fall asleep next to me, and my daughter the right to be tucked in by me? Because then, I agree." She got everything from the upstairs and found her mother still standing in the same position. For a short moment, Tay could see the broken woman underneath the cold exterior: head bowed, shoulders sagged, shadows crowding the fragile body, but then her mother steeled herself and glared at everything that was Taylor's. No, her mother couldn't expect any sympathy from her.

"Here. And don't get any ideas. There's no need to make breakfast for us. Tamara and I will eat at the Stiles' house tomorrow. I would not be mad, though, if you're gone once we get up," she hinted and then walked up the stairs, feeling exhausted. She wanted to crawl into bed and have Mason sing her to sleep. Hell, she wanted him there, but first, she had to deal with a pretty upset sister.

Rapping her knuckles against the wood, she didn't wait for an answer before pushing inside. One lamp was burning on the nightstand, and her sister was face down on the bed, crying not so silent sobs.

"I'm sorry, Tam, but I don't want you and her in one room too long." She started sitting down next to her sister's trembling side.

"Why?" The question came muffled. "Because I might spill secrets, like you raising another woman's daughter? Or you having helped here even when our parents were too proud to ask? Or about you putting seventy grand in an account for me to do with as I please?" Tamara hadn't moved yet Taylor understood her perfectly well.

"See it as your chance at freedom. You want to spend the money here, on horses and clothes and whatever?

Your choice. You decide you do want to leave, after all? Your choice. I just want you to have the best chances possible, and while it might not be enough money for Ivy League colleges, it'll be a start to whatever you want."

"I want the farm, Tay. This one. I want the house, and I want a family here. I want her gone. The dragon downstairs needs to leave."

"Most importantly, she doesn't deserve any of our stories, explanations, or attention. Why didn't you stay at Mason's? He was supposed to keep you," Taylor pointed out, and finally, Tammy turned to her.

"Didn't want to. After I had heard that you were alone with our mother here, in this house, I needed to come. Mason was prowling the door as if he was ready to pounce it and leave, too, and it was driving me crazy. I think he's hurting for you. This is … you're not gonna leave again now that she's back, are you?"

Her sister looked so young, so vulnerable as she asked that, that Taylor had to swallow.

"Why in the world would I leave?"

"Mason would follow you everywhere, and you don't want the farm. Nothing is keeping you here now." She sobbed quietly, and Taylor cuddled up next to her sister, pulling her close.

"I have you and Tim, and while I might not love this farm the way you do, it's a family thing, and I want it to be here when either of you is old enough to take it over or sell it. I don't care which way, but until then, I'm going to keep it running as good as I can. Never again will I walk out of your or Timothy's life, Tamara. You hear me? In it for life. We're a family, and I'll be your sister when you need it, your mother when it's necessary, and your friend whenever you want it. I'm going to kick your ass when you deserve it and be proud as hell all the other times. I know you're going to insist that you're grown up and all that stuff, but it won't keep me from crying at your graduation, or wedding, or when I'll be an aunt for the first time ever. Our parents might not cherish the Collins' name, but I sure do, and it'll stay that way, too."

"You'll be a Stiles soon," Tammy remarked. Butterflies erupted in Taylor's stomach.

"That's true, but at heart, I'm a Collins, and I'll always be. Don't worry about me leaving. This is our house, our family, and we take care of it. We don't need our parents. Bonnie had a hold on me for the longest time. I'd get up with a stomachache because guilt would weigh me down each and every second but no more. I got out stronger on the other side, even though it might have taken a kick or two by a very handsome cowboy we both know." She more felt than heard Tamara giggle, and that was all that mattered really.

"I miss Dad." The sentence was uttered so low, Taylor wasn't sure if she maybe had only imagined it.

"I'm not surprised," she decided to say and then sat

up. The sooner she'd get to sleep, the quicker the morning would come.

"Stella's making pancakes for Tim and Becca tomorrow. I think we should be back in time for that, too," she suggested, and Tammy sat up, too.

"I think you're right," she agreed. "Tell Mason hi," she then added with a wink.

"Lock your door. I'd rather not have Bonnie sneak in on you tonight to try to tell you whatever. Unless you're ready to talk to her." It was pretty obvious that Tamara wasn't ready because she stood as Taylor stood.

"Love you, sis. So much, it hurts," Tamara whispered and then squeezed her tight.

"That's just the headache from our mom showing up." Taylor winked, kissed Tamara's cheek, and then she left, vanishing in her own bedroom and locking the door behind her.

She didn't bother to undress, but instead fell on the bed and got her phone out of her pocket.

"Mason," she whispered the moment he had picked up.

"I love you. I love you so damn much," he replied as a way of greeting and finally tears spilled down Taylor's cheeks. They were freeing, as if all the evil thoughts and pain her mother had put into her ran out, cleansing Taylor inside out.

"Serenade me, Mason," she pleaded. "Make me feel

as if I am by your side."

　　She heard him shifting and sheets rustling, picturing him on his bed, one hand resting on her side while he got comfortable, then he started singing, and she cried silently while he sang her country songs about hope, passion, love, and a future.

twenty-three

Mason hadn't closed his eyes all night, singing to Taylor until she had fallen asleep. His heart was aching at everything her mother had most likely said to her, and he hurt for all the things Taylor had already been hearing at their house. His mother had been kind enough to repeat it all for him, and he just wanted to hurt someone, even though he wasn't the type to hit women. Or people, in general, if he could avoid it.

His daughter came down the stairs, and he only knew because of the low *thump* the stuffed animal made on each step as it was pulled down. Becca looked ready to cry, and it made Mason kneel. He wore sweatpants and a shirt, not sure if he'd stay inside the house if he dressed in jeans and his boots. The chances of him running out and going over to Taylor's farm were just too high, and he tried everything to avoid that.

"Hey, baby," he greeted her, and she wiped her wrist under her nose, eyes still lowered to the floor while her curls twisted and turned in all directions. Rebecca was a picture of misery, and it didn't help Mason's mood.

"Hey, Daddy," she replied, sniffing.

"What's up?" he wanted to know even though he could guess very well.

"Nothing. I'm fine," she answered, sniffing another time.

She passed him, avoiding his hands, and then pulled out a chair in the kitchen.The stuffed rabbit - or whatever it was, Mason couldn't tell for sure - landed on the table as she scrambled up on the seat, her pink PJs riding up to reveal a fake tattoo that was already rubbing off again. It was something Taylor allowed her to have whenever Mason was not there.

Once Becca was up, she rested her head on the tabletop, sighing.

Next up, Tim came down the stairs, still in PJs, eyes downcast, walking by him without acknowledging Mason. He, too, sat down on a chair and rested his head on the table. Mason couldn't resist, pulling out his phone to film that misery-times-two.

"Hey, buddy. What's up?" he asked, having a hard

time to keep the smile out of his voice.

"Nothin'," the boy drawled. "I'm fine." Long sigh.

"Becca, wanna have pancakes?" he inquired.

"Nah, not hungry," his daughter gave back, sniffing.

"Do you miss Mom?" he wanted to know, and his daughter turned to him. Her eyes filled with tears, and the corners of her mouth pulled so deep, Mason was sure she was trying to form a circle.

She nodded and Mason stopped the video, hitting send to make sure Taylor saw it. He just knew it would draw a smile from her lips.

"She's coming back," he reassured the children, and Becca wiped underneath her nose with the ear of her rabbit.

"Sure?" she asked, and Mason nodded. He missed Taylor just as much as the other two did.

Stella came in and arched a brow when she saw the table. Mason shrugged and then leaned against the wall, watching. His mother patted Becca's hair and then leaned in to kiss the top of Timmy's head before she pulled out a chair, too.

"Wanna help me prepare breakfast? We can put chocolate chips into the pancake batter," she offered, and Mason knew that usually this was a special treatment.

"I'm not hungry," Tim replied, his voice subdued. It almost was as if Taylor had been gone a year instead of barely twelve hours.

Mason's phone vibrated in his pocket, and he got it out, seeing that it was a video Taylor had sent him. He played it loud enough so the two at the table would hear it. Taylor waved frantically at him, beaming.

"Hi, my loves! Tammy and I will be with you in a bit, and I sure hope there's pancakes and bacon on the table when we get there. Becca, help Grandma with the batter, and Tim, make sure you show Mason how to make the bacon crisp. Mason, I love you. See you in a bit!" She was perfect; there were no other words for it.

Tim and Becca jumped off their chairs and started talking over each other in excitement.

"Upstairs, change your clothes first," Mason ordered, and the two ran past him, laughing and now bubbling with happiness. He shook his head and joined his mother in the kitchen.

"It was quiet last night with her gone," she commented.

"Becca got used to Taylor telling her good night. She had the biggest problem falling asleep for the longest time. Tim asked me a million times if his sisters would be okay, and I didn't know what to tell him. It's terribly hard saying the right things, but Taylor looks good. I mean she looked super happy over the last months, too, but it's as if a weight has lifted off her shoulders. I wonder what happened with Bonnie yesterday."

Stella lowered her eyes, focusing on the flour beneath

her hands as she talked. "Taylor is a strong woman, and as much as Bonnie probably thought it would be easy to bully her, your girl has her own mind now. And she took on the responsibility of her siblings. So trust me, nothing will come between them and her again. Ever. Especially not a neglecting mother. Taylor is a woman; the woman you always knew she could be. Only now, she knows it as well," his mom explained.

It didn't take long, and the kids charged back into the kitchen; two whirlwinds ready for action. Tim helped Becca up on the counter and then took the pan Stella offered.

Mason decided to wait outside. He wanted a second alone with Taylor, even if it was just to kiss her and make sure that she knew he loved her more than anything and was ready to defend her against whatever came.

As he stepped outside, he had to stare for a second. Soft white flakes floated to the ground, covering it slowly, just in time for Christmas. He knew Taylor had wished for that, and somehow, heaven seemed to send a sign, telling them that everything would be okay.

"Peaceful, isn't it?"

Mason turned, surprised to see the woman who always occupied his thoughts standing next to him.

"Hi, where...?"

She pointed at his truck and then grinned. "I cheated and let it roll to a standstill. You looked so peaceful; I didn't want to disturb you," she explained, and he took her hand, before deciding differently and pulling her into his arms. With a little nudge, she jumped, wrapping her legs around his hips, and Mason loved feeling her so close. He drowned his right hand in her hair while holding her around the hips with the other. Mason breathed her in as if he hadn't seen her in forever, and frankly, that was how it felt, too. One look at her face, and he knew things were different. She looked lighter, beaming, and it was as if finally nothing was haunting her anymore.

"Did I mention that I love you?" he wanted to know, kissing her neck where he could reach it, and she nodded.

"You might have a time or two," she teased, her voice sounding muffled with her nose buried against his shoulder. She held onto him as tight as he held onto her, and it made his heart melt.

"What do we do if we ever have to be separated for longer than a night and you're home alone? Or I am?"

"It'll be hell," she agreed before he had even said it, and they both laughed. He finally put her back down on her feet, framing her face. He searched her eyes, wondering what had gone down but not daring to ask.

"You know, I'm not gonna bite, even if you get curious," she promised, and he captured her lips in a kiss, taking his time to taste her and make sure she knew exactly how much he had missed her. She molded herself to his body, not leaving an inch of space between them, but then she pulled back and leaned against the wooden handrail framing the porch.

"Okay, tell me then," he demanded softly, and she crossed her arms.

"She was a bitch, as expected. But it's funny, when you're ready to let go, how it hurts a lot less. I'm not sure what she wants, besides finding a way to make her life better, but that's okay. She was gone this morning before Tammy and I got up, and while I'm sure she's not gone for good, maybe she understood that approaching us on more civil grounds would get her further." She shrugged and then crossed her arms in front of her body. Something else was on her mind, and Mason stepped closer, rubbing her arms.

"What else?"

Taylor lowered her eyes and then took a deep breath. "Tamara told me last night that she misses Dad. I wonder if maybe I should try to find him. Not that I'd know where to look," she admitted, and Mason rested his forehead against hers. As much as he wished he could do magic, finding her father seemed almost impossible.

Taylor felt Mason sigh and knew he felt bad for not being able to help her. "This wasn't about making you feel guilty," she pointed out, and he gave her a weak smile.

"It's just that when I finally have you around and can offer you the world, things come up that I cannot do a

273

damn thing about. I can easily take over all the farm work on your farm if you need me to, and I can clean out ten bedrooms if that's what's asked, but I cannot keep your mother from being spiteful or make your father reappear," he whispered, and she laughed.

"And here I thought you were a man who liked challenges," she teased, only to cuddle into his arms a second later. "Besides, I don't need you to do any of that. I just need you to listen when I complain about my mother or contemplate my father," she admitted, and he kissed her forehead, nodding.

"And I'll always be there to do just that." Taylor had no doubt about it.

"So ... plan for the day; I need to get into town, sign the accounts and the transfers, and then I need to buy some last-minute gifts. I think it's best to act as normal as possible," she told him, and he squeezed her hand.

"First, you need to see some people who really missed you." He winked, and she burst out laughing another time.

"What the hell was that? Becca looked as if someone had died." She giggled at the memory of his daughter's face.

"You should've seen her walking down the stairs with that face, pulling her stuffed bunny after her."

"Rora."

"What?" he asked, confused.

"That stuffed bunny's name is Rora." Mason's brow

furrowed in doubt, and she shrugged her shoulders. "I told her that all stuffed animals needed names, and she asked me for examples. I could only come up with Roger Rabbit. So when she wanted to name it that, I told her that surely she could come up with her own name."

"And Rora is what she came up with?" he asked skeptically, and she nodded.

"I think it most likely was my intonation. I always put the focus on the first two letters of the names. She just went with it. And decided the bunny was clearly a girl then and surprise, Rora loves doing tea parties with Becca's dolls."

She couldn't decipher the emotion in Mason's eyes, but it looked as if he was ready to devour her.

"She needed you in her life," he finally stated, and Taylor nodded, cocking her head.

"You both did, cowboy. We knew that already," she pointed out and then sashayed inside, knowing that Mason was watching her every step.

"Tay!"

"Mom!"

Taylor all but stumbled as Tim and, just shortly after, Becca threw their arms around her legs.

"We missed you so much," the girl nearly sobbed, and Taylor picked her up.

"I prepared the bacon exactly how you like it, but Mason left me alone, so I had to do it by myself," Timothy explained and threw an angry glance at Mason, who had entered the house behind her.

"Sorry, buddy, I needed a second alone with Taylor."

"I know, to push your tongue into her mouth," the boy stated, rolling her eyes.

"Timothy Collins," Taylor called, outraged, while she could hear her sister's giggles in the kitchen. She must've slipped inside during the turmoil.

"That's what they say in school. But I don't get what should be nice about it. It's all gross and eww." The boy shook his head, faking a shudder, and then he left to head back to the cooking.

"Oh no," Taylor groaned. "We're getting there. Puberty's coming!" She hid her face in her hands, already dreading all the talks that would come with it.

"You know, I can always have those talks with him," Mason offered.

"Or I could."

Taylor spun around, staring at the shadow in the door that Mason had left open because they hadn't entered the house far enough before the kids had ambushed her. Everything she had been ready to say was stuck in her throat as her sister rushed passed her, falling around the man's neck.

"Dad," her sister squealed, and Taylor could only stare.

"Mister Collins," Mason greeted him politely, almost

stiff.

"Mason, I thought we were on a first-name basis already." Her father smiled insecurely.

"Why don't we finally close the door and all settle down in the kitchen and have breakfast? Heavy talks happen best on a full stomach," Stella announced, joining them in the hall. Taylor couldn't get around noticing that Tamara all but clung to their father while Taylor had no idea what to think.

"We were, Mister Collins, but until I know you won't act like your wife did around your daughter, I think I'm going to stick with politeness," Mason replied, and Taylor went to his side, pushing her hand into his to pacify him. Whatever her father wanted, there was no need to cause a scene when Tamara clearly was over the moon to have him back.

Wayne Collins reclined his head in a small nod. "I can respect that, boy. I'm still gonna stick to calling you Mason." He grinned, and the corner of Mason's mouth lifted infinitesimally.

"Fine with me," her fiancé agreed and then leaned in to kiss Taylor's hair. "Mom and I'll prepare the table. Mr. Collins, you're welcome to join us. The kids tend to prepare too much and eat too little." Mason smirked, and Stella nodded in agreement.

"Thank you so much. I've been driving all night and wouldn't mind some food," her father admitted, and

Taylor wondered why but decided to agree with Stella. Some things really were better settled with food in their stomachs. Additionally, Taylor wasn't ready for discussions or confessions. There had been too many in the last few days anyway.

Mason left and took his mom with him, following Tamara, who'd left after a quick kiss to her father's cheek.

"You're beautiful, daughter," her dad finally said, looking at Taylor.

"Life has been treating me well for the last months," she agreed and then gave him a smile. "It's good to see you. Seems Santa granted one of the Collins' girls her Christmas wish."

Her father stepped forward and opened his arms, and as much as Taylor didn't want to, she longed for a hug because, contrary to their mother, he seemed to have come with the intention of making peace.

"Daddy," she whispered and then let him pull her close, breathing in a scent that should be familiar but wasn't. It'd been too long since they'd seen each other.

"He watches over you like a hawk," her father whispered, and Taylor didn't even need to ask, guessing that while Mason had been willing to give them space, he worried things would escalate after all.

"He should; he promised to marry me and therefore be there through the good, the bad, and the disaster," she replied in a hushed voice and then remembered whom she

278

was hugging. He was one-half of the reason she stayed away from home for twelve years. Clearing her throat, she stepped back.

"Mason Stiles, you want to marry my daughter?" Wayne called out, and Taylor turned to her fiancé, who leaned against the doorframe.

"Doesn't want to, Dad. He has to. It's fate. There was never a way around it," Tamara interrupted and then took their father's hand and led him away in an obvious attempt to dissolve the tension in the room.

Taylor followed until she stood in front of Mason.

"Some people need forgiveness, huh?" she asked, and he brushed his lips across hers.

"I ain't gonna forgive him unless I know he's here to be nice and not tell you how to live your life. I'm happy, though; you figure that letting it rest is the best course of action for you. You've been troubled enough by the past," he agreed, and she gave him a smile.

"Let's have breakfast. My pancakes are probably cold already."

He laughed and then kissed her nose. "Stella kept them warm just for you." He winked, and she couldn't help but think that maybe in the end everything would work out all right.

twenty-four

The sisters had agreed to keep Wayne around. After a rather busy Christmas Eve that hadn't been the least bit awkward, contrary to what Mason had expected, everyone had settled down for the night. The house was more than just a little filled, yet Mason couldn't deny that this felt more like Christmas than anything else ever had. Their little weird patchwork family had fused seamlessly, and he couldn't help but be glad about that. Becca was currently asleep in Stella's bed, only too happy to be sharing a bed with her grandma. It was a means to an end because Tamara needed a bed, and they had feared that the kids would've kept each other awake all through the night. Midnight was creeping up, and this was the first time

Mason had been alone with his future wife in a couple of days.

She stood by the window, watching the snowfall outside. Her expression was serene and made Mason breathe a little easier.

"Just a few more minutes and we can bring the gifts down," he commented.

"And eat the cookies?" she wanted to know, turning in his arms.

"That, too." He laughed, cuddling her closer.

"Are you okay?" he wanted to know, and she nodded against his shoulder.

"Surprisingly, I am. I can't even tell you why. It just feels as if nothing bad is coming anymore. Call me naïve, but it doesn't feel as if Dad's here to cause trouble. In fact, he has been nothing but awesome, hasn't he?"

Mason had to agree. Wayne had helped wherever he could, preparing the turkey together with Stella, had wrapped gifts with Becca and Tim, and all around had made sure to stay out of their way. Besides that, he had dropped by the Collins' farm and taken care of the horses and cows together with Daniel, the only farmhand who didn't have a family.

"Oh, which reminds me, he asked Stella if she was okay with Daniel coming by for Christmas dinner. It seems that otherwise he'd be alone at home, and Wayne obviously didn't want that," Mason explained, pulling back to watch Taylor's face, not being surprised as it lit up.

"Oh God, yes. I'm so happy he made that suggestion! Stella was okay with it, right?" Now came the part that actually made Mason choke.

"Well, Stella actually said it was our decision since soon this would be your house and your home. After all, you're becoming a Stiles," he whispered, seeing her eyes widen.

"No, Mason! This is your mother's house, and I'd never ever..." She shook her head at a loss for words, and Mason framed her face.

"She *wants* this to be our house, and says she'd be more than happy to find a cute little apartment in town," he explained, and Taylor stepped around him, still shaking her head.

"No, Mason, no way. This is her home, the place where she lived with your father, and where she raised you. No, I'd feel terrible to know that I forced her out of her home."

"Forced her? Taylor, no way in hell did you force her! She wants this for us because we have our own family now," he protested. He was surprised that Taylor took the news every way but well when he'd been over the moon with the prospect of making this their very own home – even though he had reassured himself ten times at least that it was really okay with his mom.

"If Dad hadn't returned, I'd have suggested she

moves into that house, but now ... no, she's staying right where she is," Taylor insisted, and Mason rested his forehead against the cold glass, sighing.

He loved his mother, he really did, but if she was ready and okay with moving out, he was totally on board with this being his house.

"Look, we –"

"Let's go and bring the presents down," she interrupted him, and he groaned. Taylor was too stubborn for her own good, and sometimes, Mason wished she'd be just a little more compliant.

Before she had reached the door, Mason pulled her back.

"Hey, I want to give you somethin' before everyone else does. You are the biggest gift for me in my entire life, and therefore, I decided that today you'll be getting the first gift I get and the last. Just give me a second."

"You gave me everything, Mase, I don't need more from you," she whispered, and he already heard that her voice was thick with emotion. He knelt next to the bedside table and pulled out a slender package.

He smiled to himself, knowing that Taylor would scold him for the money he'd spent. But she was worth that and so much more.

"You shouldn't have," she started before he had even handed her the little box.

"I should have," he gave back and then let her open

the first gift of the season.

"Mason," she whispered, her fingers trembling as her fingertips went over the silver bracelet. The charms were intricate, and Mason loved each and every one of them.

"We have a tiny truck for all the times we spent in mine. There's a pair of cowboy boots because we love those. There's a musical note because ..."

"You kept serenading me," she added, and he nodded, moving further.

"These are baby shoes because Becca is our daughter now. I picked a bow because we're going to tie the knot and the sign for eternity because I want to spend the rest of my life with you and last but not least..."

"A heart because that's where we'll be forever connected?" she suggested, and he nodded.

"Exactly."

"Will you put it on for me?" she wanted to know, and he happily complied, smiling as she softly jingled the charms. "I don't know what to say," she sniffed, happy tears glittering in her eyes.

"How about thank you and let's go eat some cookies?" he suggested and then saw her nod, before she padded back to the door, her bare feet looking strangely homey on the wooden floors. "Damn, I cannot wait until you are my wife," he growled, making her throw him a glance over her shoulder that told him how much she couldn't wait for that either.

Taylor grinned to herself as her newest possession tinkled like little bells around her wrist. Nothing she could say to Mason would make him understand how much she loved the gift, but she figured that being a mom and the best damn woman he could wish for was better than anything she could ever buy him.

Grabbing the gifts from the laundry room on the way to the living room, she paused as she heard murmured voices coming from there. The glow of the Christmas tree lit up the hallway, and Taylor loved it. She wished it would be Christmas every day because there were no other reasons to have the lights on at all times.

Peeking around the corner, she saw her father sitting on the sofa, twirling a long-stemmed wine glass in his hand. It was empty, and Taylor took the moment to watch his expression. He looked worn out, tired even, and not as vibrant as he had back when she had left the farm. Across from him sat Stella, telling him in a hushed, but animated voice about a trip she had taken with Becca on one of the horses. Seemingly, it had ended with both of them soaked. Her father smiled and then lowered his gaze, something flashing in his eyes.

"When Taylor was really little, she loved being on a horse with me. I think she was a better rider at five than I ever was."

"Should you be eavesdropping?" Mason playfully

scolded from behind her, making her jump, but Taylor just gave him an irritated look, focusing back on the talk in front of her.

"She loved being outside so much. I never worried that she could leave the farm," her father just added. "One time, we found an injured squirrel, and it bit her four times before realizing that she was just trying to help. Taylor was too stubborn to just leave it be." He chuckled slightly.

"She's still stubborn," Stella pointed out in an obvious attempt to soothe his heartache, and it made Taylor wonder if she had come up before in their discussion.

"I..."

She decided not to listen any further, figuring that if he had something to say, she'd rather hear it directly from him.

"So you think Santa left any cookies?" she asked, loud enough to alert the other two to their presence. She arched a brow at Mason and saw humor sparkle in his eyes. While cookies were left for Santa, someone had to eat them to keep the illusion alive ... and Taylor clearly was willing and ready. The conversation in the living room instantly ceased, and Mason shook his head. She rounded the corner and acted surprised as she saw the other two. "Oh," she made, and Mason passed her, kissing her hair with a chuckle.

"Hey, Mom. Mr. Collins?"

"Someone wants to play Santa." Stella grinned, and Taylor nodded.

"Actually, I just want to eat the cookies." Taylor laughed and then leaned in to kiss her dad's hair. "Hey, Daddy," she whispered. Having let go of her anger made her feel grown up and smart, and it warmed her heart; even though she was determined to one day get the whole story. She had mentioned that while she forgave him, she wouldn't forget. His only reply had been that he'd make it right. Somehow, the words had held so much conviction she had instantly believed them.

"Hey, sweetheart," he replied, shifting in his seat. "We're sharing a bottle of wine and old stories. You care for some?"

"Wine or old stories?" she teased while kneeling down next to the tree to put all the gifts under it. She couldn't believe how many there were as she had to go back two more times, but then she figured that for Tamara, it had been important to buy many because it was her first real family Christmas in a while. Stella had compensated all the years that she didn't have a big girl to spoil, and well, Taylor's father clearly had a guilty conscience. And the other presents most likely were from Mason. "We need to tell them that this is not going to be the norm," Taylor fussed then, and Mason laughed, settling down on the recliner as he watched her.

"They deserve to be spoiled once for Christmas," Stella mumbled.

As Taylor arranged everything to her satisfaction, she scooted over to Mason's side, pulling the plate of cookies and the glass of milk closer. "Passing on the wine and the old stories. But I do take those goodies here." She winked.

"I'll take more of the wine," Stella decided, and Taylor's father poured them some more of the nearly clear liquid.

"Stella, Mason mentioned you thought I should decide if it was okay to have Daniel over. It's not my house, and I sure as hell don't want it without you in it, so your house, your rules. If you think he should be here, then by all means," Taylor mumbled around a mouthful of cookies. She knew it wasn't polite, but she hoped it would lighten the mood at least a little.

"Taylor..." Uh, she didn't like that tone.

"No, don't Taylor me. It's your house, Stella. Your home, your life."

Stella turned to her father, rolling her eyes while Mason started to rub her neck, almost making Taylor purr.

"See, stubborn," Stella mumbled, and Wayne laughed quietly. "Where do you wanna live then, Taylor? You, your family, and I? Or you, your dad, and your family?"

So he planned to stay. Taylor wasn't exactly sure how she felt about that. "I don't care, but I won't be the reason you leave," Taylor fussed, and Stella sighed.

"You aren't. It was always my plan to give Mason this house and everything. And I won't be out of this world. I plan to find a space in town, so I'll be just around the corner, and..."

"Are you gonna keep Timothy here, or do you want me to take him?" her father interrupted, and Taylor stiffened. She hadn't even thought about that. Stella watched her father with a calculating expression, and Taylor got up, walking over to the fireplace.

"She is his legal guardian," Mason pointed out, clearly knowing very well that Taylor wasn't ready to give him up.

"It's his choice, Dad. Wherever he wants to stay, he'll stay," Taylor decided.

"See, you'll have a room problem then," Wayne went on as if she hadn't spoken.

"Won't. I already talked to a contractor about making the house a little bigger. It'll give us more space here, and the chance to add at least two rooms upstairs," Mason injected, and Taylor turned to him, surprised. "I couldn't wait," he admitted sheepishly, and she went over, sitting down on his lap. He kissed her shoulder, and she shook her head.

"See, Stella? There's enough room for you here. And about Tim ... we'll decide that after the holidays. I just want peace for a few days," she whispered and then cuddled into Mason as if he could make all her problems vanish suddenly.

"Of course, daughter. I'm sorry. Either way, I was about to suggest that if Tim stays, maybe Stella and I could open up a shared house of sorts. I suck at cooking, but I'd be willing to pass on the rent then. Of course, we don't need food every day. I just ..." Her father blushed, and Taylor bit her cheeks not to burst out laughing.

"I actually like that," Stella exclaimed, looking excited at the prospect.

Taylor knew that those two had been in school together and close when Taylor's parents were both still around, but she wasn't sure this was really what Mason's mother wanted.

"Maybe we should go to sleep," Mason just then suggested, as if feeling her discomfort. "The morning will come early enough, and no life-changing decisions need to be made tonight."

"True," Stella agreed and then emptied her glass of wine before getting up as well.

"I'm gonna get you some blankets, Wayne. You will stay, right?" she wondered, and her father nodded, accepting the offer gratefully.

"Good night, Dad. Stella?" Taylor kissed them both on the cheek and then waited until Mason, too, had kissed his mother. He was a little too quiet for her taste, and she couldn't wait to pick his brain. He closed the bedroom door behind him quietly while Taylor put on the lamp on the nightstand, holding out her hand for him.

"What's up?" she wanted to know, and he moved back until he was seated against the headboard, then he drew her close.

"Did you know that my mother and your dad were friends in high school? He was the year above her, yet they hung out a lot. Maybe it's not such a bad idea. First, neither of them would be alone, and second, Mom would still be on a farm, in a house."

"Mason, my mother is in town," she reminded him and then felt him nodding.

"I didn't have the feeling that your dad planned to share that house with her. Besides, you're the rightful owner, and I didn't have the impression *you* wanted her in it. Stella and your dad can welcome their grandkids, have sleepovers even, and if you're worried about Tamara, I planned to offer her a room here."

"She wants our farm, Mason," Taylor whispered, and her fiancé brushed his lips across the top of her head.

"And she will get that, too. Your property, remember? And no one says your dad has to leave for that. God, Tay, don't be so serious. If my mom wants to do that, she will. She's a lot like you in many aspects of life. You won't get to her to do a damn thing she doesn't want. Trust me on that. And you won't be able to change it if she wants it," he insisted.

"I just want everyone to be happy," she mumbled, almost feeling bad for that wish.

"And that's what makes you so amazing," Mason promised and then moved her until he could kiss her. Taylor willingly melted into him until breaking away with a groan.

"It'll be a really short night," she reminded him, and he nodded, turning off the lamp and then pulling her with him until her head rested on his chest. She'd always loved that because there was no better lullaby than Mason's steady heartbeat.

twenty-five

"Mommy! Mommy! Mommy!" Mason smirked, refusing to open his eyes and let his daughter know that he was awake.

"MOM!" The girl screamed, yet Taylor only snuggled closer to him, making his daughter stomp her feet.

"Your daughter demands you," he whispered ever so slightly, and Taylor pulled back enough so she could glare at him. He bit his cheeks, loving the expression.

"Oh, today it's my daughter, huh?" she hissed, and he laughed, kissing her forehead.

"Only until after the gifts are unwrapped," he teased, and she gently punched him while their blanket was pulled from the bed.

"Come on, Mom! Santa ate all the cookies."

"Santa did, huh?" Mason asked, arching a questioning brow at Taylor, but she just rolled her eyes.

"I really don't like you this morning," she mumbled and then moved out of bed. "Sit down, Becca. I need to brush my teeth first," she then ordered while Mason moved until he was resting against the headboard, watching his two girls. Becca eagerly followed Taylor's instructions and then crawled over to him, kissing his cheek.

"You can go back to sleep when Mom's done," she promised, pulling the blanket up on his chest.

"No way," Taylor called from the bathroom, glaring at him through the open door.

Mason chuckled and then got up as well, deciding to join her in the bathroom. Becca hung her little legs off the bed, swinging them while humming softly.

"I never knew you were grumpy in the morning," Mason teased as he stepped closer to kiss Taylor's neck.

"I am after barely more than three hours of sleep," she gave back, still closing her eyes as his lips touched her skin. He loved seeing them both in the mirror because it made him feel as if he could see not only them therebut also all the happiness and their promised future. It was almost magical.

"I'm gonna make sure you get time for a nap," he promised, drawing her in before she could leave the bathroom to join their impatient daughter.

"Don't make promises you can't keep," she fussed softly, and he shook his head with a smile, brushing her hair back to frame her face and then kiss her deeply. She tasted of toothpaste and more. God, how he loved her.

"Tay, can you *please* finally come?" Tim called, entering the bedroom. Becca was off the bed in a flash, grabbing his hand.

"Grandma is downstairs," she explained. "We'll wait next to the presents," she stated loudly, and Taylor rolled her eyes.

"Hold on, I'm coming. But we will wait for Daddy," she told the kids, then left the bathroom, giving Mason time to brush his teeth and maybe throw some water on his face. He knew he should be exhausted, but he wasn't. He was happy because he knew Tamara had everything she had wished for, and therefore, Taylor was relieved. It was crazy how selfless that woman could be. After he had been finished, he walked over to the nightstand, checking that the other wrapped gift was still in there. It was going to be the one Taylor would get that night, and while he was more than curious to see what she'd think, he promised himself to be patient. As much as life was about sharing, he was selfish and wanted her happiness and wonder only for himself.

He took the stairs extra slow, hearing Tim and Becca complain while Taylor clearly practiced patience, breathing in and out very slowly. Rounding the corner, Mason spotted his mom on the recliner, Wayne on the sofa, and Taylor as she pulled one gift from Becca to put it back, only to repeat the procedure again the next second.

Tamara came in after him, half-asleep still, and Mason pulled her into his side, kissing her hair. "Hey, girl," he greeted her and smiled as Tamara hugged him tight.

"I like morning cuddles." She grinned, looking instantly more alert.

"Everyone's here! We can unwrap presents now!" Becca squealed, and Taylor dropped to her knees next to the tree, looking up at Mason with a questioning expression on her face.

"We do Christmas the way Taylor did it when she was a child," Mason decided, and Taylor pressed her lips together to hide her smile.

"Becca's not gonna like that," Tamara predicted, and Mason shrugged, grinning from ear to ear. Nothing rushed them, and he always had loved the Collins' tradition.

"What does that mean?" Becca asked. "Mom?"

"It means that everyone gets to open one present now, then we'll have breakfast, read a story, and then all the other presents can be opened," she explained, and Tamara had been right. The little girl's lower lip started to tremble, making Mason cover up a laugh with a cough.

"I don't like that," Rebecca whined, and Taylor pulled

her close.

"You can sit in my lap, or Grandpa's, or Grandma's, while I read. You'll see, you'll like it," Taylor promised, and Mason wished he had implemented that tradition last year already, even though she had been too little to grasp it all then. At least now she would know it.

"Can we pick the gifts?" Becca asked, her tone sounding almost bored.

"Yes," Taylor agreed, pointing at a few gifts that were all marked with Becca's name. Naturally, his daughter picked the biggest, and Taylor shook her head, staying close as the smallest of them all tore open the wrapping.

"Mom, it's a unicorn. It's a unicorn! Look, it's a unicorn!" Taylor pulled the stuffed animal out of the box and placed it on its feet. Beneath them, almost hidden, were tiny wheels, making it possible to move forward with it in a riding motion.

"Wow, I cannot believe Santa brought you that," Mason exclaimed, disbelief coloring his voice. Becca had wanted one since her last birthday, but Mason never found one that satisfied his need for fluffy yet safe, or the wish for purple glitter hair on it. This one, though, was perfect.

"Why not?" Taylor asked, irritated.

"Best gift ever! I don't need the others," his daughter announced, settling down on the little unicorn, moving her hips as if she was on an actual horse.

"It was impossible to find one like that. I wonder how

Santa knew she wanted one," he replied, and Taylor came over while Becca made circles around the sofa. Mason brushed his thumb over her forehead to ease the frown while Tamara moved to her dad's side.

"I saw it and knew it was perfect for Becca. She's so in love with everything fairytale, I thought it was the best choice," she whispered ever so slightly. "I'm sorry."

He kissed her forehead. "For what? Making it impossible for the rest of us to shine with our gifts?" he teased and finally Taylor relaxed.

"I hoped she was going to love it," she admitted.

"Love? She's gonna sleep on that thing." He laughed and then kissed her nose.

"Can I pick now?" Tim asked, having been surprisingly patient.

"Sure can," Taylor answered and walked back to the tree while Mason settled down next to his mom's recliner.

"Best Christmas ever," she whispered only for Mason to hear, and he nodded.

"I never knew it could feel like this," he admitted just as quietly and then felt how his mom took his hand.

"As an only child, it wasn't ever as busy as this one is," she agreed, and he kissed the back of her hand before suddenly seeing only green and gold wrapping paper.

"Your gifts," Taylor announced.

"We can't pick?" Mason pouted, and Taylor just arched a brow at him.

"Ah, Santa brought me my own cowboy boots and hat! Does that mean I can finally become a real cowboy?" Timmy asked, and Mason looked at him as Taylor stood back.

"Mmmhmm, but a cowboy needs a horse, doesn't he?" Stella asked, and Tim's jaw dropped.

"No. I can be a learning cowboy first and ride with Mason on his horse," he pouted, clearly thinking they were going to take away the stuff he had just gotten.

"Fine," Stella agreed as Taylor shook her head ever so slightly, reminding Mason and his mom that the rule was only one gift for now.

"Taylor, this is ... I cannot believe ..." Tamara was a blubbering mess after opening her own present, finding a sign that read TamCo-Ranch on it, stating clearly that Taylor had every intention of giving the farm to her sister.

"Mason," her mom whispered, her breath hitching as she tried to suppress a sob. They had gotten her a framed picture that had the word family written in many languages around the metal, and inside was a picture of Mason, Taylor, Becca, Tamara, and Timmy.

"You shouldn't have, daughter," Wayne said, his voice rough, as he found a picture of his three children in his gift.

"Breakfast, finally," Taylor called out, clapping her hands. Mason had to laugh but still held her back as she wanted to walk into the kitchen.

"You get one gift, too," he reminded her, but she just stole a kiss and then shook her head.

"I have everything I could wish for," she told him, but he still handed her the first gift he found with her name on it.

"Open," Tamara demanded, and Taylor did. It was a necklace with a locket that you could open, and Tamara had put in a picture of her and Tim, and one of Mason and Becca. It was beautiful.

"Thank you," Taylor mumbled as Mason brushed her hair back and placed the jewelry around her neck. "Now breakfast?" she wanted to know, and he laughed, nodding. Everyone got up and started moving, but Mason didn't let his fiancée go.

"You're pretty amazing," he whispered before he kissed her deeply. She leaned into him, nodding slightly, agreeing wordlessly.

Mason didn't need words. All he needed was right there in his arms.

————

Taylor was glad once all gifts were unwrapped; Tamara was off with an adult coloring book, Becca riding her unicorn, and Timmy running around in his boots and hat. He looked adorable and even though he was more than happy, Taylor knew that before long he was going to cry his eyes out.

"I'm gonna take him out alone. Do this man thing

with him. Male bonding and all," Mason mumbled next to her, now dressed in jeans, a shirt, and about to pull over a jacket.

"Can you at least take pictures?" she pleaded, and he took her phone, nodding.

"Are you gonna be okay with preparing the food?" he wanted to know, pointing at the turkey in the oven and the vegetables that clustered every surface available. Taylor looked around, feeling happy and content.

"Definitely. Stella promised she'd help, and so will Tamara. You want to take him out already?"

Mason grinned, and Taylor wondered what Tim would say about *Pomeo*. The poor pony had gotten its name from being a pony and charming the ladies like only a Romeo could. It was smaller than most, and the former owner had decided to focus on more pristine horses, wanting to get rid of Pomeo as fast as possible. Mason had been lucky, getting the horse for less than a steal. Otherwise, Taylor wouldn't have agreed anyway.

"Sure do. He's going to be so excited," he explained.

"Let him do the work. It'll be his responsibility, after all," she insisted and then sighed. "You know, Becca will want one soon, too."

He nodded and then kissed her cheek. "We'll be fine." She knew that but figured he could already keep his eyes open for another bargain.

"Comin', cowboy? You need to help me water the

horses," Mason called, and Tim was by his side in no time, looking ready to work. The two left, and Taylor turned on the radio, humming along to the country Christmas songs playing. She had gotten out a cutting board and was starting on the carrots when she heard the door open and close, guessing that Mason or Tim had forgotten something until her mother's voice made her skin crawl.

"I want the keys to my house." Taylor forced herself to put down the knife before lifting her gaze.

"Bonnie," she said slowly, speaking quietly so as not to alert Stella or her father to the new presence in the house.

"I've given you a day to calm down, and you're still being ridiculous, playing family here. I want the keys to the farm, and I'm gonna take Tim home. He's my son, and I don't care what rights you think you have to him. I gave birth to him. And I worked my ass off on that farm. You fled the moment you could," her mother snarled, and Taylor took a deep breath.

"As did you, and you haven't looked back once, the way it seems. The farm is not yours and neither is Tim. Just go and live your life the way you always wanted. Free of the farm, free of the girl you think neglected you, free of the daughter who resents you for making her grow up too fast. You have no right to anything on this farm or any person living there," she gave back calmly, resuming her task of cutting carrots, even though her hands were shaking with anger. She was determined not to let her mother ruin Christmas.

"No right? I have every right," her mother all but screamed, and Taylor's eyes surveyed the room, glad when she couldn't spot Becca even though the unicorn stood right in her field of vision.

"Actually, you don't, which is the reason why I, too, had to neglect our kids and leave the farm. If I would've known that you'd be back one day anyway, I wouldn't have left in the first place." Taylor's jaw dropped as her father came in, a serious expression on his face, his eyes dark with untamed hatred.

"Wayne." His presence more than surprised her mother, and Taylor realized that for once, Sunrow hadn't been gossiping, and his father's presence hadn't made town news yet. Her mother's stunned expression was evidence enough of that.

"Bonnie." Her father hefted a slim briefcase onto the table, and while Taylor had seen it around the house, she hadn't thought about it closer until he pulled out a pile of papers with pretty green arrows marking something. "Those are the papers signing away all rights to everything on that land, including, but not limited to, the kids. I've wanted to divorce you for a long time. In fact, I should've done it the moment you told Taylor to leave if she wouldn't take over the farm, but I've been too chicken to do it. I won't say I regret having Tim, because I don't, but I do regret having lost countless nights of sleep over you. Sleeping next to you was almost hell for me. I regret, too, never having insisted on you signing over the rights to the boy, either, but that's no longer necessary anyway."

"Why would she have to sign over ..." Taylor trailed off as her father's words clicked into place. He had hated her mother, and he clearly hadn't slept with her anymore, yet they had gotten a brother ... one who most likely shared only fifty percent of their DNA. Wayne Collins' pained look said it all, and Taylor swayed on her feet, feeling someone push a chair against her knees, which she happily sat down on. Glancing over her shoulder, she spotted Stella.

"Why? You don't want him anymore?" Bonnie spat. "No one wants him."

Wayne lowered his eyes with a slight smile. "Taylor did. She has full custody of him since we both left. Even though ..." He turned to her, and she wondered what more there could be. "Tamara and Tim were both taken care of, even if you hadn't returned. I knew you'd come back, but for the slight case of no one being able to reach you, orders were in place, and my lawyer knew that. I hadn't planned to be gone that long, but ... your mother was elusive. I followed her through a few towns, ready to turn around and come back, but then I got another hint of where she was and ... well, one thing leads to another, and this whole ordeal took longer than I thought. After all, I didn't know she'd return," he admitted, talking to Taylor as if Bonnie wasn't in the room any longer. "Eventually, I figured I should be home for Christmas, and when I got here, my lawyer called to tell me that Bonnie, too, was back for whatever reason," he finished.

"She came back because of Taylor," Stella injected, and Taylor nodded, knowing it was true.

"I did not," Bonnie protested while Taylor watched her father fan out papers.

"I don't want anything extra from you. The boy is Taylor's now, Tamara is grown, and the farm will belong to me. You will sign this, and you'll have to go back to your birth name, no longer being Collins after it, or I will call the police, and they'll take you in," he stated calmly, and Taylor couldn't believe a word he said.

"Why would they do that?" her mother asked, looking more like an evil witch than the woman Taylor remembered tucking her in at night.

"Because the police are after you and they'll get you for fraud. After all, the money you took from your mother's life insurance because she's supposedly dead wasn't legally obtained. Your mother agreed to show up in court if need be unless you sign. She wasn't okay with the name change because she doesn't want you to have her name, either, but she understood it was important for her grandchildren," he went on, and Taylor got up, not being able to sit any longer. "She, too, had agreed to watch over Tamara and Timmy," he added toward his eldest daughter, and Taylor hugged herself, wishing Mason were there even while she was glad that Tim was not there to hear that.

"Sign here, here, and here," her father instructed, and Bonnie did, not even bothering to read the papers. Taylor couldn't decide if she was grateful or not, but she knew that she wanted her mother out and that she needed time to think. This was more messed up than ever. Maybe she should've talked to her dad right after his return, just so none of this could've surprised her any longer. Instead, she walked over to her purse, got out a wad of cash, and handed it to Bonnie.

"This was originally to pay you so you'd leave, but now, see it as the start of a new life. Get out of town and don't ever return here, Mother. Ever. I don't want to see you, and neither does Tamara. I don't think Tim is an issue, either. Just leave and don't ever return."

"Your father never took your side, yet you forgive him so easily?" Bonnie screamed, fury turning her beautiful features a weird shade of purple.

"My little sister forgave him, and she really was the one who had reason to hate him for life, so I follow her lead. You, on the other hand, weren't forgiven, and therefore, that's what we stick to. Go now, Mother. I have stuff to do, and we'll be having guests soon," Taylor whispered, her head spinning.

"I'll spend my life making it up to them, but I sure as

hell don't want you around. Let me escort you off the land," Wayne offered, and Stella was instantly by his side.

"Yes, let's make sure that you find your way," Stella added and then took Bonnie's arm, not even giving the woman any chance to say something different.

As soon as those three were gone, Tamara came into the kitchen, carrying Becca. Taylor's little sister looked guilty, clearly having known something she didn't know.

"I didn't know how to tell you why Dad left. And I didn't know someone was going to watch over us until you already promised to drop everythin'. Hate me, but I wanted you back, Lori. I couldn't pick up the phone and tell you to stay where you were because I wanted you to return. And about Tim ... I didn't know how to tell you, either. I wasn't exactly sure, but I guessed that he wasn't fully our blood, and I just ... I'm so sorry."

Taylor went over, seeing how Becca's lower lip trembled. "I'm not blood, but you love me, right? I'm your girl." Taylor laughed through her tears and then took her daughter, kissing her hair.

"Always, baby. You're mine and will always be mine, too. And so is Tim." She wasn't mad at Tamara even though she might have been after freshly returning. Now, though, she couldn't help but think that everything was exactly the way it was supposed to be. Putting Becca down on her own feet, she asked her to go and play while she prepared the food.

After the girl had rounded the corner, Taylor moved back to the counter, pointing at her sister to sit.

"You knew he didn't run?"

"I know he didn't neglect us the way it looked. The lawyer said he'd be back, and I could count on it, but it would take a while. I couldn't tell you because I somehow didn't believe it was true, and because I wanted to live with you. Don't hate me, please, and don't hate him. He tried, and he and Mom fought a lot. It was horrible, and I started doing more around the house, hopin' Mom would leave and work outside then, and I just ... I'm so sorry!" She was outright crying now, and Taylor went over, kissing Tamara's hair before hugging her.

"I'm not mad. I'm ... numb right now. Overwhelmed, but not mad. Trust me. Can you just take care of chopping and..."

"You'll go and see Mason? You've always done that when things got too much." Her sister smiled, and Taylor nodded, taking a deep breath. She just needed a hug and then would have to get going. They were having Daniel over in less than four hours, and somehow, she had the feeling she hadn't achieved anything yet.

Changing shoes, she stepped outside, taking a deep breath before heading toward the barn.

———

Mason had known that something was off when his mom and Taylor's dad had escorted a rather unhappy

Bonnie off the grounds, but the exhausted faces the two wore when they joined him and Tim in the barn told him even more. It didn't take long until he spotted Taylor through the open barn door, her face lifted toward the sky as if the falling snowflakes could clear her mind. Stella seemed to notice his glance, and after shooting a look over her shoulder, she took a deep breath and forced a smile.

"Tim, how about we go inside and warm up? Your cheeks are all pink," she suggested, and the little boy looked at him, holding onto the pony as if his life depended on it.

"We're done for today, cowboy. You did well," Mason told him and then playfully nudged his chin.

"Okay, let's go, Grandma." Tim grinned. "I have some other cool toys to play with!" He took Stella's hand and his father's, and then he went inside with them, animatedly chatting about his new best friend and missing Taylor by the door because of it.

Mason opened his arms for her, and she instantly crossed the distance between them, holding on tighter than usual.

"I'm afraid to ask," he admitted, and she took a few deep breaths, trying on words and dismissing them before she finally pulled back.

"Tamara knew Dad was coming back. In fact, she knew, too, that someone was assigned to take care of them, but seemingly, the lawyer was told to keep it under wraps unless it was absolutely necessary."

Mason stayed quiet. As much as Taylor had suffered, he couldn't say anything negative about her being back. "So?" he finally prompted as she didn't say more.

"So what?" she wanted to know, clearly waiting for a reaction from him.

"Taylor Collins, you will not hear from me that I'm mad at Tamara. If anythin', that girl deserves a badge for having gotten you back," he burst out, feeling hurt because she shouldn't be mad either. She was with him now, wasn't she? And happy, too.

She only shook her head. Still searching her face, he realized she wanted something different.

"I didn't know, Taylor. I wouldn't have guessed, either. I promise, if I'd have had the tiniest inkling that this was the case, I would have told you." Her furrowed brow remained only a few seconds longer, and then a smile replaced it.

"You would've told me even at the risk of me leaving again?" she wanted to know quietly, and he closed his eyes, trying to imagine that scene.

"Yes," he finally relented. "It would've broken my damn heart, but yes. You shouldn't have been forced back here."

"I wouldn't have left," she promised, and now, it was him who pulled back to get a better look at her face.

"You wouldn't?" He couldn't believe that.

310

"The moment I sat in your truck, I knew I never fully left. You've always had my heart, Mason. I never lived after I left. I breathed and ate but never lived. Seeing you again was confusing, but I knew that moment in your truck that I needed to be around you, even if just as friends. You, Mason Stiles, always belonged to my life and will always belong to it."

In the spur of the moment, he backed her up until her back hit the wall, then he kissed her until his head was swimming from the lack of oxygen.

"While that was nice"—she smirked, then turned serious again—"there's more. My father left to divorce my mother. She signed the papers inside and no has no right to Tim or the farm ... or the Collins name."

"She didn't have a right to Tim anyway," he pointed out, remembering that Taylor had gotten full custody.

"Luckily, because it turns out my dad doesn't have much right to him, either. He's only my half-brother, Mase. Tamara guessed but didn't know how to tell me. And now, above all, he's been adopted by his half-sister. I can't decide what I am to him now," she admitted, and for the first time, he saw tears come to her eyes.

"You're Taylor to him, and you'll always be his big sister," he guaranteed her, and she nodded through her sniffles.

"I guess, but why the hell is life such a mess? I thought we'd be done. All I want is peaceful Christmas and

-"

"I guess I should go then," a voice interrupted her from the door, and as Taylor's face split into a beaming smile, Mason had never been more glad to see his ex.

"Ash! Of course, not! I should've remembered to invite you, but things were crazy and... what are you doing here?"

"I was lonely," the other woman admitted, lowering her eyes to the ground.

"Well, good for us then that we have enough room and food for everyone," Mason remarked, returning the pony to its stall before he hugged Ashley and then pulled Taylor back to his side.

Things might have been chaotic, but at least everything was finally settled. He knew Taylor would've wished for a different solution, and less heartache, but it was only uphill from there on, that much Mason was sure of.

"Thank you for taking me in," Ashley mumbled.

"You're family," he stated, chuckling as both women simultaneously teared up.

"He's right," Taylor agreed, and Mason had to admit, if one person knew what it meant to turn people without blood relations into a true family, then it was Taylor soon-to-be Stiles.

epilogue

Taylor crawled into bed shortly before midnight, exhausted to her bones. Mason lit a few candles until Taylor easily could've read a book.

"You're not done yet. I promised you I'd have the first and the last gift for you," he reminded her, and she nodded, sighing on purpose, before winking at him. She actually, too, had one last gift for him and pulled it out of the nightstand on her side. It was nothing big, but she had no doubt he'd still love it.

He joined her on the mattress with a parchment roll, tied together with a red bowtie, and Taylor had a feeling that her gift would be tiny compared to his.

"You first," she insisted, handing him the envelope.

He eyed her suspiciously, then looped a finger under the side and tore it open. The pictures tumbled into his lap, and Taylor watched him stare down at them without lifting one up or dropping the envelope.

"We figured you need new pictures in your truck, so Becca and I took some. We might have gone overboard, but you can always pick your favorites." She shrugged and then gave him a wink. 'Overboard' was exactly right: There were more than fifty photo booth photos of her and his daughter, but Becca had been especially cute that day and, well, Taylor was in love with her.

One by one, Mason looked at them, shaking his head and clearing his throat a few times.

"Wow, that's freaking amazing," he whispered, collecting a pile of them in his hand. "How am I ever going to decide?" He shook his head, probably already giving up the task, but Taylor just took the pictures from him, cuddling into his side to look at them, too. It took a while for them to look through each and every one, but she didn't mind. She loved them, and whichever he didn't take, she'd put up in her truck, if she'd ever get a new one.

"Thank you, Taylor, honestly. Those are ... my two favorite girls in the world." He kissed her softly, and Taylor wanted to melt. "Now you," he insisted, but she shook her head.

"I got a lot already. You're spoiling me!" She didn't want anymore since she felt as if she could never again get even. She knew – technically – it wasn't a competition, but she didn't want him to think she needed gifts to be happy.

"Well," he mumbled, turning the parchment over in his hand, "let's say actually it's a gift for me then, okay?" He met her eyes, and she just sighed, moving his arm until she rested her back against his chest, then told him to unfold it.

He did, ever so slowly, and Taylor's heart stopped as she read the first words. She spun in his arms so quickly that she bumped her head against his lips, making him gasp.

"I'm sorry, I'm sorry, I'm sorry, but Mason … is that what I think it is?" She could barely see him through a curtain of tears.

"It's not, since, of course, I could never take the official documents, but I still wanted you to know they are ready to be signed by you whenever you want to put your name under it and make it official," he promised, speaking ever so quietly, as if he could scare her away. Instead, she threw her arms around him, and in a flurry of arms, legs, and kisses, she made sure he knew how gracious and happy she was, while a parchment fell to the floor, the words 'adoption paper' looking like a dark shadow on the crème colored sheet.

The End

And now, turn the page for a Taylor and Mason short-story featured in Tales of the Night – an Anthology

carolina girl

A short story prequel to Call Me Michigan

"Mason, Taylor went inside! Ugh, can you please go and find her? I guess she now thinks it's all fun and games, but we all know how much she hates being in there once she realizes that she's got lost." Nineteen-year-old Mason Stiles turned to the woman that had called his name.

"Sure thing, Mrs. Collins," he gave back, tipping his Stetson in a hello. He barely ever left the hat at home, and felt close to naked without it.

Turning, he made his way over to the Halloween

Maze that Taylor had vanished in. Taylor was the Collins'
sixteen-year-old daughter and, where it concerned Mason,
the most amazing girl in the world: she was the typical
cowgirl, complete with jeans, boots and the hat, sun kissed
skin freckled from all the days she had spent outside on a
horse with her friends and all her crazy ideas.

Mason knew how much she hated the dark and
anything scary. She was jumpy and as much as he thought
she'd considered going in something cool, she was
probably already regretting it.

Larry, the guy manning the entrance, took note of
Mason and put his name down as he entered. He took a
few steps, and already the maze forked off left and right.

"Men go left, because women are always right," he
mumbled, choosing the right just because of Taylor's
favorite saying. She was way too young to really
understand what everyone was implying with that, but
still, it made him smile just thinking about it.

"Collins? Where's your lazy ass?" he called out,
hoping to get an answer from her. It didn't take long for
him to round a corner and meet a wild cackling witch.

"Hey Lisa," he called and instantly the dressed up
woman stopped acting crazy, laughing.

"Hey boy," she gave back.

"Did Taylor come by?" he wanted to know and she
nodded.

"Yes. Poor girl almost jumped out of her skin. She

318

isn't even far in and looks ready to run away screaming." Mason shook his head, almost being able to picture that. "She turned left up there. Or better, she sprinted left up there," Lisa explained and Mason thanked her, moving along a little quicker. He had helped set up the maze, but between all the forks and turns he'd decorated he hadn't the slightest idea where he really was.

"Collins? You sitting in a corner, cryin' yet?" he asked, loud enough to be heard some feet away.

"Shut up, you idiot," she cried, and his smile vanished since her voice actually held an edge of panic.

"Where are you?" he wanted to know, trying to gauge where her voice was coming from. The sun was setting fast and he knew that in less than ten minutes the maze would be lit up by fake flames, adding to the scary secrets and shadows that would most likely give Taylor an even bigger fright.

"If I'd knew, I wouldn't be here anymore," she called back, anger tingeing her beautiful voice.

"Stay where you are, I'll come and find you," he promised. She stayed silent after that and he groaned. He couldn't remember one damn instance where that girl had actually done what she was supposed to do. Cursing under his breath, he followed the direction he thought she was in, hoping that luck would be on his side and there wouldn't be too many stray turns.

———

Taylor Collins angrily wiped at the blonde strands that kept blowing in her face, before she hugged her jacket closer to her body. It was getting colder by the minute, but that could be the fear she was feeling.

Stupid Ashley and her dares. Her best friend had dared her to either walk the maze or tell Mason there and then that she was heavily crushing on him.

"You want to tear his clothes off and give him your virginity, admit it," Ashley had taunted and though the maze had been scaring Taylor, there was nothing more terrifying than telling Mason what she thought about him. She saw the way he looked at her, thinking she was a little girl, and even though it wasn't true—she knew very well what she was feeling for him was more than a freaking crush—she couldn't get herself to say anything because she feared it would change the way he acted around her. If he ever laughed at her for what she was feeling, she couldn't look at him again. She'd lose the friendship she had with him, her safe haven when she needed it, and that was something she didn't want to risk.

Now though she wished she would've just gotten over herself and kissed him. That way …

A long scream interrupted her thoughts, as seemingly out of nowhere a zombie came. There was blood dripping from his face and he was losing teeth the second he opened his mouth. Only vaguely Taylor recognized the green eyes in the face and even though she tried to remind herself that everything here was fake, it looked terribly real.

"Braaaaaaiiiiiinnnnnnnssssssss," the zombie muttered and Taylor stumbled back, her heart in her throat until she bumped into something soft and warm.

"Blood," came another voice and she spun around, finding herself face to face with a pale complexion and a bloody lip. "Come on pretty girl, just a little scratch, you won't even feel it," the vampire coaxed as something rolled over her shoulder, hitting her boots. She looked down, seeing another one of the zombie's teeth in front of her. Her breathing exhilarated and she ran back the way she'd come, turning the moment she could. She kept running until she rounded a corner and saw no one following her.

For a moment she paused, realizing that in her blind flight she'd lost absolutely every sense of direction. Maybe she should've stayed where she'd been when Mason had called out for her. Problem was, she didn't want Mason to see how much she was affected by all this fake horror.

"It's not real," she started telling herself, walking again.

"What isn't?" she heard a voice question and then she was standing in front of a woman covered in spiders.

"Fake," Taylor whispered even though with every movement the woman made the spiders seemed to crawl more over her. "Fake," she repeated as her throat clogged. She hated nothing more than those eight-legged monsters.

"Can you please move over a little?" she then asked, her voice breaking. She just wanted to pass.

"Why, my dear? You don't like my spiders?" That woman wasn't anyone Taylor recognized, and she barely wore make up. It must have been someone from the fair, enjoying to scare little girls.

"I don't like to have them anywhere near me, no," she admitted and the stranger reached out, dropping something on Taylor's shoulder. She gritted her teeth, trying to keep herself from screaming another time.

"Look, there she issssss," came the voice of the zombie from earlier and Taylor looked over her shoulder, not being able to believe that they had followed her just to scare the shit out of her.

Without thinking she picked up her pace, closing her eyes as she stumbled into the woman with the spiders and away from the zombie. It was getting dark and lengthy shadows now offered more hiding spots for those freaks who enjoyed the horrors of Halloween.

"Stiles, where the fuck are you?" she called out, decided that he was the lesser evil. Plus, she knew he'd helped in building the thing, so maybe he knew how to get out. Fake lanterns flickered as she came to a stop, breathing heavily while resting her hands on her knees. Listening, she could hear faint screams and quiet cackling somewhere off in the distance, while directly around her silence pressed against her ears. Her heart was racing in her throat as she tried hard to get a hold of her fear.

"Collins?" Mason's voice was the most welcome thing she had ever heard, and she spun in a circle, only to realize that while he sounded close, he wasn't really.

"Here," she answered, wondering where exactly 'here' was. Had she gone far away from the entrance towards the exit or was she actually walking circles, returning to the beginning. Either way, she hoped she'd get out soon.

"If I tell you to stay put, will you?" Mason asked and a laugh escaped her lips.

"If nothing haunting comes along," she giggled and wished she could simply cross through the corn walls instead of having to run around them, but the fences in them made it impossible.

"Look, sweet cheerleader Taylor," a taunting bass crawled over her skin from behind her and she shivered.

"Tay, who is that?" Mason asked from wherever he was.

"No one, Stiles. Go your merry way, we'll just show Taylor here the true meaning of a Halloween scare," the guy replied and Taylor didn't want to look at the group that seemingly rounded upon her.

Glancing over her shoulder, she saw three guys wearing hockey masks, impersonating the true evil from the Halloween movies. It wasn't the masks though that scared her, it was the way they walked deliberately slow, as if they were ready to chase her, or even waited for it.

Swallowing her fear, she straightened her shoulders. "Idiots," Taylor grumbled, making fists at her side to keep herself from trembling.

"Just walk away, Tay," Mason ordered, his voice having taken on a weird tone.

"I hate bullies and you know it," she called back and while that was the truth, it didn't change the fact that she was terrified. Maybe they would leave her alone if she acted strong. Maybe she'd get away okay.

"We don't want to bully you, Taylor Collins. You're the reason for all of our wet dreams," one of the three said. They were dressed up all the same, complete with freaking wigs, but one was smaller than the others and one bigger. The smallest scared her the most because he seemed to lead the group.

"Touch her and I swear, you'll never be happy again," came Mason's threat from her left, but it seemed he was only getting further away.

The smallest dude reached out and his glove covered finger brushed her cheek, spurring her into action. She surprised them by running towards them, crashing through the wall of guys and then running as fast as she could, not caring about zombies or spider women as long as she found someone who would be by her side if the three masked boys found her again. She kept looking over her shoulder until turning too late, running straight into a larger-than-life spider web. She knew it was fake, it even *felt* fake, but that was still too much. She finally screamed as tears pooled in her eyes and rolled down her cheeks. She was freezing, she was scared to death and she was done. She just wanted to be out of there.

————————

Mason heard and then finally saw Taylor. She was beating at her arms and head, trying to get of the soft spun cotton that covered her from head to toe. Her sobs broke his heart, and he went closer.

"Just get it off me before you do anything to me," she pleaded in a broken voice, making Mason's stomach churn with anger. He was glad that whoever those punks were, he had found Taylor before they did again.

With gentle fingers he picked everything off her and then just drew her in his arms, She had yet to look at him, but that didn't matter. He just needed her a little calmer. Her body was trembling with fear and she was ice-cold.

"Small jean jacket, huh, Collins? Exactly the right thing for a night that crosses over into November," he teased.

"I look cute in it," she mumbled against his chest, her fear clearly dissipating while her body relaxed under his hands. He couldn't deny that the jacket highlighted her beauty, but he was more worried about her catching a cold.

"Hold my jacket," he ordered and then handed it to

her before pulling his hoodie over his head. "Do me a favor and pull that over your cute jacket, Collins," he ordered and she complied only too readily. It made him smile. Pushing his arms back through the sleeves of his football jacket, he eyed her up and down. Besides freaked out she seemed to be all right.

"Thank you. Get me out of here, Mase," she pleaded, her voice soft.

"Jesus Christ, girl. You really are freaking afraid. Why did you go in here in the first place?" he wondered, pulling her in his arms another time. She went too willingly, making him realize that she was more than just grateful; she held onto him as if he could keep her from drowning.

"It was either that or doing something that scares me even more," she admitted, her chocolate eyes holding his stormy ones. He couldn't help but feel as if she was willing him to read her thoughts, to guess what scared her even more, but he just couldn't. Instead his mind went utterly blank while he got lost in her stare.

"Step away, Stiles, she's ours." That was what pulled him back from the edge he was walking, the temptation to kiss her and make sure she knew she was his and he wanted a life with her. He was thinking long-term and she wasn't even eighteen yet. Christ, what was wrong with him?

Facing the three punks that clearly scared Taylor, he

arched a brow. Not one of them reached up to his six feet one, making him guess that they were either Freshmen or Sophomores. They obviously considered themselves strong because they had come as a trio.

"She belongs to no one but herself," Taylor snarled, making Mason smirk. She really hated it if people implied that she was anything but her own boss.

"Now the kitten suddenly has claws," one masked punk taunted and Taylor stepped forward, but Mason reached for her hand. As much as he knew that she was angry enough to claw their eyes out, he knew an easier way to get those three to leave,

"Honestly, Christian. You're what? Thirteen? Your mother would give ya a good whipping if she heard the way you talk to that lady here," Mason stated and the smallest of the three stiffened. Mason—one, Christian—zero. He knew he had recognized the voice earlier.

"I don't know who you're talkin' to, but it sure ain't one of us," the gnome replied, because honestly, in Mason's eyes he was nothing more.

"Shut up! Christian Crow? You mother fucking bastard!" Mase chuckled as Taylor charged forward and pulled the hockey mask off his face, making the elastic tear and snap back in his face.

"Ow! You ..." Christian started, but Mason already took a step forward.

"Just drop it, Chris," the tallest dude said and Mason

arched a brow. It was now pretty easy to guess which guys accompanied this punk: his best friends Terrance and Jones.

Mason was ready to throw a few punches, but he sure as hell wouldn't start the fight unless one of the other three touched Taylor.

"One day, Collins, one day," Christian growled and even though Mason wanted to say something, he was glad when the three left.

"Ready to leave the maze?" he wanted to know, holding his hand out to Taylor. She cuddled into his hoodie hugging herself instead of taking his hand.

"Count on it," she mumbled, walking next to him close enough so their bodies were touching every other step.

Mason knew the way out, having no trouble at all to recall how to get there. He knew there were a few more obstacles to get through and since he was by her side now, he didn't mind having her scared a little bit more. After all, he could always hold her if things got too bad. Man, he sure hoped she'd be scared out of her skin.

"How are things at home?" he wanted to know, hoping to distract her and yet being concerned. He knew that things between her and her parents were strained ever since she'd announced she was going to be a nurse instead of getting a business degree to manage the family farm.

"Well, if we don't scream at each other, we're silent," she whispered and he saw how her knuckles turned white as she squeezed her elbows, hugging herself as if that would keep her together.

"They're proud of you, Tay," he commented, knowing it was the truth. Her parents loved her, but her mother wasn't the best book keeper and they couldn't bear to lose the farm because of that. All their hopes rested on Taylor's shoulders, and Mason sure knew what a burden that was to carry.

"Well, it's not the impression I'm getting," she answered with a careless shrug of her shoulder. "Either way, I'll be fine. I was thinking about applying to the University of Pennsylvania. They have the best nursing program," she then went on and Mason swallowed quietly. If she'd be accepted—which he had no doubt about—she'd be too far away for his taste.

"You're a North Carolina girl," he teased, his tone less playful than he'd hoped.

"I can be a 'lina-girl up there," she replied before giving him a smile. It had a sad edge to it, so he reached for her arm just as another arm did, too, coming out of the cornfield behind her.

She squealed and then was pressed up against him. Behind her he could see Brad, his best friend, wink at him over her shoulder. He was dressed up as a zombie and looked terribly fake.

Grinning, he pulled Taylor closer, who was now hiding against his chest, nodding at his best friend to leave, which he surprisingly did without a word.

"Scared?" he laughed, brushing a strand of her blonde hair behind her ear. It was almost as if she leaned into his touch, but the gesture was so short lived, he wasn't sure he'd simply imagined it.

"This was stupid. You think there's any chance I can just stay the way I am and you walk us out?" she wondered, still having her face firmly pressed into his chest. If you'd ask him, he'd stay that way forever, but he knew it was better to get her out as quickly as possible. Plus, they could hang out with their friends at the Halloween bonfire. Laughing, he kissed the top of her head.

"You little chicken Collins!" She playfully pushed him away, giving him one of the smiles he loved so much because it would always make his world a little brighter.

"Just tell me how to get out," she fussed, pouting. He reached out and gently touched her bottom lip before he realized what he was actually doing. God, he seriously was lost to this girl and he sure as hell didn't need any remedy for it.

Taylor watched Mason's stormy eyes go darker as he reached out and touched her. The way he was treating her there and then was so much different than his usually playful banter and teasing. Most of the time he refrained from touching her at all and while it had never really bothered her, she knew she'd now miss these gentle gestures.

"For what it's worth, I think you'll be a great nurse. But ... are you sure you wanna go away that far? I'm sure there are nursing schools closer to home," Mason stated and she looked at him from the side, smiling to herself as she realized that now the flickering light of the lanterns was less scary and more endearing. Mason looked good in the warm glow; his hair almost black, the ghost of a beard shadowing his cheeks, giving him a rugged, handsome look. His full lips and straight nose made his profile close to perfect.

"If I stay at home, I'll never hear the end of it, so I figured that if I go off, away to college, they'd be more glad to see me when I come back instead of fussing that I didn't chose their planned career path," she replied and then pulled the sleeves of his grey hoodie down until they covered half of her hands. She never had felt as protected as she did with that piece of clothing and it's owner.

Mason led her around a corner and they finally stepped free of the maze. In surprise she turned, then cocked a brow. "You knew exactly where we needed to go," she said, half in accusation.

He laughed, sheepishly lifting up his shoulders until they almost covered his ears. "If you would have waited for me like I told you, there wouldn't have been a problem," he grinned and she rolled her eyes as he reached for her hand and pulled her towards one of the huge bonfires.

"Mason, Taylor, wait up," her mother called and Mason slowed, giving Tay an apologetic smile.

'I tried,' he mouthed and she gave him a thankful smile before hanging back, letting her mother kiss her cheek and tug her closer. The mothering was nerve-wrecking at best and downright annoying at worst. Just before they'd left the house for the Halloween fair Taylor had wandered along the barn and the stables, knowing that she'd miss everything there, but not ready to devote her life to the farm because she had different dreams.

"I was so worried," her mother started and Taylor looked up, knowing that she looked a lot like her mother, yet she had the feeling that sometimes the looks were all that she had inherited. Where she was outgoing and laughed often, her mother was serious, having a no-nonsense attitude. Where Taylor had a huge circle of friends and some really close ones, her mother preferred to surround herself with only family. One day Taylor wanted to have a family, too, but for now she wanted to follow her heart, and that was screaming out for her to go into nursing.

"It was a stupid bet with Ash," Taylor waved her off, trying to step back, but her mother held onto Mason's grey sweater. "I'll be heading over to the bonfire," she added, hoping that this would get her away from her mother.

"Careful, child. We don't need to pay for Mason's clothes, too."

"What?" she asked, startled.

"If you get burns into this hoodie from flying sparks, we'd need to replace it," was the curt answer and Taylor bit her lip.

"How about I'm handing it back to him?" she ground out and her mother's expression softened while she brushed a hand over the crown of Taylor's hair as if she was six instead of sixteen.

"You'll understand one day when your own daughter constantly needs new clothes," her mother stated and Taylor exhaled quietly.

"Sure, mom," she replied.

"We're leavin' in half an hour," her mother suddenly told her and Taylor cried out in protest.

"I can drive her home, Mrs. Collins," Mason offered and stepped to her side.

"No later than eleven. And, Mason, Taylor just wanted to return your clothes to you. Bye, honey, be a good girl." Her mom patted her cheek, something wistful in her eyes that Taylor couldn't place.

"Keep that damn thing on, I have a million of them. If one gets a few burns, I'll just throw it away," Mason winked and Taylor gave him a relieved smile.

They leisurely made their way over to the fire that their friends had claimed as theirs and while Taylor wished that he'd be with her all the time until driving her home, she knew that this was over the moment Eric joined them. They'd decided to go public that evening since they had been dating in secret for more than four weeks already.

She kept her heart free for Mason, but a girl sometimes needed cuddles and Eric was the quarterback of the team, smart and hot.

He just wasn't Mason, but sure the next best thing. Turning, she tried to find out if Eric was there yet. She couldn't find a trace of him and smiled slightly. It meant she had a few more minutes with Mason just the way she wanted, especially as he sat down on a log and pulled her to his side.

"You're parents would forgive you, too, if you stayed close to home," he suddenly picked up the topic from earlier, and she turned to him, watching him in the firelight. Maybe she should've told Mason how she felt, because the way he looked at her now she almost thought that he, too, wanted them to be something other than friends. Clearing her throat, she decided to take the risk.

"Mason ..."

She was interrupted as a busty brunette pushed her way between them. To Taylor's dismay he allowed her onto his lap, his eyes looking down her neckline. "Jane," he said as a way of greeting. "You're kinda in the way," he then added to Taylor's surprise and Jane's anger.

"What? She's still a baby," Jane whined and he laughed.

"She's still a friend and I was talking to her," he gave back.

Friend-zoned. Again. Taylor was so sick and tired of that.

"Oh, I found the prettiest girl in the whole town," she suddenly heard as strong arms wrapped around her from behind. Her tension relaxed a little and she shook her head, biting her cheek.

Her heart didn't beat for Eric the way it did for Mason, but there was no denying that Eric still made her stomach tickle in a good way.

"Hey boyfriend," she said deliberately and then got up to turn in his arms.

"Hey Stiles," Eric greeted Mason, making Taylor almost proud as his eyes stayed firmly on Jane's face while telling her hello, too, just before returning to her face.

"Bennett. Didn't know you were doing exclusive," Mason replied coldly while Eric beamed.

"Just with Taylor. She's something else," he answered and then kissed her nose softly.

Before they left she was sure she heard Mason reply, "she sure is," but then maybe Taylor just wanted to hear that.

———

He should've gotten rid of Jane the second she had

sat down on his lap. He knew that. No girl liked sharing attention, even if they were just friends. Mason wouldn't lie, he had felt as if they had made headway out of the friend-zone that night. The way Taylor had looked at him just before Jane had arrived made him think that maybe, just maybe he should risk it all.

Now though his heart lay crumbled inside his ribcage. Eric wasn't a player, everyone knew that, and the boy had been crushing on Taylor for months. He was a good guy, and he should be. Mason had taught him all he knew about football and since Eric worked on the Stiles' farm during the summers, his dad had taught Eric hard work, too. He actually was the perfect choice for Taylor, just a year older, but that didn't matter. Mason didn't want to see her in anyone else's arms.

"Mason?"

The brunette in his lap was still there and he got up, dumping her unceremoniously on the ground with that movement.

"Ass," she cursed before leaving while Mason went over to one of the coolers someone had brought along. He decided against the beer since he had to drive Taylor home, going for a coke instead.

"I just saw Bennett and Collins. The new it-couple, huh? Heads are turning just because everyone wants to catch a glimpse. They look good together," his best friend suddenly said, appearing next to him.

336

Brad really was the best friend anyone could wish for. After all, he always made sure your feelings were protected no matter what. Or not.

"Just perfect," Mason snarled and Brad moved so he actually was in his line of sight. Mason debated about turning away, but figured it was childish.

"Come on, you said you wanted to give her time to grow up and make her experiences. You wanted to be her last, remember? Besides, I think I have something to still make you smile."

Brad held out a photograph to him and in the light of the bonfire he saw Taylor wearing a white-knitted sweater, her eyes closed and her hair gently blowing in the wind. The picture captured everything she was in his eyes: strong, thoughtful, gorgeous.

"I want to be her first, her last, her everything," Mason replied quietly.

Brad took a deep breath, turning wordlessly as if looking for something, pausing eventually. Mason followed his eyes and saw Taylor wrapped into Eric's arm. She was staring intently into the fire while he watched her, clearly head over heels in love with her. It couldn't be more plain on the other guy's face.

"Unless you man up, you won't be her first, trust me," he commented and Mason gritted his teeth. It was true.

"Remind me again why you don't take the plunge?" Brad asked after they'd stared at the couple for a long moment; Mason turning the picture over and over in his hand without looking at it. Without thinking, he slipped it in the back of his jeans, ready to keep it forever and longer.

"I'm scared. I'm stupid. And she's so fucking young, Bradley."

"She's more grown up than some of the girls coming home from college," Brad pointed out and Mason nodded.

"I love hanging out with her, talking to her, laughing with her. She's one of my closest friends, and she's started showing up in my barn every now and then. When things get too crazy at home, she's fleeing and I'm her destination."

"You need to go off to college soon, Mason. You can't stay around, waiting for life to happen while you watch her grow up. I'd say you march over there and kiss her senseless, but I caught something about you friend-zoning her earlier."

Mason spun back to his best friend, blinking. "Who said that?" he inquired and Brad rolled a shoulder in a careless shrug.

"Jane mentioned something like that. She was pretty pissed because you turned her down, but she told the others you turned down Taylor even harder."

The friend comment. God, Mason really was the biggest ass out there. No wonder she had jumped onto the opportunity to call Eric boyfriend.

"Jeesh," he groaned and Brad laughed, slapping him

SAM DESTINY

on the back hard.

"That was a sign. You, my buddy, aren't ready for her yet," he joked, but Mason couldn't really find anything funny about it. Noticing his unhappiness, Brad punched his shoulder, handing him a beer from the cooler.

"Let's go watch the witches dispel the dark shadows and bad ghosts," he suggested and while Mason took the can, he dropped the beer back in the cooler before nodding. The dancing of the 'witches' was a traditional thing in their hometown, Sunburn, North Carolina. It was always fun.

Following his best friend and a group of other people, he walked over to the biggest of fires, his eyes finding Taylor through the flames across from him. She gave him a soft smile before suddenly sobering and then turning into Eric's embrace. The star quarterback kissed her hair and mumbled something soft. Mason forced himself to look away as mad cackling interrupted the conversations around the fire. Everyone waited and dressed up ladies, one uglier than the next, came and started to move to a song that picked up, playing in speakers somewhere behind them.

Daring another glance, he found Taylor watching him instead of the movements in the circle, and as much as he tried to look away, his body didn't listen. She held his eyes just as he held hers. Eventually she shook her head, biting her lip before reacting to something Eric whispered into her ear. The smile that grazed her lips was genuine and she even looked mildly happy as she leaned into him, letting Eric hold her tight. Maybe Brad was right and it had been some weird interference of fate that he'd said what he had earlier. After all, he still could be her friend and he, not Eric, was taking her home. That was something he was sure of.

Taylor thought about letting Eric take her home, but then she decided that she wanted to be friends with Mason if nothing else worked, and for that she couldn't avoid him.

"You lost Jane," she commented, biting her tongue the moment the words had left her lips.

"I shouldn't have given her the chance to sit down in the first place," Mason replied, not starting the truck even though eleven was approaching fast. She didn't care; it wouldn't be the first curfew she couldn't meet.

Silence descended, as she couldn't decide how best to answer. As much as she wished she could ask what he meant, she knew as well that her chance had passed earlier. Maybe, if they hadn't been interrupted, this evening would've taken a different turn, but then, Mason hadn't even bothered to protest the baby comment, and there had been no hesitation when he had called her a friend.

"I don't wanna drive you home, Tay," he suddenly whispered and she couldn't help but smile. She didn't want to go, either, and he seemed to know that.

"Then don't. We can always drive to the edge of a field and hang out on the back of your truck," she grinned, pulling the sleeves over her hands, just to remember something. "By the way, I actually got a spark on your sweater. There's a tiny hole right above the left cuff," she remarked and he took her hand, turning it over until he found the tiny hole she was referring to. Lifting the Stetson off his head he placed it in the backseat and then arched a brow at her. God, he was beautiful, the dark hair stuck to his head before he combed his fingers through it, making it look all messy; his blue-grey eyes shining with humor as he inspected the sleeve and then brushed his thumb over the hole. Even though there was cotton material between her pulse and his thumb, he must've felt it jump.

"Tiny being the operative word," he chuckled and then pulled the cuff over her hand just the way she liked it before letting her hand go. The strange tension between them had lifted and she allowed herself to relax against the back of the seat, turning towards him.

"What're you up to next, Mason? High School is over, you worked your dad's farm for a year, so there must be something you want to do," she inquired and then saw him turn away from her before he pushed out of the truck. Puzzled, she followed him, realizing that the improvised parking lot had almost fully emptied while the stars now shone brightly above them.

She looked up at them while Mason leaned against his truck. She hesitated, then walked over and leaned against the metal, too; close enough to absorb his warmth.

"You're gonna think I'm ridiculous," he finally whispered so low, she wasn't sure she had heard him right over the crickets.

"I think that anyway," she teased, wanting to make him smile. It worked, but the curve of his lip was short lived.

"I want a family. I don't mind hard labor, Collins, and you know that. I'd work my ass off to have my son and my wife at home. I don't need a higher education. I just want to be happy. No divorces, no split Christmases for the kids, just one happy family."

"It's not all flowers and rainbows."

"Taylor, marriage isn't about sunshine. It's about dancing in the rain and weathering the storm when it comes. There'll be fights and discussions, screams and tears, but by the end of the day I want to be the only one kissing them away. That's what I want."

She moved so she stood in front of him, grabbing his chin to force him to meet her eyes.

"It's a perfectly fine dream," she started, her voice cracking. Wasn't he just the guy every woman out there was searching for? "But Mason, you're more than that. You're smart and witty, and unless you pull out a possible wife right now," she whispered, praying to whoever was listening that he wouldn't do that now, "you need to do somethin' for yourself. Maybe one day you'll regret not going further. Apply for college, do somethin' you always wanted to do, and if then a farmer's all you want to be, good. No regrets, Stiles. Plus, as much as I like the image of you sweaty and half naked wearing that Stetson of yours, I can see you helping people. Come and go to nursing school with me," she winked, only half joking. Going away seemed less scary if he was by her side.

"You really think I'd be smart enough for that school of yours?" he wanted to know, no longer meeting her eyes.

She placed her hand above his heart, clearly catching him by surprise.

"You're amazing enough to do whatever you set your mind to," she promised, never having meant anything more than those words right there.

———————

Sixteen going on thirty, Mason thought as he felt the heat of her hand penetrate through his jacket, seemingly burning the place above his heart. Taylor could be all cheerleader, careless and fun, but then she had those moments, just like this one, where she was more grown up than most girls his age. Listening to her now, he almost believed it, too.

"You're too smart for your age," he grinned somewhat embarrassed.

"Yeah, still a baby," she declared coldly, stepping

back and tucking her hand under her elbow. "Which means you should take me home."

Too late he realized what he had said. "That's not what I meant, Taylor, and you know it," he growled, but she just hoped into his truck, making the vehicle dip a little.

He went to the driver side and got in. "You're right, you know? I do need to try before I say that farming is my life," he decided to agree instead of apologizing again. He patted the seat next to him and she hesitated only a second, then scooted over until she sat next to him.

"Good choice," Taylor mumbled gently and he had to agree. It was weirdly deliberating to think that there was more out there. And Brad had been right, too. He needed to go and just hope that once he returned from there, Taylor would still be around and in his life.

"Thanks for kicking my ass concerning this," he whispered, finally starting the car as she just yawned, nodding. It was half past eleven already, but he knew Taylor didn't care much about being late. She never did.

It wasn't the first time he drove her home, and he knew it wouldn't be the last, either, but when she rested her head against his shoulder that night, it almost felt as if there was something more between them.

Something he hoped would be everything he wanted one day.

acknowledgements

First and foremost I want to thank my best friend, Yvi, who is always there when I need it and who keeps loving my stories. I personally think we all need someone who loves our stuff no matter what. ;-) You're my superstar and I look up to you ... and always will.

Second, and nearly as important, Terra and Aimie. I cannot pick one to be more important than the other. T, you always, always, always manage to make me smile and calm me down again. Aims, you always understand. I don't know; you just get me even when I'm being impossible. Thank you for that. I love you, ladies, so so much and I know that one day I will hug you very super extremely tight.

My Betas, Kay, LucyLou (who is so much more than just my beta), and Jacklyn: You rock my world, even when sometimes you have to tell me that my books don't work just yet. Thank you for always being honest.

Jenny Sims, thanks for making my wrongs right. I learned so much from you you have no idea! Thank you. Seriously.

Leigh, you are the best and the fastest and the coolest. Thank you!

Dearest CS chicks, you manage to make me smile, and you help whenever I need it. Thank you. <3 Keep at it, you all do so great, I am honored to know you.

My aunt, who, even though she cannot yet read this since it's not her language, has always supported me and never once stops to think about it. She just does, and it means the world to me.

And last, but not least, my readers. You, the one holding this ebook or paperback right now. Thank you. Come and stalk me ... or talk to me.

Love,

Sam

about the author

Once upon a time there was a young girl with her head full of dreams and her heart full of stories. Her parents, though not a unit, always supported her and told her more stories, encouraging her to become what she wanted to be. The problem was, young Sam didn't know what she wanted to be, so after getting her A-levels she started studying Computer Science and Media. After not even one year she realized it wasn't what her heart wanted, and so she stopped, staying home and trying to find her purpose in life. Through some detours she landed an internship and eventually an apprenticeship in a company that sells cell phones. Not a dreamy career, but hey. Today she's doing an accounting job from nine-to-five, which mainly consists of daydreaming and scribbling notes wherever she can.

All through that time little Sam never once lost the stories in her heart, writing a few little of them here and there, writing for and with her best friend, who always told her to take that last step.

Only when a certain twin-couple entered her mind, bothering her with ideas and talking to her nonstop did she start to write down their story - getting as far as thinking she could finish it. Through the help of some author friends, and the encouragement of earlier mentioned best friend, little Sam, now not so little anymore and in her twenty-seventh year, decided to try her luck as an Indie author. She finished the story of the first twin, Jaden, and realized she couldn't ever stop. So, it really is only after five that the real Sam comes out. The one that hungers for love, romance, some blood, a good story, and, at the end of the day, a nice hot cup of Chai Tea Latte.

And if the boys are still talking to her, she'll write happily ever after.

Find Sam online:

Website: http://www.samdestiny.com
Facebook:
https://www.facebook.com/SamDestinyAuthor

Instagram:
https://instagram.com/authorsamdestiny/

Pintrest: https://www.pinterest.com/samdestiny/

Goodreads:
https://www.goodreads.com/author/show/8443592.Sam_Destiny

Twitter: https://twitter.com/SamDestinyAuthr